A HOUSE AND ITS HEAD

Ivy Compton-Burnett once wrote: 'I have had such an uneventful life that there is little information to give. I was educated with my brothers in the country as a child, and later went to Holloway College, and took a degree in Classics. I lived with my family when I was quite young but for most of my life have had my own flat in London. I see a good deal of a good many friends, not all of them writing people. And there is really no more to say.'

Ivy Compton-Burnett died in 1969 and in her obituary *The Times* wrote: 'Her work, from the first appreciated by a few discerning admirers, was for many years dismissed by the critics and by the general public as the object of a modish cult. The bare, stylized dialogue needs a closer attention than most novel-readers are prepared to give. But the fine comedy and the deep humanity of her books in later years achieved a wider recognition', and Pamela Hansford-Johnson said of her: 'Writing of a dying age she stands apart from the mainstream of English fiction. She is not an easy writer nor a consoling one. Her work is an arras of embroidered concealments beneath which the cat's sharp claws flash out and are withdrawn, behind which the bitter quarrels of the soul are conducted "tiffishly", as if cruelty and revenge and desire, the very heart itself, were all trivial compared with the great going clock of society, ticking on implacably for ever behind the clotted veilings.'

In 1925 she published *Pastors and Masters*, which began the series of novels in which she created a chilling world of late Victorian upper-class people; other titles include *Daughters and Sons, Brothers and Sisters, Elders and Betters, Manservant and Maidservant, Two Worlds and their Ways, Darkness and Day, Parents and Children, Mother and Son, A Family and a Fortune, A Father and his Fate, A Heritage and its History, The Present and the Past* and *A God and his Gifts*.

Ivy Compton-Burnett

A House and its Head

PENGUIN BOOKS

Penguin Books Ltd, Harmondsworth, Middlesex, England
Penguin Books, 625 Madison Avenue, New York, New York 10022, U.S.A.
Penguin Books Australia Ltd, Ringwood, Victoria, Australia
Penguin Books Canada Ltd, 2801 John Street, Markham,
Ontario, Canada L3R 1B4
Penguin Books (N.Z.) Ltd, 182–190 Wairau Road, Auckland 10, New Zealand

First published by Victor Gollancz Ltd 1935
Published in Penguin Books 1958
Reprinted in Penguin Modern Classics 1982

Made and printed in Great Britain by
Richard Clay (The Chaucer Press) Ltd,
Bungay, Suffolk

CHAPTER I

"So the children are not down yet?" said Ellen Edgeworth.

Her husband gave her a glance, and turned his eyes towards the window.

"So the children are not down yet?" she said on a note of question.

Mr. Edgeworth put his finger down his collar, and settled his neck.

"So you are down first, Duncan?" said his wife, as though putting her observation in a more acceptable form.

Duncan returned his hand to his collar with a frown.

Duncan Edgeworth was a man of medium height and build, appearing both to others and himself to be tall. He had narrow, grey eyes, stiff, grey hair and beard, a solid, aquiline face, young for his sixty-six years, and a stiff, imperious bearing. His wife was a small, spare, sallow woman, a few years younger, with large, kind, prominent eyes, a long, thin, questioning nose, and a harried, innocent, somehow fulfilled expression.

The day was Christmas Day in the year eighteen eighty-five, and the room was the usual dining-room of an eighteenth-century country house. The later additions to the room had honourable place, and every opportunity to dominate its character, and used the last in the powerful manner of objects of the Victorian age, seeming in so doing to rank themselves with their possessor.

"So you are down first of all, Duncan," said Ellen, employing a note of propitiation, as if it would serve its purpose.

Her husband implied by lifting his shoulders that he could hardly deny it.

7

"The children are late, are they not?" said Ellen, to whom speech clearly ranked above silence.

Duncan indicated by the same movement that his attitude was the same.

"I think there are more presents than usual. Oh, I wish they would all come down."

"Why do you wish it?"

"Well, it is not a day when we want them to be late, is it?"

"Do we want them to be late on any day? Oh, of course, it is Christmas Day. I saw the things on the table."

Ellen also saw them.

"Oh, you have been down first, and put your presents at the places!"

Duncan moved his neck with an air of satisfaction in the ease he had attained.

"I think they will all be down soon," said his wife, her manner seeming to carry comfort.

"Will they?" just uttered her husband, looking at the wall as if something on it struck him.

"They won't be very late on Christmas Day."

"Why should they be late on Christmas Day or any other? What reason would you suppose?"

Ellen did not say.

"Have you any idea what purpose is actuating them, the three at once? It must be something important."

"Well, the mornings are getting dark."

"The mornings are getting dark! The mornings are getting dark! Do you mean they are so sunk in lethargy and self-indulgence, that they need a strong light to force them to raise their heads from their pillows? Is that what you mean?"

Ellen, uncertain how much she had meant of this, was silent.

"I don't think they will be very late this morning."

"Only rather late, in concession to a standard of civilised decency."

8

"I know they are looking forward to their presents," Ellen advanced in the culprits' favour.

"We hardly expected to have to force them upon them."

"I am sure they do not think of it like that," Duncan was assured.

"I expect they do not," he said, with a little burst of bitter mirth; "I suppose even they are not quite so sub-human."

"They could not be a better nephew and daughters than they are."

"We see they could be on this occasion," said Duncan, biting his thumb-nail and speaking absently.

"I believe I can hear one of them," said Ellen with simple relief; "I am sure there was a sound on the stairs."

"A sound on the stairs! A remarkable thing to hear at this time in the morning!"

"It is Nance; I know her step. I am glad that one of them is down."

"Glad? Why?"

Ellen gave no reason.

"It is a natural thing for a young woman to come down-stairs in the morning to have her breakfast," said Duncan, seeming to disclaim any less tangible purpose in his daughter. "Well, Nance, you have condescended to join us?"

"If that is the word you would use, Father. I felt simply that I was joining you." Nance embraced her mother and went to her seat, obeying the unrecognised family law, that the father should not receive a morning salute. "I have never taken my place before such a pile of gifts. Do I fall upon them, or wait for those who delay longer than I?"

"Have we waited for you?"

"I observed you had, Father, was indeed struck by it. But was the process congenial enough to be emulated?"

Nance Edgeworth was a tall thin girl of twenty-four, with her father's head placed rather squarely on her shoulders, her mother's features set a little awry on her face, and an expression that was her own.

"Have you seen anything of Grant and Sibyl this morning?"

"No, Father. It is not a time of day when family intercourse flourishes."

"I asked you, Nance, if you had seen anything of them."

"No. My life to-day has hitherto been solitary. Ah, the things that I needed, that I was without! I hope to find cause to sustain these cries of joy. Do I hear the laggard footfalls on the stairs?"

"This listening for footfalls seems a foolish thing in adult human beings," said Duncan with a little laugh. "Why should not people come down in the morning?"

"I can think of no reasons, Father. And apparently they could think of none that held weight for long. Happy Christmas, sister and cousin!"

"Happy Christmas, Father dear," said the younger daughter, caressing Duncan's shoulder, as she went to her seat, a nearly grown girl of eighteen, with a fair, pure, oval face, a curved, red mouth, a childish nose and chin, and blue eyes set unusually close, and thereby gaining charm. "So it is the day of days at last."

"It is, indeed, the Day of Days," said Duncan, altering the weight on the words. "I was beginning to think it had escaped your memory. You might have been eager to begin a Day, which can hardly be long enough for the thoughts it must bring. Grant, have you not anything to say to us this morning?"

"The very thing," said his nephew, bowing round the table. "A happy Christmas to you all."

"Thank you, Grant," said Duncan, not failing himself in courteous response.

"Pray don't thank me, Uncle. You are welcome to my words."

Grant Edgeworth was a spare, dark youth of twenty-five, with a delicate, olive face, lively, almond eyes, keen but emotional lips, that twisted on the verge of a smile, and an odd feature that ran in his mother's family, a lock of pure white hair in the front of his smooth, black head. He was the orphan son of Duncan's brother, and heir to the entailed estate. He had had his home with his uncle since his parents' death, loved by Ellen next to her own, and at once accepted and resented by Duncan in the stead of a son. He was reading for the Bar, but in an easy spirit, as his future was secure.

"Yes, it is the Day at last. Can anyone tell me the meaning underneath it?" resumed Duncan, hardly showing the natural confidence in his own training.

There was silence.

"Can no one tell me? Will no one? We are not ashamed, I hope, of acknowledging the Truth, which we are all celebrating with gifts."

It almost seemed that Duncan had made a suggestion, and there was still silence.

"Nance, will you tell me what Day it is?"

"The day of the Birth of Christ, Father," said Nance, forcing a natural voice.

"Yes," said Duncan. "Yes. Sibyl, can *you* tell me what Day it is?"

"The Day of the Birth of Christ, Father," said Sibyl, in a fuller tone, perhaps feeling confidence in the answer, after his confirmation of it.

"Grant?" said Duncan.

"Oh, I agree," said Grant, making a gesture towards his cousins, and causing his aunt to laugh before she knew it.

Duncan simply turned from him.

"Nance, I should like to hear you say it as Sibyl did."

"No, you must pass my individual performance. You asked for it."

There was a pause.

"I hope that my allowing you to treat the occasion as a festival, has not blinded you to its significance?"

"It is the usual way of treating it."

"And does it blind people to the underlying meaning, do you think, Nance?"

"I think up to a point it does."

"Can you tell me why you were late this morning? I suppose you had a reason?"

"None worth stating, Father."

"Sibyl?" said Duncan, turning from his elder daughter.

"Oh, I am a growing girl, Father," said Sibyl, with her head to one side.

Duncan just shook his head, and turned to his nephew.

"Grant, why were you late this morning?"

"I felt a disinclination to rise, Uncle, so strong that it overcame me."

"You came down for your breakfast and your presents."

"Oh, yes, for those."

Duncan dropped his eyes with something like a smile on his lips. He was a man who liked the companionship of men, and in spite of his bitterness at having no personal heir, had come to find something utterly satisfying in the company of his brother's son. The same words on the lips of Nance would have struck him as essentially different.

"Ellen," he said in an easier tone, "would you say these young people feel as they should on fundamental things?"

"Oh, yes, I think they do; they are all very good."

"Well, that is the right proof of it. If that is so, I can have no more to say. Now, I have not thanked my wife for her gifts, my children not the last or least."

Duncan rose and embraced his wife, who met him with a change of expression that told its tale. Sibyl stopped him on his return, and drew his face down to her own.

"Well, Nance, haven't you a kiss for your father on Christmas Day?"

Nance raised her face, and Duncan, turning from her to Grant, in vague consideration of a substitute for the caress, caught sight of a volume at his place.

"What is that book, Grant?"

Grant uttered the title of a scientific work, inimical to the faith of the day.

"Did you remember that I refused to give it to you?"

"Yes, Uncle. That is why I asked somebody else."

"Did you say I had forbidden it in the house?"

"No, or I should not have been given it."

Duncan took the book, and walking to the fire, placed it upon the flames.

"Oh, Father, really!" said Nance.

"Really? Yes, really, Nance. I shall really do my best to guide you—to force you, if it must be, into the way you must go. I would not face the consequences of doing otherwise."

"Would not the consequences be more widely distributed?"

"I shall really do what I can to achieve it," went on Duncan, as if he had not heard, "and I trust it will not be impossible. I do not do it in my own strength."

"How untrue!" murmured Grant. "As if more strength than he has, is possible!"

"I regret my choice of word," said Nance.

"What did you say, Nance?" said Duncan, whose slight deafness was more intermittent than was realised.

"I said I regretted my choice of word, Father."

"Yes," said Duncan, easily; "you are getting into a missish turn of phrase."

"I did not know you objected to the book, Duncan," said Ellen. "I have not read it myself."

"So, Grant, it was my wife, whom you chose to lead against me!"

"I wanted to read the book, Uncle."

Duncan set his foot on the volume, and thrust it further into the flames.

"What are you laughing at, Nance?"

"The scene makes me hysterical, Father. I shall gather up my presents, and bear them to safety."

"You will sit down, Nance, and remain in your seat,"

13

said Duncan, accurately forecasting what would take place.

"Have you read the book, Father?"

"From cover to cover. And on every page there is poison. My volume met the fate of this one."

"You are qualified to understand its influence. And you thought burning was the only thing?"

"Grant might have known its nature from the title?"

"That was just it," said Grant.

"He is a better judge of titles than you are, is he, Father?"

"I don't know, Nance, if you think I find it congenial, to have this hour of peace and pleasure turned into a bout of family strife? I don't know if you think it is what I incline to?"

"I believe I was feeling it was rather natural to you, Father."

"Father, you like my books, don't you?" said Sibyl.

"We are sitting a long time over breakfast," observed Ellen, inattentive to what passed.

"We are not merely having breakfast this morning," said Duncan, with extreme sharpness. "There must be certain things that cannot be done up to time."

"Are you going to give the servants their presents afterwards?" said Sibyl. "I always think you do it so perfectly, Father. It is a thing some people would make so awkward."

"There are no presents for the servants this year," said Ellen, stumbling over the words, and withdrawing her eyes from her husband. "I mean, I have not got them; I have not been able. I was just going to ask Father for some money for them." Her eyes came to rest on her daughters.

"I do not like this giving of money to people who have served us personally through the year. We should choose their present for them as individuals. I believe I have spoken of that before."

"Yes, but I could not get them out of the money for the Christmas expenses. I had thought about it, and planned what they would like; but the other things came to more than you thought, than we thought when we went over them together."

"All that money gone on a few domestic expenses! It marks the difference between people. It would take me a longer time to spend it on better things."

"The money has gone on many domestic expenses," said Nance. "You forget the sacredness of the home, Father. You and I will stay away from church, and consider the quarter's bills, and arrange an allowance for Mother on the basis of them."

"And how long has it been your business to talk of an allowance for your mother, or any other affairs of people above you? You need give no thought to any allowance but your own. As long as you need that, you are in no position to."

"It has been my business since I saw it was imperative. For some time now."

"And are you the head of the house, or am I?"

"Oh, you are, Father; and I want Mother to be." Nance put her hand on Duncan's. "Do stop trying to be a man and a woman as well."

"Oh, you come bamboozling me," said Duncan, accepting the pressure, but giving no further sign. "So I make it a business of mine to try to be a woman? As it is one of yours, see you attend to it."

"Well, what are we to do about the presents?" said Ellen, with the open sigh which was her common sign of weariness.

"Why, call up the servants, and say that we were not able to choose their gifts this year; but that we hope they will spend what we give them on something they wish, and regard it as a present from us. It is easy enough to do it. It offers no difficulty. A gentlewoman should be able to do anything."

"It seems as good a method as the other," said Nance. "But a gentlewoman is not able to spin gold out of straw; it required a full princess to do that."

Duncan took his purse from his pocket, and handed it to his wife.

"Grant," he said, as though the matter had scarcely engaged him, "there is something to be said between us, little though I like it for the day. Am I to believe it was you, who chose to make an exhibition of yourself with a maid-servant behind the house? I find it hard to think it."

"I am glad of that, Uncle."

"Surely you have enough decency and dignity, enough respect for your aunt and your cousins, for womanhood in general, to hold you from such a depth? I am unable to think my training has brought you to it."

"I am glad, Uncle."

"It will go hard with me, if I have to believe it. But do not stoop to deceit. If that is of any good, you have stooped far enough."

"Well, what am I to do?" said Grant.

"I should have been able to repudiate such a rumour. But in face of what I have known of you, I could not. I found myself in that humbling place. I cannot discuss such a matter before my daughters."

"I am very glad," said Grant. "I feel great respect for womanhood. More than you do, perhaps. I was beginning to think you could discuss the matter before them."

"Now in a week we shall enter the New Year," said Duncan, his attention for the company. "Have you your resolves ready for it? Nance, can you tell me one of yours?"

"Your hopes seem to centre on me, Father, your first-born. I have been resolving to be more independent in the coming months."

"Sibyl?" said Duncan, passing easily from Nance.

"I have not been resolving anything like it, Father. I have been seeing I shall always be dependent."

"Well, you will both be dependent, whether or no you

want it, and whether or no I do, as far as I can see. Grant, what resolve have you to tell us?"

"Aunt Ellen and I have not made any, Uncle. We are not the slaves of convention."

"And what have your aunt's resolves to do with you? If she is well enough without them, who would say the same of you? So make a resolve, when I order you, and tell us of it."

"What are your resolves, Father?" said Nance.

"Good enough, good enough. Who are you, not to be sure of it? And if you are to be independent, what is it to you? Grant, I require you to oblige me."

"I will oblige you, Uncle. I have no false shame. I resolve to give more time to the place."

"You think that stage has come? So the place has so much to do with you? You are putting me in my grave. What else am I to expect? Now what is the matter with the girl, Sibyl?"

"I don't like you to talk like that, Father. I can't get used to it."

"You are a good girl," said Duncan, in a mechanical manner, as though accustomed to such moments. "I will cease from any talk that troubles you. Now let none of us be behindhand in leaving the house. Grant, I hope you are giving me your mind?"

"I am not thinking of going to church, Uncle."

"I said I hoped you were giving me your mind: I did not ask what you were thinking of. Why should I be concerned with it?"

"I was not meaning to go to church, Uncle," said Grant, already using the past tense.

"I said I hoped you were giving me your mind," said Duncan, as he rose and left the room.

"I am in a simple position," said Grant: "I do not dare to remain at home."

"I find myself without the traditional courage of womanhood," said Nance.

"I enjoy church on Christmas Day," said Ellen, putting her hands over her eyes. "Most of our friends will be there, and it passes the morning."

"Grant," said Sibyl, swinging her chair towards him, "I believe I could get you that book from the rectory library."

"It has a place there, and Father devoured its every word, and Grant took risks to get it," said Nance. "I am glad of my approaching independence."

"It was wrong of you not to tell me, Grant," said Ellen, almost with indifference. "Of course I should not have given it to you. Now there is that expensive book wasted."

"It keeps the home fires burning," said Grant, "if Uncle is speaking the truth about his copy."

"Well, that had been put to its intended purpose," said Nance.

"Poor Father! He is rather one by himself in the house," said Sibyl. "I hope he knows what we all feel for him."

Ellen raised her eyes with a faintly grieved expression.

"If he does not know what you feel, it is not for want of being told," said her cousin.

"He and I have always been friends. I have known his look for me all my life."

"He cares much the most for Aunt Ellen."

Ellen's eyes filled with tears, and she spoke at once.

"Here is all this money for the servants! They will be so pleased."

"Can you take what you like from the purse?" said Sibyl, addressing her mother for the first time that day.

"Father never speaks of what I have taken, when he leaves me his purse."

"A disregard of material things happily works both ways," said Nance.

"We ought to be ready to start in half an hour," said her sister. "I think we owe it to Father not to be late."

"There is no reason why we should be late."

"I suppose there is not," said Grant, walking round the room with the successive demeanours of his acquaintance entering church. "It seems there must be. There is always a laggard."

This was true, and on this occasion it was Ellen.

Duncan stood in the hall, with hat and book, in an attitude of being on the point of leaving the house. The young people stood about, still and silent, until Grant and Nance met each other's eyes, and broke into laughter.

Duncan breathed more audibly and maintained his position, but as the laughter increased, he dropped his book, and signed sharply to Grant to retrieve it. Grant took a moment to follow, and Sibyl was before him; and Duncan idly dropped it again, and motioned his nephew to obedience.

Ellen came hurrying down the stairs, her avoidable haste acting in its normal way upon her husband He remained as he was, until she came up, and then without turning his eyes upon her, walked from the house.

CHAPTER II

Duncan and Ellen proceeded to church, unconscious that it was the only occasion in the week when they were seen abroad together. Grant followed with his cousins, adopting the bearing of his uncle, and somehow contriving that the sisters appeared to reproduce his aunt's.

Ellen went first into the family pew, and was followed by her husband. Sibyl sat by Duncan, Nance by Sibyl, and Grant took his place at the end of the line, in readiness to emerge and hand the plate, a duty imposed by his uncle.

The parson conducted the service in a cold, impersonal manner, making it as brief as he could. He was a strong, solid man about thirty-eight, with face and hair and eyes of much the same pale colour, high, marked features, and a set, enigmatic expression. His discourse took the line of a lecture rather than a sermon, and was to earn a parishioner's comment, that faith as deep as his would hardly appear on the surface. In fact, his concern with his faith was limited to this level, as it was years since it had existed on any other. His scepticism had not led him to relinquish his living as he had a slender income, and a widowed mother to support, and no other means of reconciling the conditions. He hoped his duties would be less well done by a stupider man, as a believer would probably be; and his views, though of some inconvenience to himself, were of none to his congregation, as they were beyond the range of its suspicions. Even his mother, who lived in his house, assigned his unguarded words to modern breadth of mind, and either gave them no ear, or gave it with enjoyment, as although herself a believer, she had a dislike for her beliefs.

Old Gretchen Jekyll sat in the rectory pew, a ponderous woman in the seventies, in conventional widow's dress, with round, black eyes, like the eyes of no one else, features resembling her son's, and a benevolent, dominant expression. Half a dozen young boys sat under her eye, the pupils of her son, who added to his income by conducting their education. Her daughter, Cassandra, was with her, a tall, handsome woman of thirty-nine, with a finer form of the family face, her brother's clear, pale eyes, and hair prematurely grey. She was governess to Duncan's daughters, and still had her home in his house.

Gretchen marshalled her flock out of church directly the service concluded, her expression indicating that decorum might no longer be hoped. She paused at a customary spot in the churchyard, with an odd, fierce look that came of self-consciousness, frankness and penetration, and accorded with her talk.

"Well, Mrs. Jekyll," said Duncan, in a tone unheard in his family, though often by them, "I shall not wish you a happy Christmas, when you possess yourself of a member of my house."

"We must have some family life on Christmas Day," said Gretchen, staring into his face.

"It seems we must," murmured Grant.

Gretchen smiled with grim understanding.

"I seemed to grasp the essence of it this morning," said Nance. "Unless the vision comes with every absence of Cassie's, and Time, the healer, does its work in between."

"No one puts in a claim for the rest of us," said Grant. "We are left to the reality of our own homes."

"The rest of you can afford to remain in them," said Gretchen.

"The deceitfulness of riches," said the doctor of the neighbourhood, rubbing his hands, a short, plump man of fifty-five, with dark, bright, close-set eyes, overshadowed by a heavy, hooked nose, a sculptured mouth and chin, and a bland, amused expression.

"Other things can be deceitful," said Gretchen. "I find they are."

"Riches as I have seen them, are straightforward enough," said Dr. Fabian Smollett's cousin and wife, a woman of the same type and height and age, who with her spaced, blue eyes, serious mouth and straightforward expression, appeared to be normally different.

"Why is Christmas a family festival?" said Grant. "It should surely be of general application?"

"Or what was the good of the message to all mankind?" said Fabian.

"Things tend to become rooted in families," said Florence his wife.

"People think they keep them to themselves in that way," said Gretchen.

"And so they do," said Grant.

"Oh, I have caught my hair in a bush!" said Sibyl, in a voice that attracted attention.

"Ah, we must not be hanging you up like Absalom, Miss Sibyl," said Fabian, disengaging the hair.

"Thank you so much, Dr. Smollett," said Sibyl, with a full voice and smile.

"Stand further away from the bushes, Sibyl," said her father.

"Reginald," said Gretchen, in rolling tones, "will you remember you are near a place of worship?"

Reginald, qualified to interpret these words as a request to cease to whisper, complied with the request.

A lady bustled forward and put a coloured tract into his hands, as a legitimate object for his attention. Miss Rosamund Burtenshaw was regarded as having as much connection with the church as the rector, and really had more. She was a short, buxom woman of forty-four, with a high, set colour, unvarying, hazel eyes, strong, stiff clothes, and a manner suggesting that what she said would occasion mirth. Her father came behind her—his custom in every sense—an older, easier, masculine edition of her, with a dragging step and an idle but interested gaze; whose likeness to his daughter, rather than hers to him, caused surprise that two such indefinite sets of features bore such a definite resemblance. The fact that Alexander had followed no calling, was a ground for speculation, and the reason was seldom guessed, that he had been driven by no actual need.

His niece, Miss Beatrice Fellowes, more generally seen as cousin to his daughter, was a big, angular woman of thirty-eight, with awkward hands and limbs, a good-tempered, trivially moulded face, obstinate, red-brown eyes, and hair and dress conforming to some unknown standard of unworldliness, which her cousin showed herself able to ignore.

Miss Burtenshaw had retired from missionary work owing to the discomfort of the life, a reason which she did not disclose, though it was more than adequate; and was accustomed to say she found plenty of furrows to plough in the home field; and Beatrice made her home in her house, almost unaware that it was her father's, and at once served, admired and emulated her.

"Cassie, are you coming to luncheon?" said Nance. "You have no conception of the festival, as celebrated by ourselves, with Father as director."

"Poor Father!" said Sibyl; "I am afraid he is disappointed in us."

"I can hardly believe that possible," said her sister; "I don't pretend to follow his line of thought, if he is."

"Why, do you think you are perfect?"

"As a daughter I do, absolutely. I can't take any other view."

"Think how much better we are than he is," said Grant.

"If there is room for improvement in you, improve, Sibyl," said Nance: "I can see none in myself."

Fabian stood by, laughing to himself.

"Did you observe with what boyish dignity I handed

23

the plate?" said Grant. "And I put in my own contribution last, when most men put it in first. Because who am I, but a youth who is not all bad? Cassie, if you do not come to luncheon, you will offend one of these little ones."

"I will come; I will leave my home for another on Christmas Day."

"That is good news," said Ellen, her tone drawing Duncan's eyes.

"What have you to say to that, Mrs. Jekyll?" said Beatrice.

"Luncheon makes no odds," said Gretchen, her eyes roving over her flock. "Our family life has to wait until the boys are in bed."

"So the boys have no family life at all," said her son, joining the group. "And we maintain they have every advantage."

"The rector is himself this morning," said Miss Burtenshaw, looking at Oscar, and moving her feet.

"Ah, but they have a substitute for it," said a friend who accompanied Oscar, a tall, stooping man about fifty, with a small, mottled face and an affectionate manner. "You don't need to say it for yourself, Mrs. Jekyll. The little lads say it for you."

Mr. Bode turned a fond gaze upon the boys, who dropped their eyes before it. His wife seemed to second his expression, as she stood at his side, a woman of moderate height and build, with a smooth, ordinary face, and a peaceful, feminine expression, of whom he was wont to say that not once in twenty-seven years had he known her to think of herself, appearing to derive the purest gratification from the circumstance. He had indeed only retired from a profession, when his wife, by suffering the loss of her parents, presented him with her inheritance.

Their son and daughter came behind them: Almeric, a tall, sallow youth of twenty-six, with a simply sensitive face, and a look of sullen self-consciousness, whose grievance against the world began with his parents' choice of his name on the day of his birth, and who had attained the stage in letters, of honest despair of contemporary work; and Dulcia, a swarthy, but fresh-looking girl of twenty-four, with a solid, open face, a large, full gaze, and a freedom from any kind of subtlety, which caused her brother not so much to form an opinion of her, as to accustom his mind to flutter away from such a thought.

"Happy Christmas, happy Christmas to you all!" said Mr. Bode. "My wife and I wish it to you all indeed."

"And your son and daughter," said Dulcia, springing forward, and causing her brother to smile to himself, for the sake of those whose eyes were on him.

"I hope you don't find it all too much, Ellen?" said Florence, in her definite, detached manner. "You look pale and tired."

"I want to say that I wish you all a happy Christmas, in the true sense," said Beatrice, speaking as if her ending cost her an effort.

"Ah, Miss Fellowes, and we wish the same to you," said Mr. Bode, rather unreflectingly facile in the inclusive wish.

"My congratulations on your sermon, Jekyll," said Duncan. "You have given us the foundation for our day."

"The foundation?" said Grant. "Is most of it yet before us?"

"The herald angels have stopped singing," said Fabian.

"You always give us something to think about, Mr. Jekyll," said Dulcia.

"I shall think about it," said Beatrice, her quiet tone seeming audible on principle.

"Yes, you are responsible for our thoughts to-day, Rector," said Miss Burtenshaw. "You have to shoulder that responsibility."

"Yes, it is a very hard day for the rector," said Beatrice, looking round. "We are apt to forget it, as we go through it, enjoying its privileges. But of course it is."

"I do not think we forget it," said Florence, speaking without raising her head, as was her habit.

"Well, perhaps you do not," said Beatrice, with cheerful friendliness. "But I confess it has sometimes escaped my memory."

"The rector looks tired enough by the evening to remind us," said Dulcia.

"He does not show it, when he is tired," said Gretchen.

"I will go to luncheon with the Edgeworths, Mother," said Cassie.

"Yes; we haven't so much to offer. But don't forget it is a holiday. Other people will forget it, if you do."

"The Day is not forgotten in our house," said Grant.

"I am sure Miss Jekyll will do as she wishes in that house, on this day or any other," said Dulcia, clearly. "But Mr. Jekyll cannot but be thankful when its knell sounds."

"We shall be thankful to have had the day, Jekyll," said Duncan. "In that sense we shall be thankful, when it is over."

"Ah, that is the way to put it," said Mr. Bode, feeling some way to be unavoidable.

"They talk too lightly of such a thing as its being over," said Grant.

"I think the very fact that the experience of the day is so deep, would prevent us from feeling we could live it a second time," said Beatrice. "After all, Christmas Day only came once, didn't it?"

"That was really the only arrangement," said Fabian.

"I think I may say I have found it a deep experience," added Beatrice, with a view to absolute truth.

"No, we have no need to ask for any more. We had it all done for us once," said Miss Burtenshaw, her brisk tones showing that religion was not to her a subject for hush and repression.

"Are the boys and girls doing anything to celebrate the day?" said Florence.

"We hope that Almeric and Dulcia will spend the afternoon with our young people, as they did last year," said Ellen.

"We should like nothing better, Mrs. Edgeworth. Indeed we have been waiting to be asked," said Dulcia, breaking into laughter.

"Thank you very much," said her brother.

"It is we who should thank you," said Duncan.

"That is so," said Nance to Grant. "When it happened last year too!"

"We should be dispersing for luncheon," said Beatrice, addressing the group. "The rector has his afternoon service to think of."

"He need not think of it until it comes," said Gretchen.

"Can I take the boys for you, Mrs. Jekyll?" said Beatrice, with full cordiality.

"No, no; don't put yourself about."

"I shall be going anyhow."

"Do you often go to the children's service, Miss Fellowes?" said Dulcia. "I think that suggests an interesting point of view."

"I always go. Why, I can hardly say. It may be just to get something more to think about. And that is quite as likely at the children's service as at any other. I will call at a quarter to three, Mrs. Jekyll."

"My son can take the boys. He should be used to it."

"They might be a trouble to him. I will call at a quarter to three," said Beatrice, her manner smooth over the same trouble for herself. "And I will bring them back afterwards. Then he need not have them on his mind."

"Well, he will be glad enough not to be nursemaid for once," said Gretchen, drawing no veil over the task.

"He should not make both pulpit and congregation his business," said Miss Burtenshaw, somehow rendering her cousin's office a matter of course.

" 'Tis dogs' delight to bark and bite,' " said Gretchen suddenly. "Ernest, will you conduct yourself as a human being?"

"Reginald, show Ernest your booklet," said Miss

Burtenshaw, in a voice of full benevolence as regards this object.

"Good-bye, all!" said Dulcia, waving her hand. "Now, loitering parents, you have gossiped as much as is good or seemly."

Mr. and Mrs. Bode followed their daughter with a smile, and Almeric a moment later without one.

"Now, a happy Christmas to all before it is too late!" said Alexander.

"You were very nearly too late, Father."

"Better late than never," said Beatrice, lightly.

The Smolletts accompanied the Edgeworths as far as their gates. At the latter's luncheon table there was to be a certain lack of ceremony. It was the occasion of the servants' Christmas dinner, and the meal in the dining room was simplified and cold, with a view to the servants' rising the minimum number of times from their annual religious feast.

"A happy Christmas, Bethia," said Sibyl, entering the dining-room, where the table was being set.

The family income had lessened with the depression of the land, and the house was run on women servants.

"I wish you a happy Christmas, Miss Sibyl, I am sure," said Bethia, a woman of middle age, with bright, grey eyes, a very turned up nose, abundant hair and a self-satisfied expression.

"You were happy in not being compelled to church," said Grant.

"I should have been glad of the facility, sir. It would have helped me through the day."

"Don't you like Christmas Day?"

"Well, Miss Nance, I could hardly be heard to say I didn't like it, being the day it is. But it tends to be more trouble than usual, with a feeling there ought to be less."

"A brilliant definition of the day," said Grant. "I am glad you don't like trouble: I was afraid you did."

"Well, sir, if anything has to be done, I may as well be the one to do it."

"What a dreadful philosophy!"

"But you don't do it only for other people," said Sibyl, a child to this extent.

"Well, no, miss, I should not feel called upon to do it on that basis. The labourer is worthy of his hire, we have been told."

"Your life makes you proud," said Grant.

"Well, sir, I hope I don't feel it a cause for pride. It is not for me to feel it."

"Your hair is falling out of your cap, Bethia."

"Thank you, Miss Sibyl; I have too much hair for a cap. But it is incumbent for me to wear one, being as I am."

"It must be nice to have so much hair," said Grant.

"Yes, sir. Many a person has said they wished they had my hair."

"What are you doing in here?" said Ellen. "You know Father likes you to wait for the bell."

"I am on the point of ringing it, ma'am."

"You have a great command of language," said Grant.

"Yes, sir; I was always one for expressions," said Bethia, carrying the bell to the hall.

"Well, you are all in a hurry," said Duncan, obeying the summons. "The service must have given you an appetite."

"Yes, listening does make you hungry, Father," said Sibyl.

"We need building up after such a thing," said Grant.

"It was an interesting address," said Duncan, ignoring this speech. "Some people might have preferred more of a simple gospel sermon for the day. But I found it of sufficient bearing upon it. Jekyll may take another line this evening."

"It is a good thing we do not go in the evening," said Grant. "We suspect him of all sorts of things then. I would not witness his self-exposure."

"I happened not to think of ourselves. Other people will hear the sermon."

"I made sure you were thinking of ourselves. I believed I was in your thoughts, Uncle."

"What did you think of Jekyll's line?" said Duncan.

He and Grant addressed themselves to one of their discussions, which Grant more or less manufactured, and his uncle enjoyed; and under cover of the talk Cassandra entered.

"I admire you for daring to be late, Cassie," said Nance. "On this occasion it is a good thing you are. Father has been letting himself go in criticism of your brother's sermon."

"I have neither been letting myself go, nor criticised the sermon, Nance. It is simply senseless to say things that are not true. If you cannot make your impression without doing that, I should not trouble about it."

"I think my impression really needs troubling about now."

"Your brother's sermon struck me as an able discourse, rather than a sermon, Miss Jekyll. I listened to it with great interest."

"Oscar will forget to tell us we are sinners, and preach of what is nothing to do with ourselves. He has never guessed why we go to church."

"Remind him to be more conventional," said Grant. "I feel it is time I was warned."

" 'Out of the mouth of babes——' " said his uncle, with cold carelessness.

"I thought it was a very clever sermon," said Ellen.

"I am sure he did not mean you to think that. He only fancies we like exposition better than reproach."

"When the exposition is his, and the reproach would be ours," said Nance.

"Do come to breakfast next Christmas, Cassie," said Grant.

"Christmas is the festival of family life," said Duncan.

"It is because Miss Jekyll is one of us, that it is congenial to us to have her, to her to be with us."

"I am glad not to be in my own home. And none of the boys is homesick, though my mother does not try to make her house a home to them."

"You are making this house less of a home to us," said Grant.

"Are we not working this little joke to death?" said Duncan.

"It is only a joke, Father," said Sibyl.

"That was the word I used; little joke."

"Did you like my present to you, Cassie?" said Sibyl.

"No; I had seen you making it."

"Presents should be bought, not made," said Nance.

"You liked my present better because I made it, Father?"

"Yes, yes. But don't come bamboozling me."

"I never know why people say their friends should not spend their money on them," said Cassie.

Duncan smiled.

"I will get you a New Year present," said Sibyl.

"Thank you. You won't have time to make it."

"You can give this one to Mother. She will like to have my work."

"It is only fit for a relation; I do not mean to be as much one of the family as that."

Duncan smiled again. Cassie was a well-born woman, and held her own in his house, and his treatment of her was in accordance with his traditions.

"Are Almeric and Dulcia coming directly after luncheon?" said Sibyl.

"Would you all like to go to the young people's service?" said Duncan, his tone less simple than his words.

"It would scarcely be a generous method of entertainment," said Nance. "And if they had meant to go, they would not have accepted our invitation."

"They have all been to one service to-day," said Cassie.

"And young people have such memories, that one sermon in a lifetime is really enough."

"I should go to the schoolroom together, as you did last year," said Ellen.

"You don't mind our doing that, Father?" said Sibyl.

"You heard your mother suggest it? Your friends can be taken to the schoolroom when they arrive."

Dulcia entered this room in a hearty manner.

"We are fortunate to have something to fill up Christmas afternoon. It is an occasion which seems to partake of the nature of an anticlimax. We know it will anyhow not do that to-day."

"I believe we have offered ourselves," muttered Almeric.

"Well, it does not matter, as long as we have been accepted. And we have no feeling against schoolroom life, which cannot be said of everybody. Myself, I find that utter unselfconsciousness of this family a joy for ever."

"Father was interested enough to suggest our attending the children's service," said Nance. "We rejected that form of hospitality as unworthy of us."

Dulcia leaned back in mirth.

"Let us follow his suggestion," said Grant, improvising a pulpit, assuming the tablecloth, and regarding his audience with a mimicry of Oscar's pulpit manner.

"I hope none of you will leave this service, with the feeling that it has had no bearing upon your spiritual life. Anything that penetrates the mind, has its influence upon the whole being. To draw a line between the brain and what is called the soul, is to break up the entity that is the self of each, into parts that are inorganic and meaning-less——"

Grant continued in Oscar's tones; Dulcia rolled about in her seat; the others joined the mirth by degrees; and before the address was concluded, there was a knock at the door.

"Excuse me, Miss Nance, but the master feels there is too much noise for Christmas Day."

Dulcia opened her eyes and her mouth in dramatic consternation.

"You should not knock at the door, Bethia," said Sibyl. "You should open it and come in, like a trained maid."

"Well, miss, I have Miss Nance's instructions that this door is an exception. And what is for a trained maid, is for me to know better than you, as many would agree."

"Miss Sibyl was thinking of the other rooms, Bethia. Tell us what the master said."

"I can only say, miss, he is here to speak for himself," said Bethia, stepping aside for Duncan to pass.

"What is the reason of this clamour? Your friends can hardly find it congenial. They should have an opportunity of spending their Christmas as they would choose."

"We were playing a game, Father," said Sibyl.

"Grant, you appear to be taking the lead. Have you had time to collect your thoughts?"

"We were playing a game, as Sibyl said, Uncle."

"You are not capable of forming a reply? Nance, can you give me an answer?"

"No, I cannot. You paralyse me, Father."

"Grant, whom are you held to be impersonating?"

"Any clergyman, Uncle."

"Was there nothing else you could think of, to besmirch? You display a belated boyishness."

"Nothing else came into my mind. That is the only kind of thing we have come into contact with to-day."

"You had better have gone to the children's service," said Duncan, his tone hardly doing well by his earlier suggestion. "Nance, did this exhibition strike you as humorous?"

"Well, yes, it did, Father."

"You were in need of something to distract your mind from the thoughts of the day?"

"Yes, I think we were."

Duncan stood as if his attention were escaping.

"Make up the fire," he said, turning to the door. "Your

33

friends will be cold. Grant, it is your business, and not your cousins' or your guests'."

Dulcia looked with inquiry at her friends, her lips tentatively parting.

"Uncle is a weak character," said Grant.

"No, he is simple and strong," said Almeric.

"Are you afraid of him?" said Dulcia.

"Of course they are," said her brother. "They are not so stupid as not to be."

"Well, seriously," said Dulcia, "I think Mr. Edgeworth had a great deal of right on his side. We were making fun of serious things. I admit I was, and enjoying it too. Oh, yes, I went the whole hog; I am not backing out now. But that very circumstance helps me to see his point of view."

"But not to foresee it," said Almeric.

"Well, no one else's point of view has had any success," said Nance.

Bethia entered the room, with a hope in her face, that she was breaking in upon something calling for privacy.

"A lady has called, Miss Nance, and the mistress would like you all to go to the drawing-room."

"We are fortunate to have a tea-party," said Dulcia; "I confess we had expected to be alone."

"It is Miss Fellowes' umbrella," said Grant. "The young people's service is over."

"Dear Miss Fellowes! I am sure she does a great deal of good," said Dulcia, as though others would hardly take this view.

Beatrice rose and held out her hand with a smile, turning to include Duncan and Ellen in her address.

"I have come to bring you all a message, which you have already received to-day, the simple message of Christmas. I just want it to pass once again from me to you."

There was a silence.

"I am going round to all my friends," continued Beatrice, her voice gathering with her sense of a step behind. "I have made up my mind to do it. I wondered if I

34

should really get to the point, but I find I am making a beginning——" She looked about with a mild radiance—"Yes, I am being carried along. This is the first house I had in my mind to come to. And I do not feel any doubt of the others now." Her voice relaxed and she looked round for a seat.

"What a nice idea!" said Ellen, breaking the hush. "It is very kind of you to think of us."

"Kind indeed," said Duncan, speaking in his beard. "Let my wife give you some tea."

"I suppose I shall come in for a good many teas, in the course of what I have set myself," said Beatrice, looking up with a smile as she put down her gloves. "It is a relief to have got into the swing, so to speak. For I did not trust myself. I was prepared to find myself a backslider. I think few people can ever have set out upon a little mission with less assurance."

A faint giggle came from Sibyl, which Duncan somehow quelled without a glance.

Beatrice smiled fully into Sibyl's face.

"I wonder why evangelists always used words like 'just' and 'simple' and 'little' to refer to their business," said Almeric in a mutter to Grant. "It hardly seems for them to deprecate it."

" 'A poor thing but their own,' " murmured Nance.

"How did the boys conduct themselves at the service, Miss Fellowes?" said Ellen.

"Oh, well enough, considering their youth. It was their second dose of sitting still to-day," said Beatrice, by no means rendered intolerant by her own leanings. "I conducted them back to the rectory, and rendered to Mrs. Jekyll an account of my stewardship."

"Did you see Mr. Jekyll?" said Nance.

"That was the whole point of me, that I should not see him. If I had brought the boys within his sight, I should have failed most signally in my mission."

"Poor Mrs. Jekyll! She must have been thankful to

have them off her hands," said Dulcia. "I am so glad she had a free afternoon."

"It was a little thing to do, to ensure it. I believe her house is the next on my list; my mental list, I should say, as I have not made a material one. It will seem a little odd to be appearing there again so soon; but I am not going to worry about that." Beatrice's tone became light and almost touched with exaltation. "No, that is a very small matter to get over."

"It was nice of you to put us first on your list," said Grant.

"Well, people came into my mind in a certain order. Or perhaps were put into it in that order. We often use words carelessly, I think; I am sure I do."

"Anyhow we have nothing to be hurt about. I should like to know who is last on the list."

"Dr. and Mrs. Smollett," said Beatrice, looking at him with a changing expression. "But no distinction arose in my mind. As I say, the matter seemed out of my hands." She stood looking at Grant uncertainly, and then turned and gave her hand to each, with a full and impartial smile.

"We shall see you all in church this evening, I hope? We want very much to have a full congregation."

"You saw us this morning," said Duncan. "The evening is the occasion of our family festival."

"Well, we shall see the other members of our flock, who come from your house?"

"The servants?" said Duncan, as her meaning came. "We shall be dependent on them, I fear. They would be the last people to feel we were not."

Beatrice gave another smile, and turning with a rather subdued bearing, as if with a sense of failure, walked to the door. Dulcia sprang forward to open it, impeding Grant's advance; and Beatrice simply and gravely thanked her, as she passed through.

Duncan rang for her to be shown out, though it was the habit of his family to perform this office themselves.

36

"I hope I am not too late to wish you a happy Christmas, Bethia?" she said, not allowing herself to be influenced by Bethia's prospects for the rest of the day.

"Thank you, miss; and I am sure I wish the same to you."

"I hope you have found it a satisfying Christmas?"

"Yes, miss, thank you; and I hope you have found it similar."

There was a pause while Beatrice adjusted herself to intercourse on the same ground.

"Good-bye, Bethia," she said in a gentle tone.

"Good-bye, miss."

"The impertinent woman!" Duncan was saying. "Why is her position different from ours? I hope our friends will appreciate her hints upon their households."

"I think she meant it in a friendly spirit; I am sure she is very kind," said his wife.

"I quite agree, Mrs. Edgeworth," said Dulcia, rather loud. "I think what she did must have called for a good deal of courage. I found myself admiring her, in spite of myself."

"You do injustice to yourself," said her brother.

"She is attending to her own eternal welfare," said Grant, "and leaving nothing undone that comes in her path."

"Happily she has not much imagination," said Almeric.

"She is not without a skill of her own. Did you see me the victim of it?"

"You looked as foolish as you deserved to, Grant," said his uncle. "She was your guest, and entitled to courtesy at your hands. I felt I had to blush for you."

"You certainly kept back all you had to say, Father," said Nance. "We did not have to blush for you."

"It is a pity, Nance, you did not use your wit when the guest was present. You are the elder daughter of the house, and you did not open your mouth to utter a word."

"I admit I only opened it to gaze at the guest, petrified."

37

"The effect she has had on most of us, does not seem to be good," said Ellen, smiling. "And she came to do us a kindness."

"Yes, I do not think they are fair to her, Mrs. Edgeworth," said Dulcia. "You and I see what she did, quite differently. I admit I should not have had the spunk to do it, if it had been before me as my course."

"You are what she would call a backslider," said Grant.

"You would shirk," said Nance.

"No, no, I won't have it," said Dulcia. "I am not going to join. Miss Fellowes is safe where I am concerned. Now, dear Mrs. Edgeworth, thanks to you we have had a Christmas afternoon, which does not compare unfavourably with the morning. And I protest that Miss Fellowes' visit constituted one of its advantages." She laughed at this opinion.

"It has been good of you to spare us the time," said Duncan.

"Oh, I think it is a time most people would spare, Mr. Edgeworth. We were only too fortunate in being able to dispose of it."

"That is so," said Almeric.

As the guests were led to the hall, Dulcia turned back and ran up to Duncan.

"Mr. Edgeworth, I am at one with you about the game upstairs! I could not go without telling you."

She ran back after her friends.

"Dulcia has as much courage as Miss Fellowes," said Grant. "The heroism of woman is a fact."

"Where are you all going?" said Duncan.

"To the schoolroom, Father," said Nance. "We thought you had had enough of us."

"Come back to your mother, and engage in rational intercourse. I have seen the effect the schoolroom has upon you."

"That manner of intercourse is difficult in family life."

38

"My good girl, you have had guests all the afternoon. Can you never make a remark to your own family?"

"I do occasionally drop a word of my own, Father. I wonder you do not notice it."

"We shall soon reach the climax of the day, the feast," said Grant. "Miss Fellowes would only allow us one kind of support."

"I do not ask you to accept religion in that form," said Duncan.

"Not in its true sense," said Nance.

Duncan's voice changed.

"Well, Nance, send the servants to church, and attend to the dinner yourself, if you would like."

"I should not like, Father; any more than we should like to sell all we have, and give to the poor."

Duncan walked to the bell and rang it, and stood awaiting the result.

"Bethia, Miss Nance would like to say something to you."

"No, the master is mistaken, Bethia."

"We wondered if you would like to go to church this evening," said Ellen.

"No, thank you, ma'am; I am aware I cannot absent myself. Somebody else would only have to do what I should be doing; and that is not the best religion. Did you ring for anything, ma'am?"

"It was a sort of joke they were having," said Ellen. "That is all, Bethia, thank you."

"You were trying to put me in an awkward position, Father."

"I was trying to bring home to you the logical consequences of your attitude, for your own sake."

"It was not for my sake, as I need not explain."

"You forget to whom you speak. My position does not admit of this careless and clodhopping dealing. I beg you will remember it."

"No one's position should admit of such dealing. And

I believe your position would be most people's choice."

Ellen put her hands to her face, and gave a yawn of utter weariness.

Duncan cast her a look, and strode from the room.

"Dear, dear, it is a tedious time, Christmas," said his wife, pressing her fingers on her eyes.

"And every year we are betrayed into looking forward to it," said Nance. "I wonder if we are cured this time."

"I wonder what it is like in other houses," said Grant.

"Father may be different at dinner," said Sibyl. "I remember he was last year."

"You are young for the bitterness of memory," said her sister.

Duncan came to the table, as Sibyl had foreseen, bent upon giving a convivial end to the day.

"Well, I am glad we were not brow-beaten. We deserve our Christmas feast. What would you say, my wife?"

Ellen was sitting in a trance, and recalling herself, looked apprehensively at her husband.

The latter dropped his eyes.

"Well, this is a noble turkey," he said, with another effort. "Have you all made up your minds which part is to be yours?"

"We ought to have asked someone to share it," said Ellen, with the random speech of exhaustion.

"You pretend to no feeling for your own family and your own home? Our friends have not asked us to share their dinner."

"I suppose the Burtenshaws are not having one," said Grant.

"Are we to have the pudding on fire?" said Sibyl.

"If you think it worth while for the family."

"I think it a sight to exhibit to the neighbourhood," said Grant. "I remain young at heart."

"I see we are to consider ourselves in relation to the neighbourhood," said Duncan, smiling at his wife.

Ellen raised her eyes, and sought a response in vain.

"We have brought these young people up to be too dependent on society," said Duncan in a sort of burst.

"I don't think they have very much. They so often see the same people."

"I beg you will not contradict my words. It is more uncouth than can be borne."

"We cannot always think alike."

"It would be odd if we did so."

"We are fortunate in our parents," said Nance. "It is best for the children that they should be different."

"And we may be fortunate in our children," said Duncan. "Have you all had a happy Christmas?"

"Yes, very happy, Father," said Sibyl.

"Yes, Father," said Nance.

"You do not sound sure of your mind, Nance."

"Well, perhaps it was a rather rash opinion, Father."

"Do you mean you have not enjoyed your day?" said Duncan, honestly incredulous.

"No, of course I don't, Father," said Nance, thinking better of the risk. "The day will live in my memory."

"Have you had a happy Christmas, Grant?"

"It has been a most terrific occasion, Uncle."

"And you, my wife?" said Duncan, smiling, and not waiting for the answer that went without saying, and might be annoyingly expressed.

CHAPTER III

"Why, have you forgotten something?" said Gretchen, as Beatrice again entered her house.

Beatrice placed her umbrella in the stand, with her eyes upon it.

"Yes, I have forgotten something," she said, resolutely lifting her head. "At least I have not forgotten; that is not true. I have left something undone; and I want you to let me make it good."

Gretchen did not speak.

"It is not true at all: I thought of it, and put it from me, which is even less to my credit. But I hope you will give me another chance."

Gretchen was still silent.

"It seems rather foolish to shake hands again so soon," said Beatrice, performing the ceremony, and illustrating her opinion of it. "I expect you think it strange to see me a second time, but I am sure you will forgive me, when you hear my reason."

She followed Gretchen with her step resolutely free, and her lips just moving in rehearsal of her words.

"I have come," she said, standing just inside the door, and glancing at her audience, which consisted of Gretchen and Cassie, "to bring you once again the simple message of Christmas. I daresay there seems no reason why I did not give it before——" Her voice rose and ran on more freely "——but you had friends with you; and although that was not a reason why I should be prevented, was indeed a reason why I should go on, I confess I was prevented. I feel we cannot give or receive the message too often."

"We have had enough of it in this house," said Gretchen.

"You may have had enough of giving it. And you are greatly privileged in being able to give it so often."

"Do you find it so much of a privilege?"

"But have you——" Beatrice held to her course, and brought her face nearer to Gretchen's— "have you had it fully yourself? Have you and yours——" She seemed to put her eyes on Cassie, without turning towards her "—fully received it?"

"Why should you think we have not received it as much as you?" said Gretchen.

Beatrice took a step backwards, her eyes on the latter's face.

"There are many reasons," said Cassie. "But Miss Fellowes can hardly state them."

"I feel you have done so much," went on Beatrice, with great gentleness, "and I have done so little; and I wished, before the day was over, to do my small part towards the whole."

"You have just got it into your day," said Gretchen, glancing at the clock. "Well, what is it, William?"

A boy appeared and delivered a message, and was about to withdraw.

"What have you forgotten?" asked Gretchen.

"Good-night, Mrs. Jekyll. Good-night, Miss Jekyll. Good-night, Miss Fellowes. Thank you for taking us to the service."

"The child has had the Christmas message, and knows it," said Gretchen.

"Thanks to Miss Fellowes," said Cassie. "We do leave such things to her. It is no wonder she has to reckon with it."

"Good-bye, Mrs. Jekyll," said Beatrice, rising and holding out her hand, in recognition that attention was no longer for herself. "Thank you very much for letting me see you. Good-bye, Miss Jekyll."

"You sound as if you were setting an example to William," said Cassie, escorting her to the hall.

"She made a poor thing of her business," said Gretchen. "And she looked as if she thought so."

"It must be hard to have a faith that would remove mountains, and then find it does not remove them."

"It did not remove anything."

"You and I must be classed as mountains, Mother."

Oscar came into the room.

"I met Miss Fellowes in the hall. Why did she come?"

"She forgot something," said his sister.

"To do her duty by us, or rather yours," said Gretchen.

"Much of my duty I am pleased enough for her to do."

"I don't know if you will be pleased by this. She came to bring us the message of Christmas."

"The simple message," said Cassie.

"And did you repudiate it?"

"We made it hard for her, Oscar, Mother, especially. Where she most naturally looked for bread, she was given a stone."

"Did you not offer her tea?"

"Mother was waiting for you, and continued to wait."

"If she is so engaged with spiritual things, she need not put people about over the material. Why should she attend to the higher needs of the place?"

"Well, no one else attends to them," said Oscar: "she must feel singled out."

"She would be the last to like it, if anyone did."

"People never like other people to do their work; I cannot understand it," said Cassie.

"Neither can I," said her brother.

Gretchen sat in pride and silence, listening to her son and daughter's talk.

Beatrice directed her steps to the house of the Bodes. The husband and wife were at tea, and their son and daughter had returned. Beatrice shook hands with the four.

"Well, we soon meet again; I hope you will not be tired of the sight and sound of me," she said to the young people. "I have come to ask you all to let me bring you again the message of Christmas——" She varied her words for the sake of her former hearers "—the simple message, which is the meaning of the day to us all."

"Ah, now that is nice of you, Miss Fellowes," said Mr. Bode, rising a second time and taking her hand. "That is a thing we can't hear too often. We are always the better for it."

"I made up my mind to do it," said Beatrice, looking at him with a sort of glow on her face; "to do it for all my friends. I asked myself if it were feasible; and then I think I just made up my mind——" She gave a little unsteady laugh "—to do it, whether it was or not. And now I am glad I have done it; though there have been one or two moments when my confidence has failed."

"Well, I think it is fine of you, Miss Fellowes," said Dulcia. "I thought so at the Edgeworths', and I think so now. I don't give a fig who hears me. I did not there, and I do not intend to be induced to."

"Ah, our girl knows what is what," said her father.

"It is nice to feel our young people have you amongst them, Miss Fellowes," said his wife.

"Well, I hope the young people do not regard me as a preaching busybody," said Beatrice, with a light and fortunate confidence on this point. "Well, if they do, they will just have to: I am not going to undertake to reform."

"I do not think so, Miss Fellowes," cried Dulcia. "At the risk of being told by you to swear not at all, I swear on my life it is not the case."

"And here is somebody else who does not think so," said Mrs. Bode, putting her arm in her son's, "though his masculine self-consciousness prevents our hearing his opinion."

Almeric drew away from his mother, the quality she referred to threatening to overwhelm him.

"Almeric, you want to get Miss Fellowes some tea," said Dulcia, in a voice of grave reprimand.

"I can't claim this is my first tea this afternoon," said Beatrice. "I am not going to make the attempt."

"You must need something, Miss Fellowes," said Mr. Bode with extreme concern.

"You must, Miss Fellowes," said Dulcia.

"Well, anyhow it is pleasant to have it," said Beatrice, slapping her gloves lightly on the table. "I am not going to take up the position of indifference to the good things of life. And tea is a stimulant, they say, and helps one about one's business. I have found it has to-day, though I ought not to need that kind of support. I confess it has helped the flesh to be less weak."

"Tea is a stimulant, they say," murmured Almeric.

"What did you say, dear?" said Mrs. Bode.

"Nothing, Mater."

"Well, I must even be going about my business. It is a pity we cannot be spirited from place to place. The time spent on the way seems to be time wasted. But we do not wish to be spirited, as it is not the arrangement for us."

"If you cannot spare us any longer, Miss Fellowes, we will not ask it," said Mr. Bode.

"Would you like Almeric to escort you anywhere, Miss Fellowes?" said Dulcia, bringing no words from her brother, as she deprived him of them.

Beatrice shook hands with Mr. and Mrs. Bode and turning to Dulcia, found her arms flung about her neck, and returned the embrace with deliberate affection.

"Good-bye, Almeric," she said, her tone holding only friendliness.

"Good-bye."

"Good-bye, good-bye, Miss Fellowes," said Mr. Bode, attending her to the hall, and returning to his family. "Ah, that was the kind of tea party for Christmas Day."

"Look at her, dear Miss Fellowes, going along in her dear, single-hearted way, and with her dear, single-minded look!" said Dulcia from the window.

"I do not need to look," said Almeric. "I can remember. I could not forget."

Beatrice proceeded to the small but chosen home of the Smolletts, and came upon this couple in their hall, about to go out to dinner.

"Why, how do you do, Miss Fellowes?" said Florence. "It is nice to have a Christmas call."

"Now, a very happy Christmas to you, Miss Beatrice, if it is not too late."

"I am glad you do not feel it is too late," said Beatrice, in a quiet tone that was naturally rather drained of energy. "I have been fearing you would. I have come to bring you again the message that Christmas gives. I hope you will let me offer it to you?"

"Thank you, Miss Beatrice, thank you," said Fabian, with his eyes on the horse, and a feeling of having supplied the initiative. "And indeed we return any message you so kindly bring."

"You can wish for us nothing we do not wish for you," said his wife in her hearty manner.

"Well, we will receive and accept the message together," said Beatrice, doing what she could with the position. "For I do not think the two things are quite the same, do you?"

"We will, Miss Beatrice; we do. We accept and receive it, thanks in every way to you. Yes, the good wishes of the season. And now may we keep you a little longer by driving you home? You will allow us? Thank you very much."

"It would be very kind. I confess my energy is flagging a little. But is it on your way?"

"Our way is yours, and yours ours, until we see you at home. And Miss Rosamund is well?"

"Yes, very well. She has been resting this afternoon. She did not feel there was anything to take her out."

"Ah, that is what you must do. Miss Rosamund chooses the better part. She does not think too much of other people."

"It is difficult not to do that," said Beatrice, with an uncertain smile, not disputing the suggestion. "They seem so much more important than oneself, somehow."

"You must not let them be. We are all equally important," said Florence. "That is quite far enough to go."

"Yes, yes; self first," said Fabian, lifting the rug. "Now let me move across to help you, Miss Beatrice."

"Good-bye, and take care of yourself," said Florence.

"Ah, a good girl," said her husband, readjusting the rug, and putting a cigar between his lips. "She would be different, married; but why bother about the difference?"

Beatrice rather soberly opened her gate, and walked up the path to her uncle's cottage. She found him smoking in his chair, and his daughter reading on the couch.

"A nice scene of rest and leisure," she said.

"I have finished my letters, and helped to set the supper, and sent the maid home," said Miss Burtenshaw, giving the background to the picture; "and am now feeling justified in having what she calls 'a good lay down'. Have you had a successful pilgrimage?"

"Yes, I hope so. Some of it was very satisfying. I think it had its measure of success. I did not find what I had set myself, quite easy to carry out; and less so in some houses than in others. But the hard moments were more than compensated for by the good ones. For those were very good. I must just try to forget the others. It is a small price to pay, that little bit of self-control."

"Who were the successes and who the unsuccesses?"

"Well, I do not think I will say that. Perhaps it would not be quite fair. And of course the unsuccesses were my own failures: that must not be forgotten."

"Yes, well, that is so in a way, isn't it?" said Alexander.

"We can work together better for people, if we give each other full confidence," said Miss Burtenshaw, her colour proving a power of variability.

"I did not feel I was withholding anything that could

be of use to you. If that is so, I will tell you, of course. I think the friends whom I failed to help, were Mrs. Jekyll; and perhaps Dr. and Mrs. Smollett, who brought me home."

"That was heaping coals of fire upon your head," said her cousin in her normal manner.

"And I think those who found my message helpful, were the Bodes; with the exception perhaps of dear Almeric. It has struck me that Dulcia is of those who would go far at our side."

"Dear child, we will spare her some work indeed," said Miss Burtenshaw, putting the matter as she saw it.

"Of course it was not my message: I should have said the message I felt myself entrusted with," said Beatrice, in a light parenthesis.

"How did things go at the Edgeworths'?" asked her uncle.

"Well, that is a good word," said Beatrice, including her cousin in her smile. "Things 'went'; but I cannot say in what direction, because I do not know. It was with dear Mrs. Jekyll"—she spoke with the permissible humour— "that things did not go at all. I confess they remained at a standstill; that my little effort—well, great effort it was for me, or at any rate considerable—was wasted; if we are right in using the word of honest effort in a sphere of which we understand little."

"Oh, we are not right," said Alexander, who accepted the influence of the house, rather than the effort of resisting it. "The bread was cast upon the waters, to return after many days."

"I am not always sure that the rector has full sympathy in his home life," said Miss Burtenshaw, not feeling this to be the case elsewhere.

"I daresay he has not, my dear. A woman like you would be the thing for him," said her father in a tone of agreement.

"Well, perhaps that is hardly for outsiders like us to

49

say," said Beatrice, as deaf to Alexander's words as her cousin, though they were spoken rather loud.

"I think it was quite a permissible speech."

"I am sure it was, if you felt it to be. I should have spoken for myself, I retract what I said, as regards you."

"Don't bicker, girls," said Alexander.

"I am sure I have heard you say the same thing, Beatrice."

"In that case, I am afraid I must have said what I did not feel to be within my province."

"I am afraid you must. But I don't know why we are having a disagreement over a trifle, on Christmas Day."

"Neither do I," said Beatrice, whose regard for truth could not lead her to explain that she disliked to connect her cousin with Oscar, as much on Christmas Day as on any other. Indeed this regard left her inner life as much concealed as other people's.

CHAPTER IV

"Are we not to have breakfast this morning?" said Duncan.

"What did you say, Uncle?"

"No breakfast, did you say, Father?"

Duncan put his hands beneath his coat and his legs apart, and looked down at his feet.

"I expect Mother will be down soon," said Sibyl, summing up the position before she thought.

"Your mother's punctuality is a disadvantage rather than otherwise," said her father in an almost amused tone, "if we are to be led to depend upon it, and then played false."

"Played false after twenty years," said Nance. "It is a grievance we cannot be armed against."

"Consistent unpunctuality is the thing to aim at, as no one can be punctual," said Duncan in a muffled voice.

"Mother was not well last night, Father. She may not be coming down."

"Wasn't she?" said Grant and Sibyl.

"No, not at all," said Nance, looking at her father. "Cassie and I sat with her until she was asleep."

Duncan swayed slightly to and fro, his hands wavering about his pockets.

"Father, I wish you would answer me."

"Did you ask me anything?"

"People generally make a comment, when they hear someone is ill."

"Well, I will comment in the usual way," said Duncan, almost pleasantly. "How is your mother this morning?"

"I have not heard; I do not know, Father. I have only just remembered she is not well."

Duncan fixed his eyes on his daughter, his brows slowly rising.

"I will go and see how she is, Father."

Duncan turned his head slowly after her, his brows remaining at their angle.

"Shall I go for you, Nance?" said Grant.

"It is Nance's anxiety," said his uncle, his voice seeming to follow the movement of his brows. "It is in her imagination that the trouble lies. You may tell your mother, Nance, that we are waiting for her."

"I shall not couch the inquiry in those terms, Father."

"You saw my wife last night, Miss Jekyll?" said Duncan, in a tone of easy continuation. "Nothing amiss, is there?"

"There is something amiss, but I do not know how much."

"Well, nothing; or you would know," said Duncan, his voice settling on to a comfortable note.

There was silence.

"People little know the inconvenience this sort of casualness causes," said Duncan, glancing at the clock.

"They may be preoccupied with other things," said Cassie.

"Perhaps Mother is not well enough to come down," said Sibyl.

"Not well enough to come down! When the people— the daughters who knew she was not well, did not trouble to inquire after her!"

"She may want a tray taken up," said Grant.

"She certainly would have wanted one, if it had been as Nance said."

"Why should Nance want to prove that Aunt Ellen is ill?"

Duncan just raised his brows and threw out his hands.

"It could not be of any advantage to her."

"It would make us all seem as if we were heartless, or selfish or something, I suppose. Though even on that basis, she had not decided much about it." Duncan gave a little laugh, as though he could not help it.

Nance returned to the room.

"Mother does not feel any better. She thinks she will stay in bed."

"She is not sure?" said Duncan.

"Yes, she is sure, Father. I might have put it differently."

Duncan glanced at her, and walked to the door.

"Ellen! Ellen! When are you coming down? Do you realise we are waiting? I don't seem to be able to get a message through."

"It is Mother who failed to do that. Father would only have to walk up one flight of stairs."

"What did you say, Nance?" said Duncan, looking back.

Nance repeated her words, and caused her father simply to resume his position.

"Is Aunt Ellen really ill?" said Grant.

"She looks unlike herself, and says she cannot eat.'

"We had better observe the futility of taking up a tra,

"I will get it ready," said Sibyl, going to the sideboard.

Duncan returned to the room.

"She will be down in a few minutes," he said in a careless tone.

"Father, is she fit to? Did you over-persuade her?"

"You are not even yet sure of your opinion of her fitness."

"Did you over-persuade her, Father?"

"That is the safe part of the question. I did not persuade her at all. I do not persuade pople. I called out to her, and inquired when she was coming down; and she answered, 'In a few minutes.' "

"I hope she is equal to it."

"You are not convinced that she is not?" said Duncan, looking at Nance in a rather quizzical manner. "It shows how little meaning your words have."

"I wish her words were allowed to have some meaning, Father."

"I wish they were," said Duncan, turning to Sibyl. "My good child, I beg you will cease to fidget with that tray. You heard your mother said she was coming down. You might have lost your senses."

Ellen entered the room, and walked to her seat, seeming to focus all her attention upon reaching it, and leaving the door open behind her.

"Mother, are you ill?" said Sibyl, as Grant went to shut the door.

"You cannot attain to conviction about that, can you?" said Duncan, not turning his eyes to his wife.

"I was getting ready a tray for you, Mother."

"You were," said Duncan, repressing a laugh. "And you are right to say so. It would not occur to your mother as likely, when you knew it would not be needed." He glanced up under his brows at Ellen.

Ellen looked at the tray, as if it would have met her need, and seemed about to speak, but did not do so.

"Well, now the truant is here, we may get along," said Duncan. "People who don't want any breakfast, generally want a good one, in my experience. It seems to be a symptom of their state."

Ellen looked at her husband, and in an unfamiliar way, as though it were a normal thing, sank into tears.

Duncan plied his knife and fork, keeping his eyes down. Sibyl got up and put her arms round her mother, who made an almost fierce movement to be free.

Duncan changed his plate, thinking better of his choice of food.

"What time will you be ready to start to church, my wife?" he said, the easy term of affection placing the occasion.

Ellen gave him a glance, and fought with her tears.

"She is going to bed, of course, Father," said Nance. "She is ready to go now."

"Then why does she not go?" said Duncan, helping himself.

"Because you make it impossible, Father."

Duncan flung out his hands, and rising in such a way as to give the table a shock, strode towards the door.

"Father, you have upset the coffee!" said Sibyl.

Duncan made a sign to Bethia, without a glance at the table, and went on his way.

"Every Sunday breakfast seems the worst," said Nance. "But I imagine we have attained the climax now."

"I am so silly; I wish I were not such a fool," wept Ellen, using a term strange on her lips.

"Sibyl, tell someone to see to Mother's room."

"Mother likes to have me with her. Someone else can go."

Ellen took a hand of each of her daughters, and spoke and wept at the same time.

"I can't help what Father says: I must stay at home to-day. People must sometimes be ill. I have been ill less often than I ought in my life, because Father hated illness. I must sometimes be like other people. This house has to be so different from other houses; and lately I have felt it is too much for me, all this difference."

Cassie signed to Grant to carry the message, and Ellen was taken to bed. It was settled that Grant and Sibyl should go to church, and Nance remain with her mother. Cassie was, as usual, to join her family. The question of consulting Duncan did not present itself as possible.

Duncan appeared in the hall at the customary hour. He perceived his companions, and guessed how matters lay; and taking his hat, walked from the house, so suddenly that he left them behind. They hastened to catch up with him, and presently he paused and looked back.

"Nance is not coming to church, Father. She is staying with Mother."

Duncan remained as he was, his eyes straining towards some object not imagined by his companions.

"You felt you could leave your mother, did you?" he said, as he turned to proceed.

55

Sibyl was at a loss for an answer.

"It is a mistake to have too many people about," said Grant. "Nance is to send for the doctor, if she feels there is any need."

"What doctor?" said his uncle, after a pause.

"Smollett, of course, Uncle. What other doctor is there?"

"Why, many others, I have believed. Smollett is not the one I should choose, if I saw reason for uneasiness."

"Which one would you choose?"

Duncan hummed to himself.

"The information would be of no good to you," he said in a moment, as if the answer were an afterthought.

"We have never had any other doctor, Father."

"We have never had this show of anxiety. If there is any ground for it, Smollett is not the man. But if it is merely a show, as you seem to agree, it is well enough."

There was silence.

"Oh, you must have a show about something sometimes," said Duncan, with tolerant resignation. "Your life is too smooth and easy to be possible."

"Smollett is a clever man," said Grant. "I never know why he stays in the country."

"You won't get out of it in that way, Grant. If he were good beyond a point, he would not be in the country."

"What did you think of Aunt Ellen yourself, Uncle?"

"I thought," said Duncan, after a just perceptible pause, "that she would be better about amongst us all, under observation; so that, if there seemed any reason, we could send for a proper man."

"We could not do much observation in church. And Smollett is probably as good at it as we are. And this plan has the advantage of allowing the patient to keep her bed."

"Oh, no, he is not, Grant," said Duncan, glancing with interest at a tombstone, as he passed, and lowering his voice in the door of the church. "No one can observe anyone, as well as her own family. That is why I was surprised that you and Sibyl came to church, feeling as you did."

He proceeded to his pew, protected from Grant's reply, and put the matter aside to concentrate on other things. When a messenger came, and Fabian left the church, he simply signed to his companions to keep their seats. In due course he led them to their friends, without comment upon the occurrence.

"Why, what is wrong with Ellen, Duncan?" said Florence at once. "Was she ill when you came out? She has looked very thin lately."

"These Christian names!" said Dulcia, falling against Beatrice. "They send a thrill down my spine."

"She was not quite herself," said Duncan. "Nance was to send a message, if she needed help. We must go home, and let Sibyl relieve her."

"Ah, it is nice to be wanted," said Mr. Bode.

"So you all felt you could come to church?" said Gretchen.

"No, not all," said Duncan. "We felt one of us should remain."

"I am sure Mrs. Edgeworth has everything that could be conceived of," said Dulcia, in her clear tones. "We shall only have to ask Dr. Smollett that."

"I will come in and see her this afternoon," said Florence.

"So will I," said Mrs. Bode. "I hope there will be something I can do."

"Well, Mother dear, I hope not," said Dulcia. "If there is nothing, it will show there is nothing wrong."

"Ah, that is what my wife would like," said Mr. Bode. "To do something for somebody. That is what would suit her."

"Well, I hope there is not much amiss," said Duncan; "or the gathering will be out of place. I am glad you none of you feel there is. I think the general feeling is a good touchstone."

"What a very odd opinion!" said Grant.

"I am not so sure I feel it," said Gretchen to Cassie. "Doctors are not fetched out of church for nothing."

"If they were good for much more, they would not be in church," said Almeric.

"But I repudiate your alarmist theories, Mrs. Jekyll," said Dulcia. "It is borne in upon me, that nothing much is the matter: I feel I could almost guarantee it. We should not be standing about here, if there were. I feel we should somehow be prevented." She laughed.

"We need not say that our time is yours," said Beatrice, stepping up to Cassie. "It goes without saying."

"It does not do that. But I will remember it."

"Thank you very much," said Beatrice, simply.

"I leave things that go without saying, to do their own business," said her cousin. "Or they might be the other kind of things."

"I suggest we should go home," said Duncan to Grant and Sibyl. "There is little sense in standing about gossiping, and adopting this pose of being anxious."

"I am sure there has been no hint of gossip, Mr. Edgeworth, or pose either," said Dulcia. "I have been listening to them, and I bear witness to it. Any appearance of anxiety has been absolutely genuine."

Duncan walked on as if he had not heard, but atoned to his companions by causing for their sakes an amused twitch to play about his lips.

Fabian met them in their hall with the suavity of his kind, under conditions that would indicate another manner.

"Ah, it is nice to see you all together. It is what we have been wanting. Yes, and Miss Cassie is with you. That is what is wanted too. So we will all go up to Nance. I have sent for a nurse to be of some help to her. I knew it was what you would wish."

"Have you seen my wife?" said Duncan, passing over this summary of gratified desires.

"I have been with her since I left the church. It was

wise of Nance to send for me. She has been wise and good."

"Is there anything much wrong?"

"Well, perhaps we should not say it is wrong. Nature will have her way with us."

"Is anything serious the matter?"

"Well, we use words like 'serious'. But words do not make much difference, do they?"

"They convey ideas of things. Tell us the truth," said Grant, incurring a look from his uncle for overreaching his place.

"Dr. Smollett is doing so, Grant."

"Ah, the wisest of us cannot always do that," said Fabian, sighingly speaking as one of these.

"Can you tell us what you fear the mischief is?"

"What is sometimes the mischief with us, and the mischief for a long while. But it made no difference until to-day, or until quite lately; we can think that. Yes, you will like to see her; and you need not feel it will do harm."

The family followed him to Ellen's bed, sensing the warning in the words. Nance was sitting by her mother, and the nurse was in the room, her presence striking its own note of warning. Fabian muttered to Grant, under cover of giving place to Duncan and the girls.

"A deep mischief has gone on for a long time. It seems to do its work at the end. It is months since I spoke to your uncle of her looks. There is little more for it to do."

Duncan turned his head, and Fabian came forward.

"Now, here they have all come to see you," he said, as if this fact had importance. "Yes, that is what they wanted, when they entered the house. Some of us are thought about more than other people."

Ellen was lying on her back, seeming to be sunk into the bed, with a look of having lain for a long while. Her face seemed suddenly thin and small, and her family knew they had missed a gradual change. She hardly moved her head, but turned her eyes.

"It is lazy of me to be lying here. I don't know when

I have lain in bed. It seems so easy to get used to it."

"We are all lazy," said Duncan. "Lying here does not make any difference. We are none of us going to do anything useful to-day."

"Mother dearest, do you feel ill?" said Sibyl.

"I don't feel really ill, not really," said Ellen, her voice at once perplexed and aware. "You need not stay here. You must be going down to luncheon. Bethia is going out this afternoon."

The everyday words threw up what was strange in her voice.

"You will have luncheon with us, Smollett?" said Duncan, not looking at the face on the pillow.

"If I may send a message to my wife, I shall like to be with you all." It was somehow clear that Florence would not come that day.

Duncan led the way from the room, throwing over his shoulder a glance of summons. Ellen's eyes followed him, and Sibyl noticed her look.

"Say good-bye to Mother, Father."

Duncan gave an absent nod towards the bed, as if he hardly heard, and Ellen relapsed as though meeting what was natural.

At the table Duncan talked in his usual way, forcing Grant to take his part, and appearing unaware of his daughters' silence. Afterwards he went as usual to the library, with no sign of knowing that he went alone.

"Oh, yes," he said, pausing and looking up the staircase, "come and bring me the news. We had better have it before we smoke." He closed the door without waiting to be answered, helpless in the grip of the morning's mood.

The day wore on and the cloud grew, and at last overwhelmed the house. Ellen was still and quiet, and was thought to show no change, but her first unconsciousness seemed an expected thing. She spoke at times, with a hint of awe at her state, as though the strangeness of the experience showed it to her from outside. She was pleased that the girls and Grant should come to her door, and when she no longer turned her head, would ask with closed eyes which of them it was. Duncan came at longer intervals, and returned alone to the library. At dinner, where Fabian was again present, his aloofness had taken the guise of individual anxiety.

"Do you give us hope, Smollett?"

"While there is life there is hope. And there is life still."

"Be silent," said Duncan, to the weeping Sibyl. "Do you mistake this for a time to think of yourself? Bethia, return to the room, when you are fit for your duty."

The family went to bed at night, avoiding the effort of urging each other to rest. The sisters came often in the night to Ellen's room. Duncan slept through the hours like a dead man: he had spent himself the most. Fabian and the nurse and Cassie rested and watched by turns. No mention had been made of another opinion; it was only not said in words that the time was too short.

The next day Fabian admitted a cloud over his urbanity and ease; Duncan presented an impregnable front; Nance and Grant were haggard and silent; and Sibyl was openly tear-stained and dishevelled. Duncan looked at her and did not speak: it was a small thing this morning.

The day went on, silent, swift, at a standstill, without time. The midday meal was one which was never remembered. At some time in the afternoon came Ellen's last lucid hour, and her family found themselves at her deathbed.

She turned with a smile, and a gesture towards the nurse, suggestive of some characteristic comment upon her. Her daughters made a silent response, and she closed her eyes, content to have done what was in her mind.

In a minute she opened them with a worried, almost guilty air.

"There are one or two things not paid," she said, her hurried, stumbling voice her own but for its weakness.

"There is a list in my own desk." The thought shot

through them that it would not long be this. "There are more than one or two, I think."

"That is my business," said her husband. "It has nothing to do with you."

Ellen relapsed with a smile of relief, that showed in its simplicity how she had looked as a child.

Then she turned her eyes from one to another, seeming to have just seen them.

"Stay for a little while," she said, as though she had been dull alone, and closed her eyes.

There was silence until she opened them and looked at nothing, and Sibyl bent over her.

"Mother, you know how I have always loved you?"

Duncan pushed his daughter aside, and took her place

"Loved me?" said Ellen, looking about in a bewildered way, as if she heard from a distance. "I know that Nance has loved me. I like people to show those things, myself."

There was silence, while Sibyl approached again, and Nance drew aside, as though agreeing she had had enough.

Ellen seemed to feel her husband's eyes, and met them.

"Illness is always a trouble, isn't it? Some people are always ill. Of course they can't help it, but that does not make it better."

"It is a trouble to those who are ill," said Duncan, taking her hand.

"I want to say good-night to Cassie," said Ellen, in an almost petulant tone. "I don't know what I should do without Cassie. She and Grant make things so much better for us, don't they?"

"Good-night, Ellen," said Cassie, stooping over the bed.

"Good-night," said Ellen, in a satisfied, almost social tone, and was silent.

Fabian took his hand from her wrist, and turned to face her family.

"She had her last wish. You can feel that," he said, welcoming the place of this desire of Ellen's which he knew to have been gratified. "You have been beyond praise; you have made your father proud, when you wanted to do something for him. Grant, we will leave them to you and Miss Cassie. You are both of you people who can do so much. Edgeworth, you will stay with me for a while?"

Duncan complied, something about him forbidding concern or condolence. He thanked Fabian for what he had done, and spoke some conventional words of his wife. Then he took his leave, and went to the library and closed the door.

An incident broke across the hour, and shaped its memories. Bethia came to say that Miss Fellowes had called, and begged to see a member of the family. Cassie found Beatrice and Dulcia waiting on their feet, as if they would not serve their own comfort in the conditions of the house.

"How is Mrs. Edgeworth?" said Beatrice, stepping gravely forward.

"She died a little while ago."

"I feared that might be so, when I saw the blinds drawn down. But I was so loth to give up a purpose I had come to for her," said Beatrice, firmer than usual in the face of obstacles. "May I perhaps leave my message for someone else in the house?"

"If it will do for anyone, perhaps you will give it to me."

Beatrice met Cassie's eyes in silence.

"I am simply the adjutant, Miss Jekyll," said Dulcia, as though Cassie's attention would by now be upon herself: "I am not the originator of the scheme."

"I was grateful for the support," said Beatrice. "I am so poor-spirited over the things that ought to make me the opposite. I do not make any bones about it."

"I hope it does not need so much spirit to leave a message here."

"Ah, now, Miss Jekyll, if you think that," said Dulcia, "you quite mistake the force of your personality."

"May the message be given to someone who would

63

receive it?" said Beatrice, passing lightly over her implication that this would hardly be Cassie. "To Mr. Edgeworth perhaps, as he is in need."

"Shall I give it to him for you?"

"Thank you very much," said Beatrice, in a revealingly grateful tone. "I ought not to let my work devolve upon you. But we neither of us want to be thanked, do we? It all has too little to do with us. I know I felt just compelled to it."

"That is what I feel," said Cassie.

"It is kind of you to see us, Miss Jekyll. We could not expect it of the family, and we know you feel it as they do," said Dulcia, doing justice to Cassie's kindness.

"Mrs. Edgeworth was a great friend of mine."

"We know she was, Miss Jekyll; that it was a real, genuine, equal friendship."

"Why speak of it in the past tense?" said Beatrice.

"If anyone knows it was well with her at the end, it is you, Miss Jekyll."

"She had nothing to repent of," said Cassie.

"I think we all have that," said Beatrice, with a kind of charged brightness.

"Not Mrs. Edgeworth,"

"I am sure I feel I have," said Beatrice, as though this indicated it in a general sense.

"And I," said Dulcia; "things without number."

"People are so different," said Cassie.

Dulcia took Cassie's hands and pushed them backwards, with a roguishly comprehending expression.

"May I write a note to Mr. Edgeworth?" said Beatrice suddenly.

Cassie opened a writing table.

"Confess, now, Miss Jekyll. You would like to put a pistol at our heads," said Dulcia, as her friend made deliberate preparations.

"I cannot stay with you much longer, if that is what you mean."

Dulcia looked slightly taken aback, though it was hardly an exaggerated treatment of her words.

Beatrice rose, and coming to Cassie, put a fastened letter into her hands.

"You will give it to Mr. Edgeworth? Thank you very much indeed."

"Now here is Miss Jekyll, grieved and worn and needed by other people!" said Dulcia. "And here are we, preventing her from attending to herself and to them! So if she will promise to do the first as well as the last, we will not ask another word."

"I promise," said Cassie.

"Anything to get rid of us?" said Dulcia, catching Beatrice's hand. "Now, farewell, Miss Jekyll, and in the literal sense. You have lost a friend, an intimate—we give you that fully—but the world is not dark, because of one spot. Come along, Miss Fellowes; we hold to our side of the bargain."

Beatrice followed, turning to smile at Cassie, as if she would not leave her without a sign.

Cassie was going upstairs with the note, when she met Fabian.

"Miss Fellowes wrote this for Mr. Edgeworth. She came with a message for Ellen, and found it too late."

Fabian took the note and tore it across.

"Oh, yes, Miss Cassie. Yes, you gave it to me to give to him, and I forgot. No one will be referring to it. Miss Beatrice has left it to us."

The family gathered at the evening meal, meeting no reason for breaking the routine. Fabian's absence reduced their life at once to the level of the future.

"Do you want to come to dinner, or not, Sibyl?" said Duncan.

"I don't mind, Father," said his daughter, looking at him through tears.

Duncan sat down without further sign, except that he suddenly motioned Nance to her mother's place.

"Well, we have lost one very dear to us all," he said, as though summing up the matter before putting it aside. "She will always be the dearest of my memories. We cannot look for life to be the same."

The meal shadowed forth the numberless meals of the future without Ellen. Duncan's voice seemed unfamiliar, and his figure was unreal as he left them.

"You are coming, Grant?"

"No. Uncle; I will stay with the girls to-night."

Duncan went into his room and closed the door.

"Cassie, will it always be like this?" said Sibyl.

"No, This is a day by itself. I suppose not even your father would see it as typical."

"Is Father all right alone?"

"Not if appearances are deceitful," said Nance. "But we do not consider remedying his condition."

"It is all very well for you, Nance, after what she said. There is no need for you to wish you had been different."

"No other success in your life will count," said Grant. "You may from this day cease from effort."

"If you don't like sitting in Mother's place," said Sibyl, "we can all sit nearer together, and leave it empty."

"Its emptiness would hardly be a solution."

"It would be better for us, than seeing someone else in it."

"It would be worse than seeing Nance in it," said Cassie. "Father settled the question, and on the whole opinion is with him."

"I find I am not capable of real sorrow," said Grant. "Aunt Ellen's life was not more to me than my own. And my own kind of sorrow is very uncongenial."

"I wish I could joke," said Sibyl. "Cassie, shall I always feel I was not good enough to Mother?"

"No, not always. Not very much longer."

"Are the ennobling effects of sorrow temporary?" said Nance. "I admit I have not felt them. I have only been surprised and sorry not to see them in Father."

66

"It would be a great thing for us, for Uncle to be ennobled. It will be too bad, if he is not a changed man. Surely he will not allow Aunt Ellen to have died in vain."

They went from one thing to another, reckless, confused, hysterical; and hardly noticed when someone opened the door.

"It would be well not to make so much noise," said Duncan. "If you wish it for yourselves, you can hardly do so for the servants. I chose not to employ one of them on the message."

"Cassie, shall we ever live down this shame?" said Nance.

"What does it matter what we live down, when Mother is dead?" said Sibyl, rushing to the door. "I can't stay with you; I am going down to Father."

She broke into the library, where Duncan was by himself.

"Father, you and I must grieve for Mother alone. No one else seems to miss her. We must feel she has left us to each other."

Duncan looked up and around, as though a wave were breaking over him.

"We will not wear our hearts on our sleeves," he said.

CHAPTER V

THE NEXT DAY Duncan showed his usual demeanour, or, if his family had been in a state to observe him, a strained and exaggerated form of it; compelled his nephew to normal intercourse; and continued to discountenance signs of grief. If anyone failed to appear at a meal, he seemed to see nothing. It was as if he could not free himself from a spell.

"Nance, either leave the table, or remain at it. Feelings so indefinite that you cannot decide on them, need not be shown."

"I am getting a tray for Sibyl, Father. She feels she cannot come down."

A violent spasm crossed Duncan's face at sight of the tray.

"Put that thing down, and come to the table," he said, and continued to eat.

He sat in silence at the following meals, the occasions on which he met his family. It was known he had arranged for his wife's burial, though he had said no word. At dinner on the third day after Ellen's death, he spoke in a changed, almost cheerful manner.

"It is a good thing your mother did not have to keep up and about on that last Sunday. It might all have been much worse, both in itself and for us to look back on."

"Keep up and about?" said Nance.

"Yes, keep up and about, Nance. What did you think I said?"

"That could hardly happen in a civilised household, Father."

"Oh, yes, Nance, it could. Little you know what besets the sick member of many households, almost of most. Harassment, questioning, exaggerated concern, anything and everything that can keep the sick one from the peace she craves, and which is her chance of life! You have no conception of the pressure and the strain. I thought I saw it all coming in this case; but I think I contrived it should be averted: I think and believe I did. We may feel that the end had to come."

"I should not have thought too much of that sort of thing would do so much harm," said Nance, who had passed from the numb of shock to active grief. "Less indeed than too little."

Duncan drew himself together with a violent movement, almost glaring at his daughter, and rose and left the room.

He returned, appearing in the last stage of a spasm of coughing, and continued to speak under its cover.

"Yes, your mother had as little cause for suffering in her life and her death, as is possible for a human being. We have that to think of."

"Not more cause than had to be, for deep suffering, perhaps."

"Well, all suffering is deep," said Duncan, with a note of contempt. "Suffering that is not deep, should not bear the name. I was not speaking of a hitch in the housekeeping, or a spar at the breakfast table."

"I am sure you were not speaking of the last," said Nance, who was struggling in the inevitable, bitter survey of her mother's life. "You hardly could have been. Though things of that kind are sometimes said to be the worst."

"The worst? My dear Nance, you can suggest that, at this moment of your life?"

Nance made no reply.

"You took that message I gave you, Grant?"

"Yes, Uncle. They say the expense is very unusual."

"Is it a usual case, or a usual person?"

"Indeed, no, Uncle: I will take the answer this afternoon."

"Is it something for Mother, Father?" said Sibyl in a soft tone.

"It is the last thing for her. It shall be done as well as the other things. As it has been, so it shall be. Thus it was in her life, and in her death it shall not be different. Do you not all feel with me? Do not you, Nance?"

"I don't feel strongly about it, Father, as long as it is all done suitably. It can make no difference to Mother now."

"Did it make a difference to her, when she had the best room in the house, the first place at church, the seat at the head of the table?" Duncan spoke with a vibration in his tones. "All the other things that were accorded her as her due? We who knew her, know that they made no difference, that she had a carelessness of such things. But it was fitting she should have them; and it is fitting now."

"I would rather she had had the money to spend on herself or on the house," said Nance, breaking into tears. "She was also so short of money; we had always to see her troubled for the want of it."

"What did you say, Nance?" said Duncan, in a shaking, incredulous tone.

"I wish she had had the money, to spend on herself or the house."

"On the house! That is to say, on yourself!" said Duncan, rising from the table. "I do not wish for any more dinner, and you need not prepare a tray for me. I neither desire nor recommend that remedy."

Nance continued as the door closed.

"So Mother's advantages begin, and we rejoice with her over them! I hope she will find it all worth while, that her fortunes after death will make up for those in her life."

Cassie got up and came to her.

"Be quiet, Nance! You know your father will hear."

"Yes, be quiet, Nance," said Duncan, looking through the door, and using a voice of calm support of Cassie. "It does not signify who hears: no doubt you wish to be heard. But I must remind you that your mother is still lying in the house."

There was silence after he had gone.

"Had you better go to him, Cassie?" said Sibyl. "He is in such a strange mood."

"He may be better with someone not too near to him."

"Trouble is said to draw families closer," said Nance. "It seems to fail in its purpose. I don't really see any good in trouble at all."

"You are soon yourself again, Nance."

"The voice of someone too near to me!"

"Trouble is also said to break down family reserve," said Grant. "Let us be on our guard, lest it really does that."

"Well, Cassie, go to Father," said Nance.

"Yes, Miss Cassie. You will have a talk with Mr. Edgeworth. He will be better for it," said Grant, in Fabian's manner. "You will go and have a word with him."

Cassie went to the library.

"The girls are concerned that you have eaten so little, Mr. Edgeworth."

"The girls! What do I want with the worrying of girls? It is not what I have been used to: I have been used to something different. How should children know their father?"

"They cannot know you as your wife did, of course."

"She knew me, Miss Jekyll; she knew my ways?" said Duncan, with sharp and simple eagerness. "You knew it from living with us? You had sense as well as eyes and ears. People need not reach each other in one way?"

"Indeed they need not," said Cassie. "We all know that."

"What does it matter what you know? What can people know of what is hidden from them? Why should they know?" Duncan put his arms on his desk, and Cassie, as she left him, saw him fling himself forward over them.

The days went by until the funeral, seeming one day, seeming an endless stretch of days. Duncan sat alone, speaking to no one, barely replying when addressed. His concern was with the preparations for the burial, and none knew these but himself.

He appeared at the board for his family and friends, composed, courteous, conventionally clad, and gave himself to his part. He listened in a controlled manner to Oscar's address, stirring not a muscle, when his daughters were moved to tears; stood at the grave as a figure of stone; and left the churchyard as he had entered it, aloof amongst his kindred, silent, as if he were alone.

The mourners drifted together, as though unaware what they did.

"Do we get our entertainment out of it all?" said Gretchen.

"I think we have got something out of it, Mrs. Jekyll," said Dulcia. "Not entertainment, of course; we take that as it was meant; but the spectacle of honest grief, controlled from regard for dignity and the feelings of others, has given us a lesson. I stand confessed as at once inspired and subdued."

"The confession is useful," said her brother. "We had no clue to your feelings."

"We have none to yours either, old boy," said Dulcia, slapping his arm. "I am not going to have people think you what you seem."

"You were wise not to bring your little lads, Mrs. Jekyll," said Mr. Bode.

"I should never take a child to a funeral," said Beatrice, looking round.

"They have done nothing to cause it," said Gretchen. "Why should they suffer it?"

"I always say Mrs. Jekyll is a real child-lover at heart," said Dulcia.

"It has been so terrible to be able to do nothing: I have felt so helpless," said Mrs. Bode, in some consternation at having been unable to prevent Ellen's death.

"I am sure Mr. Edgeworth is shaken to his depths," said Dulcia. "I suspect a great deal beneath that stony exterior."

"We owe you our thanks, Jekyll," said Mr. Bode, "for

doing what had to be done, as we should have chosen."

"We are not ungrateful," said Miss Burtenshaw, in a terse manner.

"Thank you, indeed, Rector," said Dulcia. "Most of all for those who have gone on before."

"It was a beautiful address: I enjoyed, appreciated it very much," said Mrs. Bode, defining her exact feelings.

"Beautiful is hardly the word, Mother. Strong, characteristic, subtle," said Dulcia. "Forceful, if you must."

"No, Mrs. Bode must not," muttered Fabian.

"There are evidently words," said Almeric.

"I am sure the family appreciated it," said Beatrice. "Of course they could not give any outward sign."

"They could hardly desire it should have to take place," said Oscar to his mother. "I did not look for them to applaud."

"We saw Miss Jekyll going away in the heart of the family, Mrs. Jekyll," said Dulcia. "And while grieving for her, we did justice to her inside place."

"There will be a great blank in our midst," said Mrs. Bode.

"Yes, Mother dear, but that goes without saying."

"And like many things that go without saying," said Florence, "may truly be said."

"That is so, Mrs. Smollett: I feel duly snubbed."

"Mrs. Smollett will miss Mrs. Edgeworth indeed," said Beatrice. "I feel for her so much. I think a woman's friendship is one of the deepest and most dignified of human relationships."

"Deepest? Yes," said her cousin. "It is perhaps not accorded its dignity."

"It has been so terribly sudden," said Mrs. Bode.

"We do not foresee even the immediate future," said her son.

"Now, mother and son, don't quarrel," said Dulcia. "It is a bad habit, which I observe to be growing on you."

"Little birds in their nests agree," said Beatrice.

73

"Terms are so easily misapplied," said Miss Burtenshaw. "But how the term, 'beautiful character', gives Mrs. Edgeworth!"

"Ah, that is what we have all thought," said Mr. Bode.

"Then, Father dear, I wish you had said it oftener, in justice to her," said Dulcia. "We should say these things when we think them, in all fairness."

"Did Mrs. Edgeworth feel she was near her end, the end of life, of this life?" said Beatrice to Fabian.

"She may have felt it, Miss Beatrice. But the feeling would be weak, with the weakening of everything."

"Dr. Smollett," said Dulcia, "we have thanked the rector for what he has done, thanked him in all sincerity. And no one has made any movement of thanking you, a condition which I would remedy. We are grateful from our hearts for what you have done, tried to do"—Dulcia was hampered by the climax of Ellen's illness—"for doing all for Mrs. Edgeworth that was humanly possible."

"It makes little difference which of the three it was," said Florence. "Have we not stood about long enough?"

"Standing about is not quite the phrase," said Beatrice, turning to her friends. "It has been a little more than that."

"It has been that, too," said Dulcia. "Let us not evade what is."

"It is Mr. Edgeworth who is in my mind," said Beatrice, seeming loth to leave the group. "And we can do nothing, or so very little."

"It is odd we cannot alter it for him," said Almeric.

"You did what you could, Miss Fellowes. You plucked up your courage, and faced the music," said Dulcia. "That was not square dealing."

"We have nothing more to get out of it," said Gretchen. "I don't know why we make all this of a funeral. We are all sure to have one. Mine is too near for me to fuss about someone else's. I hope you will enjoy it as much as this."

"Mrs. Jekyll, I can't keep a straight face in your

proximity," said Dulcia, suppressing evidence of this in view of the occasion.

"There do not seem to be as many funerals as there must be," said Oscar, following his mother.

"Miss Fellowes!" cried Dulcia, bounding after Beatrice; "I am going to do it. I have screwed my courage to the pitch. Turn and rend me if you must; I am going to take the plunge. May I call you by your Christian name? There, it is out!"

"I should like it very much," said Beatrice, after a moment. "I think it is a pleasant token of friendship."

"It has long been my ambition to call two people by their Christian names," said Dulcia, taking her arm and walking with her head close. "You and Miss Jekyll. But I should never dare to approach Miss Jekyll; I am not in quite such a fog about my compass."

"She is certainly an unusual woman," said Beatrice.

"There, I knew you would corroborate me. It is not everyone to whom I would unhesitatingly accord another the first place. But I knew I could depend upon you. And you do not play second fiddle with me, you know. I am glad to approach someone comfortably nearer to my own level."

"I see my uncle making signs to me."

"Then, good-bye, dear Miss Fellowes. Good-bye, Beatrice. What a delicious shiver it gives me! I do feel I have got a step further to-day."

"You and Dulcia seem on intimate terms," said Miss Burtenshaw.

"She asked if she might call me by my Christian name. And I was very glad she should. It was very nice and friendly of her."

"Oh, you are within the radius of possibility. I must admit I am too far removed by age and other things."

"It was quite pretty to see her make the approach. She was so tentative and shy over it."

"Well, why three girls can't call each other by their Christian names, beats me," said Alexander.

"Perhaps she was not exactly shy over it: that is not quite the word. But there was nothing to criticise. It was quite sensitively done.

"Father! Mother!" called Dulcia, running to catch up her family, at a fitting distance from the churchyard. "The day is to have some compensation for me! I have asked and been granted permission to call Miss Fellowes by her Christian name! I screwed my courage to the point: I thought I never should, but I did; and lo and behold, I brought it off! It is a red letter day for me in a way, in spite of the other side."

"The scale must perhaps go down on that side on the whole," said her brother.

"Ah, the advantage is not all yours, my dear," said Mr. Bode.

"Stop," said his daughter. "There are Dr. and Mrs. Smollett! I insist on joining forces. We are not going to be aloof to-day."

"My girl was not going to have you escape us," said Mr. Bode, with a needless sense of elaborating the truth.

"Dr. Smollett," said Dulcia in a straight manner, "I hope I did not do the wrong thing in thanking you for your service to Mrs. Edgeworth? I can guess how a reference to a lost case must strike a doctor; how sensitive a nerve must be touched by the lightest allusion. I hope I have not committed the unpardonable sin?"

"Hope springs eternal——" muttered Almeric, as Fabian bowed towards his sister.

"Ellen was in the last stage of her illness, when my husband was called in," said Florence.

"And I have said the wrong thing, and established myself a blunderbuss."

"You are saying the right thing now," said Almeric in a consoling tone.

"How soon do you think we may go to see the Edgeworths?" said Mrs. Bode.

"We are going to them later in the day," said Florence.

"Well, Mother dear, naturally Dr. and Mrs. Smollett take precedence of us in the line of approach. We must be content, as we are content, to follow in their wake."

"I think it is good for them to see their friends. If I did not, I should not go."

"Mrs. Smollett, I can see you going, heedless of the pain to yourself in sensing the blank in the house. One person here is alive to the truth of the intention."

"I would rather see Ellen's family than no one to do with her. The blank is all that is left."

"Ellen's family! What a beautiful and intimate sound! That is how I shall think of them. I shall not feel it presumptuous, kept to the confines of my own mind."

"It will be narrowly restricted," agreed her brother.

Ellen's family had entered the house, that still seemed to be ordered by Ellen. Duncan went alone to the library, his children hardly thinking of his doing otherwise; and the others drifted to the drawing-room, and took their usual places, their eyes on the empty place, that seemed to be finally empty for the first time since Ellen's death.

"We are supposed to make a new beginning," said Nance. "I find the ending enough."

"Mother would wish us to start again," said her sister.

"I could not bear people to do that, directly I was dead," said Grant. "It would ruin my life after death to find they were doing it."

"I shall always wish I had been a better daughter," said Sibyl. "But other people will have to feel the same. I am sorrier for Father than for myself."

"Neither you nor he is the chief person in the case," said Nance.

"Well, I would rather be myself than him just now."

"Why?" said Cassie.

"Cassie, you must know he was not kind enough to Mother. It does no good to pretend to forget."

"I should have thought it would do a great deal of good."

Sibyl was silent, her eyes on the door.

"I was not kind enough to your mother, Sibyl," said Duncan, in a tone that seemed to be drained of conscious feeling. "The thought of it will be my life: I have to prepare to live it."

"People always feel that, when someone is dead," said Nance, going to his side. "We are all feeling it. We could use your very words."

"Father, I did not mean it. I felt I had not been kind myself, and I wanted you to be the same. I wanted you with me, as I always want you. That is all it was."

Duncan put his arms round his daughters, and suddenly bent forward with his head on Nance's shoulder, too depleted in spirit to be alive to what was thought.

"My wife, my wife, whom I could not treat as if I loved you! I could not, and you are gone! I cannot have one day to make you know. I shall not have it, though I had all those other days."

"It is a common feeling, Father. It will pass, if you give it time."

"She was sixty!" said Duncan, lifting his head almost as an animal giving a cry. "You were sixty, Ellen, when you went upstairs alone, and were never to be well again! Sixty years old, and weak and ill, and you did not have your husband! You did not know I was anxious; and I was anxious, Ellen. And I did not think of you as sixty; I thought of you as when I first knew you; I thought I was old, and you were young. And I thought there was nobody like you, nobody like you."

"Father, she knew you thought it. She knew you never put things in words. She loved you for yourself, for what you were: I have heard her say she would not have you different."

"Have you, Nance? Have you heard her say it? When did she say it first? Was it a thing she said often? What were her words?"

Duncan drew his daughter from the room, and led her

to the library. It was an hour before she emerged and followed the others.

"I feel I have lost both my parents. Mother has not vanished more completely than Father. In his stead there is a man, who has been an almost monotonously amiable husband. I dread he will begin to repent of the monotony."

"Has he been telling you?" said Sibyl.

"I have been telling him. He inclined himself, as you know, to the opposite view. It is fortunate I am not a person who cannot tell a lie. I hardly remember the difference between truth and falsehood; and he is not in any way concerned with it."

"Poor Father! It is the least we can do for him."

"It was the most I could do. You don't know how much virtue has gone out of me. The virtue was Father's, but I had to produce it."

"I wish I could help him."

"You will have every chance. I have indicated the line to be pursued. I don't know if he and I can meet again, after what I have told him. If he is not shy of me, it is because he is no longer as other men. But he is no longer that."

"If we all tell him the same things," said Grant, "he will be shy of meeting all of us, and the duty will be done."

"It is Mother's opinion of him, that is in his mind, and he will not have to meet her. We shall all be pressed into the service."

But for the time Duncan's need was satisfied. He welcomed the Smolletts as the widower controlling his grief, and showing of his courtesy a use for their companionship. By dinner he had sunk again into himself, and Sibyl tried to rise to his need.

"Father, you must make an effort to eat. You have always thought of what Mother wished, and you can do this for her now."

"What are you about, telling me what I know, as if I

needed to be told? That is settled between Nance and me; and there was little need for her to come into it. I will thank you to keep off."

Duncan spent the evening alone; was heard pacing the room in the night; and sat at breakfast without a word, sunk in the silence as if in a sleep.

When he turned as usual to the library, he simply beckoned to Sibyl. She served him as her sister had served him yesterday, and left him startled by the truth of her words.

At luncheon he was still at peace, but there were signs of the creeping reaction.

Henceforth it happened as Nance had foretold. He made heavy demands in the next weeks. His horizon was filled by his own remorse, and no other aspect of the family bereavement seemed to strike him. Sibyl found the duty the easiest, and derived her reward from his dependence on herself. The simplicity with which he demanded and accepted, proved his need. Through it all he remained himself, and signs of flagging in what came to be a duty, drove him into states that resembled his old moods.

"So, Grant," he said, when his nephew had failed in some assurance, "I may sit here, as I become used to sitting, dependent on those who would have none of me. The person who knew my mind, has left us. Well, she has her due from me, and will have it. No one else thinks of how they dealt with her. Only I would have been perfect in my dealings. Only I suffer because I failed, as man must fail."

"You were clearly perfect in your dealings," said Grant. "Surely that is settled by now."

Duncan met this speech with an indifference that was almost real. Grant had from the first held aloof from his demands, and from the first his resentment had been touched with respect, as for a man whose truth went beyond that of women. To Duncan those who rendered a service, became those who existed to serve. Somehow this moment, though no one could ever recapture it, marked the end of the first stage of his sorrow, its turning point to simple grief. His nephew's facing of the truth gave him the truth as a thing to be faced. He could himself identify the instant of his release. There was darkness still ahead, but the darkest point was past.

CHAPTER VI

ONE MORNING DUNCAN'S silence had a new quality. He seemed to be waiting for someone to speak, and at last spoke himself.

"Does anyone notice a difference in the room?"

"The portrait of Aunt Ellen is over the sideboard. I saw it when I came in."

"Then why did you not speak of it?"

"I don't know, Uncle. No one else did," said Grant, not acknowledging the shyness attendant on mention of the dead.

"Did you take it from the landing, Father?"

"My dear Sibyl, from where should I take it, when it was on the landing that it hung?"

"It is nice to have it in here," said Nance.

"Nice?" said her father, contracting his forehead. "What an odd word!"

"Well, what word would you use?"

"I shall find it a support to have her portrait before my eyes."

"That is certainly expanding the phrase."

"It is not a joke, Nance."

"Of course it is not, Father. But it is not a change of oppressive import either. If it is, why did you make it?"

"You have not improved since your mother's death," said Duncan, looking with quiet appraisement at his daughter's face.

"I believe I have not. The event has been fraught with no improvement."

"I am glad you have put the portrait there, Father," said Sibyl.

"Are you, my dear? I am glad one of you is. I hoped you all would be."

"We all like to have it there," said Grant. "But it is not a good likeness, is it?"

Duncan gave his nephew a long look.

"You do not mean you are unable to supply the deficiencies from your own memory?"

"It is because I can supply them, that I do not care for the portrait. And if we are to supply the likeness from our memories, what is the good of it?"

"It would be of no use to tell you," said Duncan, returning to his breakfast.

"Did you take it down, yourself, Father? And put it up?" said Sibyl.

"Should I have allowed any hand but mine to touch it?"

"I thought I saw some plaster on the landing," said Nance.

"In what way is that on the point?" said Duncan, with strong irritation.

"It was not a contribution to the subject, certainly."

"Nance, this note is most uncongenial. I have tried not to guess what it must mean; I have tried to put it from me. I can put it from me no longer."

"It is not much good for families to put things from them."

"Families!" said Duncan, in an aloof tone. "We are hardly a family now. We lack our binding force." He gave a heavy sigh. "You do not do much to help me through the beginning of my day."

"You are attending to it yourself," said Nance. "We have done all we can for you, Father."

"Yes, you have done it, done it in a way that has showed it was a duty. It is true you have done all you can. You have let me see I am alone."

"Mother is not here to console him for her death," said Nance to Grant. "It will be his last grievance against her. Or I cannot imagine a later one."

"If his married happiness goes on increasing, I don't know what we are to do. The contrast must also increase."

Duncan signed to Grant to fetch him something from the sideboard, and continued to sign until Sibyl drew her cousin's attention. When a package was given him, he took out a scroll of parchment, and bent his head over it.

"I thought this design for the stone, and these characters for the inscription," he said, as though his companions' thoughts would be running on this line. "Have you any other suggestion?"

"Is it for Mother?" said Nance.

Duncan turned his head towards her, and did not speak.

"It is beautiful, Father," said Sibyl.

"Of course, there has to be a gravestone?" said Grant. "I thought at the time that there was a place in the family vault."

"There was a place," said his uncle.

"But you did not wish it used?"

"There were not two places."

"I do not feel I could bite my tongue out," murmured Grant. "I should rather like to think of Aunt Ellen in the vault, and Uncle outside."

"And why, Grant?" said Duncan.

"Oh, I wish I had bitten my tongue out—— Because, Uncle—because I should like her to have an especial place."

"You would not like her to have the place she would have chosen?"

"Yes, of course I should, Uncle. Of course you are right—— It was silly not to bite my tongue out, so that I should be dumb, and not expected to speak."

"It would be better, Grant, to put your tongue to uses you are not ashamed of."

"Grant was joking, Father," said Nance.

"Joking?" said Duncan, his brows taking their slow, upward line. "Joking, at this time, when we are discussing —I will not say what; I would choose to keep it apart."

"I may as well bite my tongue out," said Nance, "for all the good it seems to be. I shall soon not dare to use it."

"Here is a letter from my invalid sister, your Aunt Maria," said Duncan, in an incidental tone. "She wishes me to pay her a visit; and it may be my duty; I even fear it is. I must not become so sunk in myself, that I am careless of her need. I have made the excuse of reluctance to leave your mother: I cannot make it now."

"Yes, do go to see her, Father. It will do you good," said Sibyl.

"Do me good? Do her good, you mean? There would be little point in the visit, if my good were its object." Duncan gave a little laugh. "That need not be taken into account."

There was a pause.

"I suppose this is one of those silences that speak," murmured Grant. "I hope it does not really."

"Your mother was not easy about your aunt's isolation. I must try to recall her words. How clearly they come back to me!"

"She would hardly wish you to go just now, if it goes against the grain."

"Would she not, Nance?" said Duncan, almost gently. "I am afraid I cannot tell myself that: I happen to know, you see, what her wishes would be."

"It would anyhow be a change, Father."

"It would not be that, Sibyl. The past is outside the sphere of change; and my life is in the past. There is one thing of which I can assure myself. It cannot be worse with me."

"Is Aunt Maria's life in the present?" said Nance. "Though she is a widow, and has lost her children? We hear of the differences in families."

"She is a widow, Nance, and has lost her children. And I am a widower; and, I sometimes think, have lost my children. It seems meet we should be together."

"I believe he inclines to the trip," muttered Grant.

"Yes, Grant, I expect you do believe it," said Duncan,

whose hearing maintained its inconsistence. "Yes, you would believe that."

"Would you want me to do anything, while you were away, Uncle?"

"What you would want to do, yourself," said Duncan in his own tone. "You know you should get a grip of the workings of the place. It is for your own sake and your own future. You may stop putting it all on to me. Miss Jekyll, will you very kindly give directions about my packing?"

"You should ask me to do that, Father."

"Yes, Nance, I should. Ask yourself why I do not."

"You are not going at once, Father?" said Sibyl.

"To-morrow," said Duncan, in a faintly weary tone. "If I put it off, my resolution will fail: I almost feel it failing."

"Is Aunt Maria expecting you?"

"My poor sister!" said Duncan, almost with a laugh. "She has long been expecting me. I reproach myself when I think of it; I hear your mother's reproaches. We will telegraph, and end her suspense, and incidentally bind me to my project."

"He hears Mother's reproaches!" murmured Nance. "How different Mother is getting!"

"She is, Nance," said Duncan, in almost pleasant tone. "With every day I realise more, what were the workings of her mind; and how our two minds bore upon each other."

"It would be a shame to disappoint Aunt Maria," said Sibyl.

"Oh, I don't know. Would it? She is very used to it. I admit I am still dallying with the idea. It may get the better of me."

"The silence spoke," murmured Grant.

"I never can make out whether Father's hearing is below the average or above it," said Nance.

"You have made up your mind for some time," said Duncan. "It would have to be very much below, to prevent my realising that."

"What time does the train go, if you decide to take it?" said Cassie.

"My sister has kept me informed of the trains. The one she always recommends, is at a quarter past eleven."

"And you want to catch that?"

"I do not want to," said Duncan, leaning back. "But if we assume I am going to, it will dispose of this shilly-shallying, which need not be apparent, as well as real."

"Do you want anything done for you, before you go?" said Nance.

"If there is anything to be done, see that it is done," said her father, going to the door. "We don't want question and answer over what goes without saying."

"What goes without saying! Does it really?" said Grant. "I shall hold my breath until it comes to pass."

"You may hold it too long," said Nance: "I can't think it can happen."

"Well, I believe that would kill me, anyhow."

The next day Duncan appeared submissive to fate, and simply acquiescent in arrangements; but as the morning advanced, there was a change.

"Grant!" he called from his bedroom landing, "fetch my writing case from my desk; and put in some pens and stamps, and bring it up here! I have been calling until I am hoarse; I thought you were all stone deaf."

"It was odd to continue calling," said Grant, as he hastened on the quest.

"Grant! Grant! Don't you hear me? Can't you answer me, boy?"

"I am getting the things, Uncle! I will be up in a minute."

"But can't you answer me? Can't you open your mouth to reply, when I stand and shout myself hoarse? Are you dumb as well as deaf?"

"I thought you would know I was getting the case, Uncle."

"How was I to know, when I shouted and got no

response? How was I to guess at what moment I should pierce your senses? How was I to know you had any senses, when there was no evidence of it?"

Grant ran upstairs and offered the case, Sibyl on his heels with its supplies. Something in the zeal attending these offices, caused Duncan to meet them with deliberation.

"Pens; stamps; yes. Paper? Do I want paper? Will not your aunt have that, Sibyl? That is"—he gave his little laugh—"if I get there, and need it."

"Of course she will, Father. How stupid of me! I will take it back, and look round to see if there is anything else."

"There is no reason for hurry: I don't want the final look round made yet. We may never get to it. Who knows?" Duncan raised his arms with a yawn and a sigh. "So many things come in the way of really getting off, more than the business is worth."

He broke off, and looked up and down a newspaper from a trunk, smiling to himself at its reminders.

Grant and Sibyl went downstairs.

"Nance, we betrayed an eagerness to get Uncle off. I can hardly believe in our foolishness."

"What about putting some obstacles in his path?"

"There will be enough in it," said Cassie. "You had better avoid his path."

"There he is, calling again!" said Sibyl.

"He has soon begun to miss us."

"Has anyone seen my old gloves, that I wear in the grounds? Those that are kept in the drawer in the hall, or should be kept there? I know people are always disturbing that drawer."

"They are not there, Father!" called Sibyl, after a swift search.

"Of course they are not there!" said Duncan, coming to the stairs. "If they were there, should I ask you if you had seen them? I should simply tell you to fetch them." This was accepted as true.

"I thought you wanted them fetched, Father."

"Of course I wanted them fetched," said Duncan, moving from foot to foot. "If I did not, should I have asked about them? I should not expect them to walk to me, should I? Or to fly to my hand?"

"If they don't fly to his hand, I don't know what we are to do," said Cassie.

"Why, you have them in your hand, Father, waving them about!" said Sibyl, with an easy laugh that laid no stress on the mistake.

Duncan glanced at the gloves, and continued to wave them.

"Fetch me the scarf from the drawer, that I wear with the gloves," he said, giving a quick glance behind him, as though arrested by something.

"I believe the gloves did fly to his hand," said Grant.

"There he is again!" said Sibyl, running with the scarf. Duncan stood still, his hand outstretched, until his daughter had mounted the stairs and put the scarf into it.

"The fire in my room is smoking again," he observed, tossing up the scarf and catching it.

"We shall never get him off in time," said Nance, "if the things in one drawer prove such an obstacle. So far he is equipped with one scarf and a pair of gloves, and neither of them suitable for general wear."

"We had better resign ourselves to frustration," said Grant. "The hope has been very sweet."

Duncan entered the drawing-room, with bag and rug, using these objects to wave from his path Bethia, with some offer of assistance. He put his burdens down, and taking a chair picked up the paper.

"I should not have left the paper lying idle, when I was your age," he said, smiling. "You have very little curiosity about the nation's affairs."

"True, when they are swamped by an acute private anxiety," said Grant.

"You don't think this election business will follow that course——"

"No, Uncle, I scarcely think it will."

Duncan continued his perusal with an air of alertness and interest, pausing to comment or quote.

"Father, it is a quarter to eleven," said Sibyl.

"A quarter to eleven?" said Duncan, taking out his watch. "A shade past the quarter. My watch is absolutely right, exactly to the second. A quarter of a minute past the quarter." He smiled at the coincidence of the words, and resumed the journal.

"You like half an hour between leaving the house and catching the train," said Nance. "The cob is at the door."

Duncan glanced out of the window, and back to the page.

"He stamps and paws, that little brute," he observed, his tone preoccupied. "It will do him good to learn patience."

"Too hard a lesson for a dumb beast," muttered Grant.

"Horses are said to know the moods of human beings," said Nance. "I hope we shall not render this one unfit to take Father to the train."

"Father, William is looking through the window," said Sibyl. "He cannot get down because of the horse."

Duncan lifted his eyes, and catching the signs of the groom, rose from his seat.

"My umbrella, my rug!" he said in a quick, curt tone, turning rapidly about. "I suppose you can hand me the things before your eyes. Grant, you know by which end to hand an umbrella! You do not comfortably take the handle yourself, and offer the point! Nance, here is a list of the things I want remembered. It is clearly written. You can read it, I suppose?"

"Certainly, in that case, Father."

"My purse!" said Duncan, pausing with a jerk. "Will somebody give me my purse? Can I do without it? Shall I have to pay for my ticket, for my luncheon, for my porter? Sibyl, will you fetch it? You seem the least phlegmatic of the three."

Sibyl made a dart in a vague direction, and glanced back at her father.

"I can't see it, Father; I shall find it in a second; I shall be sure to sight it?"

Duncan stood still, his eyes on her movements, and suddenly let his possessions fall, and sat down on the hall bench.

"Well, bring the paper then," he called to his daughter, as though making provision for a period.

"Did you put the purse in your pocket, Father?"

Duncan put his hand to his waistcoat, and withdrew it, picked up his belongings, and walked to the door, in one smooth, unglancing movement.

Sibyl sprang back; Nance gathered up the rug; Grant ran out to the door of the trap.

"Good-bye, Father! Good-bye, Uncle! Good-bye, Father!"

"Good-bye, Miss Jekyll," said Duncan, turning to Cassie with deliberate courtesy. "I fear some of my responsibilities will devolve on you. And good-bye, Nance; good-bye, Sibyl. Grant, don't block the way out of the house. I may miss the train yet; though if I do, I shall be back in ample time for luncheon. Let me hear from one of you twice a week, and go to church on Sunday mornings. In the evenings do as you please."

"Good-bye, Father. Good-bye, Uncle. Good-bye, Father. Take care of yourself. You will let us hear when you arrive?"

"If I stay more than a day or two," said Duncan, pausing with his foot on the step of the trap. "If I do not, one letter will serve a double purpose. Have you any messages for your aunt? I shall be able to deliver them anyhow."

"The messages usual between people who do not meet," said Nance, "and would not know each other, if they did."

"So no message. Good-bye, all of you," said Duncan, mounting the steps.

Sibyl waved in the porch, and her father looked back and raised his hat.

"How you have the spirit to wave, when the train may yet be missed!" said Grant.

"If I had not had the spirit for a good deal, the train would not have been aimed at at all."

"The train will not be missed," said Cassie.

"Nance, we are to go to church on Sunday mornings," said Grant. "Does that mean he will be away for weeks?"

"What should I be, if I did not prick up my ears at that? Not Father's daughter."

"The trap is coming back!" said Sibyl.

"The trap? With Uncle in it?"

"Of course with him in it. They could not have got to the station and back."

"He might have been thrown out and killed. I see that his death would be the only thing."

"The trap might have headed the sad procession," said Nance.

"It could hardly be sadder," said her cousin.

The trap came up the drive, with Duncan leaning forward over the horse.

"Hold back, Williams! Do you want to destroy the beast? A horse for the sake of a train! What a muddle of values! Now pull up gently, and quiet him. Grant, come to his head, and see if harm is done. Williams, you may keep your seat, in case we want to start again.

"None at all, Uncle. He is hardly in a heat. He is fresh, and wants to get along."

"No harm done!" said Nance.

Duncan sat waiting to be asked to explain his return, and as no one put the enquiry, took out his purse and went through his change, and then leaned back and crossed his legs.

Bethia hurried out with his dressing bag, and he made a quick movement towards it, but checked himself and signed to his nephew.

"That bag is rather heavy for a woman," he said in a tone almost of interest, his eyes on the bag. "You should keep your wits about you. Well, good-bye again, if only for the moment. It will be a matter of minutes or weeks, I suppose; and it does not much matter which it is."

CHAPTER VII

"So FATHER IS still away?" said Mr. Bode in the church-yard. "It was nice to think of a change for Father. You are glad he should have it. And he writes that he is doing his best to enjoy his visit?"

"Yes, but, father of mine," said Dulcia from where she stood, "our friends are aware of Mr. Edgeworth's relation to them, without being told it so often."

"He does not write that," said Grant. "But he hopes we are leading our usual lives; so we wondered if Almeric and Dulcia would come back with us to luncheon."

"You dear things, I have longed to give a fillip to your spirits," said Dulcia, now to face with this opportunity. "I have almost felt a skunk for not suggesting my presence. It was mean to avoid a charge of forwardness at the expense of your interests; definitely second rate. I welcome a chance of atonement."

"Make the most of the time when the cat is away," said Gretchen. "It is getting short."

"Yes, Mrs. Jekyll. Yes," said Mr. Bode.

"It seems to get longer," said Grant. "The return is again postponed. Aunt Maria simply can't part from Uncle, I don't know what she feels about our separation from him."

"Well, after all, he is her brother," said Dulcia.

"Blood is thicker than water," said Beatrice.

"I don't see why blood should count more there than here."

"It is good to have things as they were," said Florence. "If we can't have it all, we will have what we can. Nance, it is your father's turn to write to me."

"Oh, he writes to you, does he, Mrs. Smollett?" said Alexander.

"Really, Mrs. Smollett, I do think it is rather a success for you," said Dulcia, with a laugh.

"We have all been wanting to do something for you," said Miss Burtenshaw to the Edgeworths; "and behold, you turn the tables and do it for us, by looking yourselves again."

"Topsy-turvy seems to be the word," said Beatrice.

"I am sure I do not look myself," said Grant to Fabian: "I am still sorrowing for my aunt."

"Ah, we are all doing that, dear boy," said Fabian, his sigh ignoring his surroundings.

"Nance," said Dulcia, thrusting her arm into her friend's, "why don't you throw convention to the winds, and ask all these dear people to your house, to some simple gathering? It would not matter what it was. It would be just a pretext for behaving naturally again, and giving them the satisfaction of seeing it. It would sum up as a simple method of doing much."

"Our house is a dreary place for even simple gatherings. It has never been the scene of any other kind."

"Don't hesitate, dear. Don't worry about its dreariness or drabness or anything about it. We just want to come and see you all getting on to your feet again. That is all we should ask of the entertainment."

"Though it be all you ask, it is hardly enough for us to offer."

"It would be enough and to spare, and would fill our cup to overflowing. We should feel greatly exalted above the run of mankind."

"I suppose it would be the right thing to go," said Gretchen.

"I think we could not hurt their feelings by staying away," said Beatrice.

"Why should we want to stay away?" said Florence. "I should find it a pleasure to go."

"So should I: I like to be asked to a party," said Miss Burtenshaw, moving her lips more than usual.

"I think we are doing injustice to Mrs. Jekyll," said Dulcia. "She was speaking only from her well-known mistrust of herself in society, which we all consider to be so very ill founded. Was that not so, Miss Jekyll?"

"I don't think she was speaking from anything in particular."

"That is perhaps enough, dear," said Mrs. Bode, moving to her daughter.

"Enough, Mother dear? Enough about anything is pretty good from you to me."

"It would be very kind of them to ask us," said Beatrice.

"I don't think they feel that," said Dulcia, as if throwing light of her own. "They only feel it will mark their taking up the common round again."

"The trivial round, the common task," said Beatrice.

"I don't know why the party should be called trivial," said Miss Burtenshaw.

"Dearest, you did not think I took too much upon myself?" said Dulcia, as she walked away with Nance.

"Of course she thought so. She is a sane person," said Almeric.

"I am not going to care about you, wet-blanket of a brother. It is only Nance's assurance that I want; and I know I can depend on that. Nance, you can tell me you are grateful to me?"

"What will be Uncle's view of revelry in the house of mourning?"

"We need not tell him," said Sibyl.

"Other people may do so," said her sister. "We cannot inform our guests it is a secret function."

"And you would rather not have it secret?" said Dulcia, taking her arm. "You would act according to yourself. We shall indeed speak freely to your father."

"You have not solved my problem," said Grant; "but rather added to it."

"Oh, he will not say anything, I stand guarantee," said Dulcia. "I'll go bail he will not raise Cain: I undertake to square him."

"What ground have you for the undertaking?" said Almeric. "I should hesitate to give it."

"You belong to the masculine half of mankind. Mr. Edgeworth has a soft spot somewhere, for a youthful member of the other half: I have noticed it."

"I believe, so have I," said Nance to Grant; "provided the youthful member is not of his own family."

"What other youthful member has he seen than Dulcia?"

"No other. It is Dulcia who has the evidence."

"Almeric," said Sibyl, "you and Dulcia are very unlike for a brother and sister."

"For any two people, I believe."

"I should never guess you were related. Do you think Nance and I are alike?"

"No, not at all."

"Nance has a much better face than mine, not just young and pretty in the ordinary way."

Almeric made no answer.

"Now here we are in this satisfying room again!" said his sister. "It is a place in which I would not have one single thing altered—except of course for dear Mrs. Edgeworth's empty chair."

"Of course, as you say," said Almeric.

"I have seldom seen a room so completely satisfying. It breaks on one like a poem, with its suggestions of a past age, and that touch of something not quite shabbiness, which only lends distinction. I admire without any reservation."

"Except the one specified."

"Do you like to have a time without your father, Nance?" said Dulcia, with simple straightforwardness.

"We enjoy being without the constraint of his presence; and we are glad for him to have a change. We are rather a rudderless household without him."

"Luncheon is ready, Miss Nance," said Bethia. "Cook is carving the chickens downstairs, in case Mr. Grant cannot manage them."

"Oh, Bethia! She is too utterly just what she is," said Dulcia. "I can't keep my composure within ten yards of her. She is almost the best part of coming here again. To think we have been missing for all these months, going about in all her inimitable Bethiadom!"

"But not quite the best part," said her brother.

"Nance, Almeric, think you and I are very unlike."

"It is a matter of common concurrence."

Dulcia glanced at Bethia, pushing in the chairs, and raised her brows round the table, before taking her seat.

"I think that whatever the one of you has not, the other has, *vice versa*. You do not interfere with each other in the faintest degree. I have never met such a case of diverse colours meeting without a hint of clash."

"I am glad there is no ground for bitterness between us."

Dulcia leaned back in mirth.

"What would happen to you, if there was something to be amused about?" asked Almeric.

"What would happen to me? I should derive from it the full need of enjoyment. I think one appreciates the humour in things better, for being able to see the humour in everything. I am glad of my capacity to laugh at all things and sundry."

"You have a right to claim that you have it."

"Now, Nance, are you thinking of my suggestion?" said Dulcia, putting her hand on her friend's. "Are you giving it fair consideration? You are going to afford us the opportunity of meeting at your house, with the purpose of doing good to you, rather than to ourselves? I assure you it is really an altruistic project."

"Then perhaps from our point of view it fails in hospitality."

"Hospitality be damned!" said Dulcia, striking the table. "What do we want with entertainment? What we want, is for the three of you to come out of your shell, and look about, and see that the world is good. That will be hospitality enough. That is all we shall ask of the simple party."

"Grant," said Nance, under her breath, "I suggest you address an occasional word to our guests."

"I am mesmerised into silence; Dulcia fascinates me like a snake. I will talk to Almeric afterwards; he comes to himself away from her."

"I don't think we will give a party," said Nance. "But we might ask our friends to come in one day, as Mother often used to. That would be just going on in the old way."

Dulcia brought her closed fist down again upon the table.

"That hits the nail! That strikes the wavering balance! There was something about the other plan, that was not what was wanted: I admit it, though the idea was mine. The essence of the situation, that something in its nature, is met by this adjustment. It is saved."

Nance rose from the table, and Dulcia followed with a promptness which accorded her her full due as hostess. The young men went into the garden, and Sibyl followed.

"Now, Nance," said Dulcia, settling herself, "can I do anything for you in the line of entertaining our mutual friends? Not that there is the slightest objection to your doing it all yourself, anything in the world against your making the little gesture. I have been longing for you to make it, have shown it to the point of insistence. I am at your service; that is all."

"There will hardly be anything definite to do. We shall just ask our friends to come and welcome them."

"And they will respond as one man, and the end will be achieved! The ice will be broken, and your future will lie clear. I have not expressed to you how I have grieved for you in these months. I don't mean we have not felt sympathetic respect for your father's sorrow; indeed there has been something about his dignified withdrawal into himself, that has been impressive. But you are young; and we have got tired of viewing you all from a respectful distance."

"It is nice to be at close quarters again."

"It is so nice that I can't get close enough. I am so glad to get a word with you, without my damping brother. And I won't fail you in the matter of doing anything you may eventually wish for the dear people whom we both love. You may depend on me, simply."

A week or two later the friends of Ellen Edgeworth came again to her house.

"This is our greatest pleasure for a long time," said Mr. Bode. "It takes us back to the old days."

"Father dear, that is just what it does not do. I thought you would get a little further than this, without coming down."

"Well, we can't give everything up, because one of us is gone," said Gretchen, "though it had better have been anyone else."

Beatrice looked round with smilingly contracted brows.

"I am glad you see the joke," said Gretchen, contriving that she no longer saw it.

"You may say it better have been yourself, Mother," said Oscar. "That is as far as you must go."

"Enough of you think that, for it to go without saying."

"Ah, Mrs. Jekyll, we would spare many people before you," said Mr. Bode.

"Now, careful, Father dear! In what sense are you using the word, 'spare'?"

"In the sense in which he palpably used it," said Almeric.

"I don't think we can fairly accuse him of ambiguity," said Beatrice.

"I take sides against myself. Puns in all their degrees are odious."

"Let us check this process of elimination in time," said Nance.

"I am prepared to admit I am a much less needed person that Mrs. Edgeworth," said Dulcia. "And I am sure many people here would tell themselves the same—Oh, what a thing to let slip, unawares! You dear, dear things!" She flung her arms round the first person in her path, who was conveniently Miss Burtenshaw. "Oh, my unwary tongue!"

"It does not matter in the least, as far as I am concerned," said Beatrice, with her eyes upon the embrace. "I do not mind at all."

"I consent to be enrolled in the army of superfluous spinsters," said her cousin.

"Superfluous, Miss Burtenshaw, with your father at your elbow!" said Mrs. Bode, gently and fully giving Miss Burtenshaw her place in the scheme.

"Oh, whatever truth there is in it, it was for other people to say it, and not me!"

"Have you heard from Father this week?" said Mr. Bode.

"Father is unfair," said Sibyl. "He has rewarded three long letters with half a page."

"He may surprise you one of these days," said Gretchen.

"I am sure they would none of them mind," said Dulcia.

"I am sure they would be very glad to see him," said Beatrice at the same instant.

"I wonder how he is amusing himself."

"He attends upon his invalid sister," said Grant. "If she has not had expert attendance, she soon will have."

"He may wish he had done it for somebody else," said Gretchen.

"I will pilot my mother to some obscure spot, and return," said Oscar.

"No, no, Mr. Jekyll, I don't think she deserves that," said Dulcia. "We none of us always conquer any little disposition to be over downright for some obscure cause in ourselves. If she is to be banished"—she took her stand by Gretchen—"I constitute myself her escort and accompany her into exile!"

"Let me be her escort," said Florence; "I have been wanting to talk with her."

"There seem to be some interesting masculine gossips going on," said Beatrice, looking from Almeric and Grant to Oscar and Fabian.

"We must not expect to be a party to every lordly confidence," said her cousin.

"I am sure they are saying nothing that we could not hear."

"Well, if that were true in every sense, they would not leave us. Oh, we don't grudge them their own kind of simplicity."

"I think it is natural that men should want to talk apart from women sometimes," said Dulcia. "After all a man's nature is different; and things that are no more than simply masculine, said in a company of men, might take on quite a different complexion in mixed hearing. And I am talking of things that might be said in all innocence."

"I must go and disturb one masculine gossip," said Sibyl. "Grant forgets he is the host."

"I suspected they will not much object to being disturbed," said Miss Burtenshaw, looking archly after her.

"I suspect they will not," said Beatrice; "I know I should not, if I were a young man."

"There are some promising sounds in the hall," said her cousin. "They suggest another fellow guest."

"I did not know anyone else was expected," said Dulcia. "It is a full extra, the excitement of a stranger."

"Is someone answering the bell, Bethia?" said Nance.

"It is only the master, Miss Nance," said Bethia, proceeding with a tray.

"What?" said Sibyl. "What did you say, Bethia? Stop and tell us what you mean."

Nance hurried to the door, and Grant to the window.

"It is true. It is a hired trap, with Uncle's luggage!"

" 'My father is come!',", quoted Nance. " 'He is in the hall at this moment'."

"Well, we are none of us doing anything to be ashamed of," said Dulcia, "I, for one, am extremely glad to see him."

"He seems to have arrived from nowhere," said Beatrice.

"He not only seems to have arrived. He has done so," said Duncan. "How are you my daughters? How are you, Grant, my boy? This is a congenial welcome."

"Father, we have asked some friends in Mother's old way," said Sibyl, pressing to his side.

"It is good to see our friends in any way. And good to see they are still our friends. We might have ourselves to thank, if they were not. Mrs. Jekyll, it is pleasant to find you in my house."

"So you have happened on to-day of all others to come back?"

"I decided upon it. And there seemed no need to send warning to my own home."

"And there was no need," said Dulcia. "We are beginning to see that. I am thoroughly glad to see this home-coming. It is a proof of so much that I always said existed in this household. I may have had to maintain it in the face of opposition, but here is the proof before our eyes! And full and satisfying proof too."

"Now I think the better part of valour will be to make ourselves scarce," said Miss Burtenshaw.

"We will not even give them the trouble of saying good-bye," said her cousin.

"Now I don't know," said Dulcia: "I believe Mr. Edgeworth would like us to stay. He said so; and he impresses himself upon me, as a person who would wish to be taken at his word. I intend so to take him, and to feel I am doing as I would be done by."

"Well, it will be of no good for us to go by ourselves," said Beatrice.

"I knew you would stay when I put it to you; and I do think I am more alive to the atmosphere of the Edgeworth family. I have always held it was much more sweet and wholesome than might be thought."

"Ah, somebody has Father back again," said Mr. Bode, as Sibyl went by on Duncan's arm.

"Now there you see borne out what I say! As simple and natural as anyone could wish."

"You left a man and woman behind, Mr. Edgeworth," said Mrs. Bode, smiling at Nance and Grant. "You could go away with a light heart."

"Well, really, Mother dear, I hardly think the words 'light heart,' go to the spot. That is reading too much into a veneer assumed for our sakes."

"I must not depute my duties any longer; Grant should be doing his own work: I have come home to fill my place."

"Like the dear, brave man he is, and worthy of the dear woman, as he is!" said Dulcia, in a glowing manner. "Yes, we can bear to see Nance in her mother's place."

"It does not take long to get over things," said Gretchen.

"Mrs. Jekyll, do you not think it a sign of depth of feeling, to force yourself to do as the loved one would wish? You are a living refutation of what you say, going, as you do, in your widow's weeds, about your daily usefulness."

"I think Mr. Edgeworth seems really cheered up by the party," said Beatrice. "I was afraid, when he came in, that he might find himself out of tune with it. But he has reassured me, and not only in the ways in which he might make an effort for a woman guest."

"It seems a spontaneous response," agreed her cousin.

"I was so sure the party would work out well for everyone," said Dulcia. "I did so earnestly recommend Nance to give it."

"It is good to serve other people and ourselves," said Miss Burtenshaw.

"Yes, I was serving myself: I have enjoyed it, heart and soul. I think a plan only works, if it is made whole-heartedly in its parts."

"Father looks well, doesn't he?" said Sibyl.

"And you looked sweet, darling, walking with your arm in his. It is where I have always wanted your arm to be. Nance, I am glad from my soul, that my plan has so signally prospered. I should have been definitely put out of countenance, if it had not. But I had no fear. Such determination as mine does not go before a fall."

"I see the portrait of your mother has been moved to the dining-room," said Beatrice: "I think it is such a nice idea."

"Father moved it himself, Miss Fellowes," said Sibyl.

"Dear Mr. Edgeworth! The new light thrown on him is all to his advantage," said Dulcia. "Not that it is new to me: I have laid claim to my personal illumination."

"It gives a wrong impression of her," said Nance.

"Well, but we can read her into it," said Sibyl, as her father approached.

"But strangers cannot."

"Father was not thinking of strangers."

"But I can understand that you think of them in a way," said Beatrice to Nance. "You like to give as true an impression as possible."

"All the little softenings and intended improvements," said Dulcia, "strike you as so much blur upon the dear reality."

"It is difficult for me to recognise any intention of improvement."

"The imperfections were to you perfection."

"We are talking about Mother's portrait, Father," said Sibyl. "You must be so glad to find it in its own place."

Duncan shook off her hand, and turned to face his guests, and spoke as if he held himself from following his own meaning.

"I will take advantage of being with my friends and my family, to announce a change which is to take place in my life. I am going very soon to be married. I will believe that my wife will meet the welcome from you, which I have met to-day."

There was silence, and Duncan moved towards the men, and spoke in his usual manner.

"Will you not come to the library, and have a cigar?"

Fabian complied at a gesture from his wife, and Gretchen understood, and signed to her son to follow.

For a minute the silence held.

"You can't any of you know what a usual thing this is," said Gretchen, in a comfortable tone.

"Well, we were all assembled to hear the news," said Miss Burtenshaw, in almost her usual manner.

"Well, to be sure," said Alexander. "Well, we none of us thought of this."

Dulcia went up to Nance, and stood holding her hand, her eyes full of tears and fixed in front.

"We must simply hope they will both be very happy," said Beatrice.

"Not a simple wish," said Oscar.

"A double one, Mr. Jekyll," said Miss Burtenshaw, facing him sturdily.

"No, no," said Dulcia half to herself; "I can't say the ordinary things; I can't."

"What we hope is, that you will all be happy together," said Mrs. Bode.

"No, Mother, no!" said Dulcia, with a quick shiver. "If you can, I can't. And neither can most of us here."

"Father must go his own way," said Mr. Bode. "He would have been a great deal by himself. You will be able to feel he is not that."

"He was left by himself," said Florence.

"Yes, Mrs. Smollett," said Dulcia.

"So that is why I should be doing my own work," said Grant. "I thought that speech a little sinister."

"You will have great opportunities for other people. I envy you for that," said Miss Burtenshaw, so accustomed to the character she bore, that she accorded it to herself.

"I do not envy them. No," said Dulcia, shuddering.

"Well, it can't be helped," said Alexander. "It doesn't do to make too much of it."

"It could have been helped," said Florence; "but perhaps there was no cause for it to be."

"Well, there is no need to behave as if one of us were dead, instead of going to be married."

"One of us is dead," said Sibyl, bursting into tears. "And it has been forgotten."

"I don't think it is fair to say that," said Beatrice. "It may have been because your father felt the miss, that he was driven to the change."

"In that case the second wife is the tragic figure, rather than the first," said Nance.

"Dearest, you have risen above it!" said Dulcia, turning to look into her face. "Second wife! What a height!"

"I hold to my position, that you are to be envied," said Miss Burtenshaw. "You are in a high place."

"Mrs. Smollett, you speak," said Dulcia. "You have the right of intimacy, of deep friendship with the dead. You speak, and we will follow."

"We can only do our best for everyone in the new conditions."

"We follow, Mrs. Smollett!" said Dulcia, drawing herself up.

"We follow!" said Miss Burtenshaw.

"We follow," said Alexander. "Yes, of course we do."

"Now, dearest," said Dulcia, taking Nance's hand and swinging it forward. "To the heights!"

"We shall be allowed no choice but to follow."

Dulcia dramatically dropped the hand.

"Mother's place will be filled!" said Sibyl.

Beatrice put her arm about her, and spoke into her ear.

"Not only Mother's," said Nance. "We cannot put it all on to her. She will suffer the least from the filling of the place."

"I am dwelling upon the possible filling of mine," said Grant. "Dare we ask Uncle the age of his bride?"

"Well, the question might savour of inquisitiveness," said Miss Burtenshaw.

"You mean, there may be an heir, Grant?" said Dulcia, in a clear, open tone.

"I had no other meaning."

"Poor, dear children!" said Mrs. Bode, wiping her eyes.

"Mother dear, to the Spartan colours! The standard is slung."

Duncan returned to the room with his friends, and after glancing about him, went up to his daughters.

"Do me the kindness of conducting yourselves as you were doing, when I arrived."

"I thought we should not escape on that score," said Nance. "We were enjoying life again."

"Well, Uncle ought to understand adaptability."

"We were," said Dulcia, looking straight before her. "We were enjoying life. We will not shirk the onus of it, its implication. It seems as it must seem."

"Good-bye," said Gretchen. "You don't want us all about. Come in to us, Cassie, and tell us what is to be told. We don't pretend we don't want to hear. You may soon be with us altogether."

"Good-bye, my dears. My heart cannot but ache for you," said Mrs. Bode.

"The colours, the colours, Mother of mine!"

"I hope it will turn out well," said Alexander. "I don't see why it shouldn't."

"Miss Jekyll," said Dulcia, "we have been saying not one word to you, who are virtually of the family, and involved in its changes! And one of the family you will remain, if I have any powers of divination; I was not speaking of changes in any ulterior sense. Now let one of your shafts of light flash forth upon the subject."

"I feel I have been receiving light upon it."

"Well, I do feel we have done something towards the end. And a good and gallant end it has turned out, too."

"Thank you for having us," said Miss Burtenshaw.

"I hope we have behaved nicely enough to be asked again."

"I am sure she does," said Nance, "when she considers who will be the hostess the next time."

"We are going to leave you with Father," said Mr. Bode. "He will have all of it to tell you."

"Good-bye, dearest. Courage!" said Dulcia. "I feel nothing can be too much."

"Good-bye," said Beatrice, pausing after the words, as though to say something further, but passing on.

"Good-bye, my dears; dear boy; good-bye, Miss Cassie," said Fabian. "We are all in it together. Florence, you forget your manners. Say what you ought."

"I am forgetting nothing: I have nothing to say," said his wife, continuing her way.

"I will take that cue, and leave without a word," said Oscar.

"I feel rather a coward," said Beatrice. "I made up my mind not to come away, without leaving them a word to hold by. I feel I have left them alone in a difficult place. I am not proud of myself."

"Well, we have all done that," said Alexander, kindly intentioned in identifying himself with his niece.

"It is of no good to cry over spilt milk," said Miss Burtenshaw. "Or over milk that has not been used at all, if you like it better."

"I do not like it better. But I see that is how it was."

"I should like to be back in that house now," said Alexander, "and see how things are going."

"Why, what idle curiosity, Uncle!"

"Well, really, Father!"

"I don't know," said Beatrice, in a quick tone; "I believe I had some thought of the kind myself. I am sure I had, even when I said what I did."

"It would be an odd person, who took no interest in his friends at a time like this," said her uncle. "I shouldn't envy or admire him; I don't pretend I should."

When his last guest had left his house, Duncan turned to his family.

"Has the last post come?"

"Yes, Father. It comes at half-past six," said Sibyl.

"When I ask you if it has come, you must know I want to see the letters."

"Your letter has come, sir: I have put it on your desk," said Bethia.

"I must see your accounts, Grant," said Duncan, turning to the door, and crushing a note of excitement. "It is the last time I shall have to depute them. Your own work calls for your time. You look passably well, you girls: you are decent-looking people. You would not make a fair impression only on your father. And you thought you would take up life again? I knew you would not need the word. Time has to go on: we have realised that together."

"I feel as if we had given Father the lead," said Nance; "that he had to be engaged, to keep us in countenance. We should certainly have been put out of it, if he had come back as he went away."

"I suppose it had to happen," said Grant. "It is odd we did not think of it."

"It did not have to happen," said Cassie. "It was not even likely to happen so soon."

"The stone has just been put on Mother's grave," said Sibyl. "I had just written to Father about it."

"You don't mean the letter will be following him?" said Grant.

"Well, I suppose it will be forwarded back here."

"The letter is not posted, Sibyl," said Cassie. "It is on your dressing table."

"The stone should strike him as a just impediment," said Nance, breaking off as her father entered.

"You are all in spirits; I am glad not to meet long faces."

"Father," said Sibyl, "you have not told us what she is like."

There was a pause.

"She is young and beautiful," said Duncan, in a tone as incredible as his words, though it changed the next moment. "What is it to anyone what she is like? It will be your business to make things easy for her. See that you attend to it."

"It is you who must be depended on for that," said Nance.

"I can be depended on," said her father, and again went to the door.

"What shall we do about Mother's portrait?" said Sibyl.

"It is a more pressing problem," said Cassie. "The gravestone is anyhow not in the house."

"Sibyl, you are a two-faced young woman," said Grant; "I don't believe you are capable of a point of view."

"I am, I am," cried Sibyl, bursting into tears. "I will go after Father, and make him listen. He shall not put another woman in Mother's place." She ran into the hall and caught up Duncan, who seemed to be wandering in a sort of dream.

"Father, Father, think while there is time! Think of the portrait, you hung yourself in its place. Do you want someone else to sit beneath it?"

"What are you talking of? There have to be things in a house, before someone comes to it," said Duncan, in a sharp but somehow unaffected tone.

"Remember the stone you chose yourself for her grave. Think of the words we put on it. Promise to wait until you see it. How can you bring a woman to a place that is filled?"

"Why should I see it? What good could I do by that?" said Duncan, with a sort of empty harshness. "Stop talking of it, and see it is attended to. That is what you can find to do about it."

"Cassie, it has come on us," said Nance. "We must face our situation with a quiet dignity. Dignity is always aimed at when circumstances preclude it. It is no wonder it comes to the mind."

"If we have done nothing, we are supposed to have nothing to be ashamed of," said Grant. "How absurd that is!"

"Ought we to do anything about the portrait?" said Sibyl, in a calm tone. "Would Father like us to move it, and say nothing?"

"We will not do it, in case he would like it," said Grant.

"It is of no good to be bitter," said Cassie.

"It is not," said Grant. "If it were, things would be different."

"Nance, will you go on sitting at the bottom of the table, until she comes?"

"It would serve no purpose to leave the place unoccupied. It will not be connected with any one person now. It seems rather especially subject to change."

"She can't be nice, can she?" said Sibyl.

"Can't she?" said Grant. "She must be hopeful and of a high courage and very affectionate, to have become fond of Uncle. And she is young and beautiful. I don't see how she could be nicer: I sympathise with Uncle in his choice."

"What? What do you sympathise with me about?" said Duncan, again within hearing.

"About the qualities of the lady you are going to marry, Uncle."

"What are they to do with you?" said Duncan.

CHAPTER VIII

"We expect a good deal of the harvest decorations," said Beatrice, from the pulpit of the church. "They are to serve the secondary purpose of a sign of welcome."

"It is no good, Beatrice; it is no good," said Dulcia. "It is dear and noble, but I can't stay the course. I would rather put flowers on the grave of the first Mrs. Edgeworth, than pile up the church with them for the second."

"I think we should try to conquer that feeling," said Beatrice, justified in her serious tone, as in herself interest and anticipation had achieved the conquest.

"A place kept vacant can after all only be a blank," said her cousin.

"A blank may be sacred," said Dulcia. "Shall I confess to a tiny feeling of disappointment?"

"The girls will find their happiness in their father's," said Mrs. Bode.

"Mother, we should hardly expect it, we who saw them share his sorrow."

"They will find their own happiness," said Florence. "We can make too much of it all."

"Here they are, the two dear, determinedly unconcerned ones, in the faithful escort of Miss Jekyll!" said Dulcia. "Coming along as naturally as if it were an ordinary occasion! There is one person here who will never feel their position is different."

"Well, you have come to the day," said Gretchen. "Are you taking the stand of looking forward?"

"The situation has its element of interest," said Nance. "Would you think it had not?"

"My dears, I am struck by a thought," said Dulcia, in a low, aghast aside. "It has come on me at this moment.

They won't have to face the last trial, to call the new-comer as they called their mother; by the simple, maternal name?"

"The newcomer is young," said Cassie, "and is to be called by her Christian name."

"The relief!" breathed Dulcia.

"That will make a pretty hotch-pot in the house," said Gretchen.

"Not to me," said Dulcia; "there will be no hotch-pot for me. For me the old dispensation will remain, clear cut, permanent, in its original lines."

"What is the Christian name of the young step-mother?" said Miss Burtenshaw."

"It is out," said Dulcia, "the word! I have feared it, and known it must come. Somehow I am glad I was not the one to say it."

"Names make so much difference, I think," Miss Burtenshaw continued on her own line. "Some people are ill done by. Personally I am grateful to my godfathers and godmothers."

"Rosamund; Rose of the world," said Beatrice, reflectively. "It is a pretty name and a pretty meaning. I like my name too. Beatrice, Blessed."

"What difference can it make to Miss Burtenshaw to be called Rose of the world?" said Gretchen, with a little burst of laughter.

"She seems to know," said Cassie. "And Beatrice is blessed, of course."

"Well, what is the name of the newcomer?" said Florence.

"Alison," said Nance. "It goes rather well with Edge-worth."

"It is dear of you to think so," said Dulcia. "And so it does."

"It is a charming name," said Beatrice. "We cannot say it is not."

"Why should we want to say so?" said Florence.

"We did not say so about the others," said Gretchen, laughing again.

"The more charm that is coming, the better," said Miss Burtenshaw, with a touch of excitement.

"You are looking very nice to-day," said Beatrice, to Nance and Sibyl.

"Darlings, I do admire it," said Dulcia. "Going out of black as quietly and unobtrusively as if it were the most natural thing in the world, when it must have gone so sorely against the grain! It is well done. And there is not a word I say, but it applies to Miss Jekyll."

"It would hardly be happy to receive a second wife, in a garb of woe for the first," said Nance. "I hope we shall shine more brightly than that."

"Here come some nice, useful men to our assistance!" said Beatrice, as a group of these persons came up the church, bearing the bulkier items of its adornment, with Grant empty-handed and lively at their sides.

"And Grant with them," said Dulcia, "looking so dear and distinguished, with his arresting, white lock of hair, as if he were the heir of all he surveyed! Which of course he still is; and may he always be."

"The future will take care of itself," said Miss Burtenshaw.

"That seems to be so," said Grant. "It is setting about it."

"Well, a light note is best," said Beatrice.

"I declare I felt a fool," said Alexander, "stumping through the village with those sheaves of corn! I could have laughed at myself; I sympathised with the urchins."

"So Father is coming home," said Mr. Bode. "Now Father will always be Father. You must not make a mistake."

"What a horrible sight a smothered church is!" observed his son.

"Almeric," said Sibyl, "how would you feel, if you were waiting to be inspected by your father's wife?"

"I suppose much as she would," said Almeric, only conceiving of the position on equal terms.

"Did you say Mrs. Edgeworth was young, the new Mrs. Edgeworth?" interposed Beatrice.

"Yes, dear, the new Mrs. Edgeworth," said Dulcia; "that is better."

"Yes, she is twenty-eight," said Nance.

"Twenty-eight?" said Beatrice.

"Twenty-eight, dearest, or thirty-eight?" said Dulcia, leaning forward.

"Twenty-eight. Why should I be ten years out?"

"Then how many years is she younger than your father?"

"Father is sixty-seven. You can do the calculation, if you distrust my figures."

"And how long is it since your mother died?" said Dulcia, dropping her voice.

"Nine months."

"Now Father is bringing you a companion," said Mr. Bode, in a fainter tone.

"Is he bringing one for himself?" said Gretchen. "He needs one the most. He has proved that he thought so."

"Better be an old man's darling than a young man's slave," said Beatrice.

"We all know our own Mrs. Edgeworth led the life she did, simply because she wished to," said Dulcia.

"Your father was not young, when he married the first time, was he, Nance?" said Florence.

"He was forty-one, and Mother was thirty-five."

"Not an early marriage," said Dulcia, judicially.

"No, rather late," said Nance. "Now we must leave you, to enter upon the new chapter in our lives."

"May it be a bright chapter, darling. You pass beyond appreciation. We shall think of you at the crucial moment, turning your faces to the music under Miss Jekyll's captainship."

"Good luck to you all," said Florence. "Send for me when I am wanted."

"I think you take it so perfectly, Mrs. Smollett, the supplanting of your old friends," said Beatrice.

"Indeed, Mrs. Smollett. Even I find it hard to come up against," said Dulcia, "further as I am from the fountain head, so to say."

"My old friend is dead. Her husband's remaining a widower would not bring her back."

"But it would keep something of the old atmosphere intact," said Dulcia, with all effort to maintain in Florence a natural bitterness. "It would not have seemed to root her out, root, barrel, and stock."

"Death seems to do that by itself."

"I have such a prejudice against a second marriage," said Beatrice, looking round. "I can never understand a woman's becoming one of the parties in one."

"You haven't seemed to feel much prejudice against this," said Gretchen.

"It seems to me that the essence of it would be the singleness of the experience," continued Beatrice without moving her eyes.

"Repeated, it would be besmirched," said Miss Burtenshaw, her colour deepening.

"I hope we shall be able to make the girl feel at home amongst us," said Florence.

"Mrs. Smollett, you set us an example," said Dulcia. "The girl, too, revealing your feeling as purely understanding and maternal! Here we are, grudging her an empty place, and blind the while to her complex and difficult part!"

"She will be safe enough with Nance."

"She will, Mrs. Smollett. Safe with Nance! With Nance, who is yielding her place to her, who is definitely stepping back! And we who give up nothing, cannot await her in common charity. It is a parable."

"Will your daughter remain with the Edgeworths, Mrs. Jekyll?" said Mrs. Bode.

"Mother, that question were better left to work out its answer."

"Does the second matrimonial venture call up the first?" said Miss Burtenshaw.

"It cannot but touch certain chords," said her cousin.

"I cannot picture Mr. Edgeworth as a lover," said Dulcia.

"I saw him when he was younger," said Florence.

"And it reminds you? You make me shiver, Mrs. Smollett," said Dulcia.

"It is common enough for people to marry twice," said Gretchen.

"Of course it is, Mrs. Jekyll. Let the poor man marry in peace," said Alexander. "Why should he not marry a hundred times, if he wants to?"

"And can find a hundred women to marry him," said Miss Burtenshaw.

"I suppose some men cannot live single," said Dulcia.

"Well, here comes a man who lives single," said Miss Burtenshaw, as Oscar and Fabian came up the church, "and another who does not."

Gretchen sent her eyes to the speaker.

"We saw the Edgeworths' carriage going in at the gates," said Oscar.

"And stood and stared after it," said Fabian, "and were pointed out to the bride."

"Did you see Duncan pointing you out?" said his wife.

"Yes, and saw her look at us. Very satisfying."

"Did you not look at her?"

"Yes. Very satisfying."

"Is she pretty?" said Beatrice.

"Did Mr. Edgeworth seem very attached?" said Miss Burtenshaw at the same moment.

"Yes," said the men together.

"As much as to the first Mrs. Edgeworth?"

"Yes."

"How could you tell?" said Miss Burtenshaw.

"Well, you must know of ways, to ask the question," said Oscar.

"Oh, I know, Mr. Jekyll," said Miss Burtenshaw, her knowledge having only for a moment eluded her.

Dulcia was silent, and Beatrice looked on with a simple grave expression.

"You have no criticism to make?" said Florence.

"None," said Oscar. "We quite understand."

"Well, our decorations are complete," said Beatrice. "Let us hope Mrs. Edgeworth, the new Mrs. Edgeworth, Mrs. Edgeworth's successor, shall we say, will appreciate them to-morrow."

"I think we had better not say that to-morrow," said Oscar.

"I should not dream of it, of course, Mr. Jekyll. I was not serious."

As Duncan's carriage passed his gates, his family gathered in the hall.

"I feel more nervous than ever in my life," said Sibyl.

"I hardly feel involved in the drama," said Nance.

"We are merely walking on," said Grant. "That is to be my permanent part. It is true it is more difficult than might be thought."

"It will be hard on Father, if we make a bad impression."

"I don't know that it will matter," said Nance. "He has reached his climax without finding any need to involve us."

"Mother would wish us to stand by him in this crisis of his life."

"In any other crisis. This may be the one that admits of doubt."

Bethia walked swiftly and silently past them, and took her stand by the door.

"Yes, there is the carriage," said Nance. "Unlike Bethia, I can bring my lips to frame the words."

"Father!" cried Sibyl, springing forward.

"Well, Father, you are up to time."

"The horses have brought you well, Uncle."

"Welcome!" Duncan was saying, in a tone they did not know, with his back turned to them. "Welcome to the house where everything is yours. Welcome home."

A tall, young woman came swiftly up the steps, and looked about her in an open, interested manner. She had fair skin and hair, liquid, hazel eyes, rather beautiful features, rounded and a little worn, becoming, individual, expensive clothes, and an air at once provincial and gently bred. She had led a secluded, oppressive youth, lost her invalid parents, and found herself without provision. Duncan had met her at his sister's house, and starved as he was of a normal life, had lost his command of himself.

"These are my daughters, Nance and Sibyl. This is Grant Edgeworth, my brother's son. You have but to say a word to any one of them, to have it followed."

"That is a rash undertaking on their behalf. Why present me as such an overbearing stepmother?"

His wife spoke in quick, soft, definite tones, and accepted the hands of Nance and Grant, and Sibyl's embrace.

"Nance, are we not to have tea?" said Duncan, using a sharp tone to cover his consciousness.

"It should be ready in the drawing-room, Father."

"You ought to pour it out," said Alison, as Nance gave her the place. "It is your established duty, not mine."

"It is your duty now, unless you are tired by your journey."

"I will put off all duties while excuse offers," said Alison, sinking on the sofa, and looking from face to face. "No doubt you are prepared to wait on a couple of an earlier generation."

"We are prepared to wait on you," said Grant, bringing her cup.

She took the cup in one hand, and reaching for Duncan's hand with the other, swung it caressingly, while Duncan's family kept their eyes from his face.

"Here is Cassie, come to be introduced," said Sibyl.

"This is Miss Jekyll," said Nance. "She used to teach us, and still keeps us under her eye."

"Will she mind having me under her eye too? It is hard to have somebody extra put in, without being consulted."

"She lets us call her Cassandra, or usually Cassie."

"What a lovely Christian name! Am I allowed to use it? Or have I to say Miss Jekyll, like an outsider. Of course that is what I am. I don't know why I should expect preferential treatment; but of course one does expect it."

"No doubt you have had it," said Grant.

"It would be kind and friendly to use the name," said Cassie.

"I have only an inferior name to offer in exchange. But pray do all use it," said Alison, rising and stooping over Duncan, with her hands on his shoulders.

"You will be treated as you say," he said.

"Won't you have some more tea, Alison?" said Sibyl.

"Oh, yes, please; cups and cups," said the other, springing back to her seat.

Grant brought the tea again and she raised her eyes.

"Of course you are all distinguished looking. You do not have to face the humiliation of being described as pretty."

"I have never suffered it," said Nance.

"I believe I have, Alison."

"Yes, I think you are pretty," said Alison, looking at Sibyl. "Yes, I am afraid you must be called pretty. It is sad for you."

"I can't help my appearance, Alison."

Duncan looked up at the repetition of the name.

"And your family portraits are as out of the ordinary as you are. More so, I think. Yes, I should call them more out of the ordinary. Who is the pale, dark lady, with the streak of white hair?"

"That is Grant's mother, my brother's wife," said Duncan. "The white lock of hair is a family feature, and keeps cropping up. Grant is a conspicuous victim of it."

"What a pleasant, easy way of becoming distinguished! I wish my family had had such a good method. They could only be distinguished in the usual ways, and so they were not distinguished. We must be careful never to add a portrait of me to the gallery. It will be easy to avoid it, as all the room is taken."

"We can make room, Alison," said Sibyl.

Duncan rose to his feet.

"Now you want a rest," he said, extending a hand to his wife, and recalling to Nance a similar gesture to her mother years ago. "I must not wear you out with my ready-made family."

Alison rose and taking the hand, went swiftly from the room at his side.

"We are so far from betraying hostility," said Nance, "that we have erred on the other side."

"Nance, it is a tragedy," said Grant. "Uncle ought to have known better. To think of that girl's future!"

"So our concern is to be transferred from ourselves? I am still thinking of my own future. It seems it will be as odd as I thought."

"Do you think she is so pretty, that she makes everyone else look ordinary?" said Sibyl.

"Not ordinary," said Cassie. "Less pretty than she is."

"I think Father is very much in love."

"I think he is," said Cassie.

"It is unspeakable," said Grant. "To wreck a young life to satisfy his senile whim! It does not bear thinking of. What would Aunt Ellen say."

"It is more than a whim," said Cassie; "and it is not senile."

"She is not any younger than we knew she was," said Nance. "She even looks older than her age. I don't see why Mother should say more now, than she would have at first."

"It would hardly have happened, if she had been here

to express her views," said Cassie. "And we don't know if she would have preferred a woman of her own kind in her place."

Duncan returned, and coming to the sofa, sat down and opened the paper, with a tell-tale movement of his mouth.

"Father, she is beautiful," said Sibyl.

"All my congratulations, Uncle."

"We could not admire her more than we do, Father."

Duncan looked up, repressing a smile.

"See that someone goes to her room to help her to dress."

"I should love to, Father," said Sibyl.

"Love to, Father," said Duncan. "Can't you open your mouth, without saying a name?"

"So should I love to," murmured Grant.

"We are to forget the habits of childhood," said Nance. "It seems a good time for forgetting our childhood altogether."

"I meant one of the maids, of course," said Duncan, and began to read.

Alison came to dinner, radiant and a little strained. She was vivacious in the drawing-room, walked to the dining-room with head held high, and paused at her place at the bottom of the table.

"Is my seat all this way from you, Duncan? That is not a good plan, when you are the only person here who wants me."

"That is your place, of course. Whose could it be?"

"Well, I suppose every other belongs to someone else," said his wife, sitting down, and then turning to Nance. "This has been your place until now?"

"It has never really been mine," said Nance, looking aside.

"Oh! It is the place occupied by my predecessor! Let me hasten to another, where it is not sacrilege to sit. I made sure that one would be sacred and empty, with a halo round it."

"That is your place," said Duncan; "the place of the

mistresses of the house for generations. You have many predecessors in it."

"But I expect most of them corresponded to only one master. I meant my immediate predecessor. Her place ought surely to be empty during your lifetime. I was not prepared for this way of treating it."

"We would rather see you in the seat, than see it empty," said Grant.

"Grant, your opinion on the point is not needed," said his uncle.

"Do you like this room, Alison?" said Sibyl, seeming to wish to change the topic, and looking round the walls.

"Yes, I like it better than the drawing-room. It is more homelike. I think I shall often sit here. What I do like about the house, is that it is so pleasantly simple and homelike." Alison had been struck by the modesty of the house and its appointments. "I had been dreading a proud, ungainly structure, with dull elaborations. I am grateful to my predecessor for her tastes."

"If they would have been so congenial to one another, it is a pity they could not be here together," murmured Nance.

"I agree that this room is more homelike," said Sibyl, still looking round.

"The portraits are less overpowering. I shall never be friendly with the relations you have imprisoned in the drawing-room. I see another of the woman with the white piece of hair. She looks quite young and amenable."

"She was only forty when she died," said Grant. "I was a boy of twelve. The white lock of hair appears in babyhood. The rest of her hair was as black as mine all her life."

"Yes, of course, she was your mother," said Alison. "And the pleasant, peaceful-looking woman over the chimney piece? She has a nice, affectionate look. I may get quite attached to her."

There was silence.

"Who is she?" said Alison.

"She was my wife," said Duncan in an even tone.

"My mother," said Nance, at the same moment.

"Oh, no wonder I felt drawn towards her! It is natural there should be a bond of sympathy between us. Of course she looks at me understandingly: I must cultivate a corresponding expression."

"There is a similarity between their positions," said Nance. "It is stronger than between those of any two women I know."

Duncan went on with his dinner, and Bethia, as if of intention, walked up and handed him a dish.

"Why do you say your clever things so low?" said Alison to Nance. "If I could make clever speeches, I should shout them abroad."

"Nance has a belief that I am deaf," said Duncan, "and forgets it is not a general infirmity."

"I suppose my colleague has always hung there, looking down on you all?"

The chance word brought silence, and Alison looked from face to face.

"The portrait has not been there long," said her husband. "It used to be on the landing."

"And when was it brought here?"

"Not long ago."

"Oh, I see. You wanted your consorts all about you. I hope it is proving all you wished. I am glad there is no blank yet in the circle."

"Alison," said Duncan, rising to his feet, "I had only my past to depend on. It seemed to be all I had. You must understand how it was."

"Oh, you poor, dear one!" cried Alison, running round the table. "Did I leave him to himself, so that he had no one but my predecessor? I am so glad he had her to turn to. So she ought to be glad he has me, and feel all is fair between us."

"I am sure she is glad, Alison," said Duncan, bringing a change to his young wife's face.

"So I give satisfaction to you both," she said, returning to her seat.

"It is certainly a success not to be the cause of their first difference," murmured Nance.

"Our friends are in luck that to-morrow is Sunday," said Grant. "They have only to wait one night before their sight of Alison."

"Great zeal has been put into the harvest decorations for her sake. I fear they will not afford her a spectacle of equal interest."

"Spectacle!" said Duncan. "We shall simply go to church in the ordinary way."

"You know you will be very proud, Father," said Sibyl.

Duncan gave a frown, and seemed about to speak, but was silent.

"Your parlourmaid eyes me as an interloper," said Alison.

"She is your parlourmaid," said Duncan.

"That was ready, Father."

"It was obvious, Sibyl."

"All the servants will fall in love with you, Alison."

Duncan made a sudden movement, that brought the meal to an end. Grant went to open the door for the women, and his uncle addressed him almost before he returned.

"You must throw yourself into your work, Grant. You may feel it a misfortune to have given your mind to the place. I am sure you understand me?"

"Yes, I do, sir; I hope you will have a son."

"That is not what I said."

"Isn't it, Uncle? Then what did you say?"

"I am talking about you, not about myself."

"I see we are less connected than we were. I hope for your sake and Alison's, that it will be as you wish."

"Alison! Alison! You had to use her name, I suppose; there seemed no alternative. But you need not reiterate it every time you open your mouth. One would think you had never heard a name before."

"I have seldom heard such a charming one. But I will not say it oftener than I can help. It will be natural at times to refer to her."

"Oh, not so often," said Duncan, tapping his glass.

"It would be a natural satisfaction to leave the place to your son. I ought to sympathise with you. I should have looked forward to doing it myself."

"Thank you, boy; thank you. You are a reasonable person to see my life is my own. Some youngsters would not have seen it." Duncan rewarded his nephew by dealings as man to man. "Do you think—would you advise me, Grant, to take that portrait from the dining-room?"

"I think it was better in its old place. The chimney piece is too high for anything above. Would you like me to attend to it?"

"Thank you, Grant, thank you," said Duncan, remembering how lately a task similar and different had been for his own hand. "I will leave it to you. Have the papers come from the station?"

"They are on that table." Grant was glad to rise and fetch them. "I hope they were in time for the speech."

The two men talked in the way that Duncan had begun to miss, and regarded as masculine, and an hour passed before they went to the drawing-room.

Alison was sunk in an easy chair, listening to Nance reading aloud. She raised her hand in warning, and Duncan and Grant sat down. Nance stopped at the first break, but Alison signed to her to continue; and Duncan found himself, for the first time within his memory, adapting his evening to his household. One of the ways in which his years were telling, was an early weariness at night, and as he sat unoccupied, the voice lulled him to sleep.

Nance shut the book, afraid of waking him, and Sibyl looked up and began to smile.

"Must we leave off?" said Alison, in an audible tone.

"The reading caused the slumber," said Nance, "and should be the last thing to stop it. We may as well maintain both. My delivery is clearly not too dramatic."

Sibyl fell into repressed laughter; Alison looked up and joined, with her eyes resting with light apprehension on her husband. Grant glanced quickly from the mirth of one face to the lined weariness of the other.

The sleeper suffered an involuntary snore, that shook him into wakefulness, and sat up and stared at his companions.

"It is time to go to bed. We cannot sit here all the evening, pretending to be occupied. It is hardly a self-respecting thing to do."

Alison stared in her turn, as she beheld what was to the rest an accustomed sight; and Duncan forced a different manner.

"We 'lack the season of all natures, sleep'," he said, while his daughters looked at him, almost in consternation at his effort. "We have a full excuse in our day."

His family rose, and Alison looked from one to another.

"I don't think I will go yet. I will stay and go on with the book by myself. I can't be torn from it at this exciting point. I don't understand how you have all got sleepy together in a moment."

"Follow at your pleasure," said her husband; "but remember your day has been equal to mine."

"I have not had the task of introducing two wives," said Alison, her eyes on the page. "That must have helped to spin things out, in spite of the fancy they took for each other."

Grant and the sisters bade her good-night, and she smiled and waved the book, and continued to read.

Left to herself, she read a page, threw herself about in her chair, read the page again, and rose and walked about the room. Surveying herself in a mirror, she was startled by the door.

"What a predicament for a stepmother!" she said, with another easy recourse to the quick, light quality of wits. "I was wondering if I looked the part, and deciding

I soon should. It will be a step to attain a suitable appearance."

Grant stood with his eyes on her face.

"Do you always go to bed at the nod of the head of the house?"

"You see we do: I came down to carry out a commission."

"Well, I will not start such a custom; it would be a most undignified beginning."

Grant sat down in his uncle's chair, and leaned back and closed his eyes. As his aspect approached that of Duncan sleeping, Alison gave a trill of mirth.

"Poor darling! What a shame, when he was tired with bringing home a wife and a stepmother, and being a father and an uncle and a widower and a husband himself! It was enough to exhaust any man. I have found two characters enough. And making friends with my predecessor. By the way, what was she like?"

"This photograph is good," said Grant, moving it forward.

"Of course the house bristled with her portraits. I hope I shan't have to be treated in like manner. I should think I am safe, as all the places are taken. She looks a more suitable consort for your uncle."

"Much more."

"Were you very fond of her?"

"Yes; I thought of her almost as a mother."

"I suppose my existence seems an insult to her?"

"Alison, I feel the existence of all of us in this house an insult to you."

"I hope you will reconcile yourself to the relationship."

"It is a thing to which I shall never be reconciled."

"I don't ask you to look on me as a mother, even though I should only be the third on your list."

CHAPTER IX

"So ALISON IS not down yet, Father?"

Duncan did not reply.

"So Alison is not down yet, Father?"

Duncan caused himself to smile.

"I can hardly say she is down, can I, Sibyl?"

"I wondered if she was tired after yesterday."

"Then you did not express yourself very clearly."

"Set us a better example, Father. Is there any reason for her not being down?"

"No doubt there is, Nance, or she would be down."

"I wondered if she would like her breakfast sent up," said Nance, finding her voice falter over the words.

Her father's sounded impeded by amusement.

"You are neither of you very good at expressing yourselves this morning."

"We'll do better, Father. Would she like her breakfast taken up?"

"I do not think any message has come down."

"Here she is!" said Sibyl.

"Here she is!" said Duncan. "And here is Grant! Here he is!"

"Good morning, one and all," said Alison, caressing her husband. "Oh, now I begin this sitting in someone else's place!"

"I have been acting as your deputy," said Nance, moving from the urn.

"Pray keep the seat; I am sure its real owner would rather you had it. After all, you are a relation of hers. But where is she? Where is my predecessor? It speaks well of her, that I already miss her. I quite share the general feeling."

There was a pause.

"I moved the portrait to its old place," said Grant. "We are used to it—it looks better there."

"Cannot she bear to see me sitting here?" said Alison, taking the seat. "I am glad she has a family who think of her comfort. If I have a successor, I don't want to spend all my time gazing down at her. I hope you will consider me as well. That space will have to be empty, Duncan, until you come to a wife who consents to occupy it."

Duncan gave a laugh as of easy amusement.

"It must be entertaining to have a succession of wives, and watch their relations. Your first two are getting on fairly well. I quite agree that the first of all was above the average."

Duncan seemed suddenly to shrink into himself.

"I wish we could know what she would have thought of you, Alison," said Sibyl, softly.

"Sibyl, have you lost your senses?" said her father, in a low, harsh tone.

"When did she flit?" said Alison. "Does she generally make her journeys at dead of night?"

"I moved the portrait in the evening," said Grant, "after you had gone to bed."

"After we were together in the drawing-room? So that is why you came down. I did not assume it was to get a glimpse of your new aunt."

"Did you not go to bed, when you appeared to be going, Grant? Even in the smallest matters, it is correct to give the right impression."

"I came down to move the portrait, Uncle; and Alison and I talked for a time."

"The portrait was not in the drawing-room," said Duncan, in an almost absent manner, looking into his cup.

"It was in the dining-room, and then on the landing," said Alison. "It appears to have missed the drawing-room out. Neither of your first two wives approves the room. It is another point they have in common."

"Are we all going to church this morning?" said Sibyl.

"It is Sunday," said her father, crushing any hope of an altered routine.

"I wondered if Alison cared to go. People are not always as regular as we are."

"She and I think alike on fundamental things."

Duncan and Alison walked to church, followed by the three young people, who had walked so often behind him and another woman. The many times of their following Ellen seemed to condense themselves into a single, overpowering memory. If Duncan had felt any doubt on this following of precedent, he gave no sign.

Alison walked swiftly into the church, and complied when her husband ushered her to the first place in the pew. The rustle that greeted her, rose and fell, and then seemed to swell and hold in spite of itself. She glanced about with an appearance of natural interest, and then seemed to forget where she was. After the service Duncan walked to the halting place, and simply introduced his wife.

"How are you, my dear?" said Gretchen. "I hope as good as you look."

"Well, if that is so, I admit we have nothing to complain of," said Dulcia, aside.

"Ah, here is someone whom you like to have with you," said Mr. Bode.

"We do, Mr. Bode," said Sibyl.

"How do you do?" said Almeric, looking at Alison's face.

"We are glad to see you," said Florence. "We have all looked forward to this moment."

"We have, but in what spirit?" said Dulcia.

"In one we could now confess," said her brother.

"Did you find your journey tiring yesterday?" said Beatrice.

"It was not such an ordeal as this, I am sure," said Dulcia, suddenly pressing forward.

"It must be dreadful to be stared at like this. Let us stand back," said Beatrice, with a movement to sweep the group backwards.

"We are not staring, because we are looking with friendly interest," said her cousin. "We will not be thrust aside in disgrace."

"We will not be thrust, but we will go of our own accord," said Beatrice, looking surprised that no one followed.

"My wife, Jekyll," said Duncan.

"What a penetrating look!" said Alison. "It seemed to go down to my soul. Of course my soul is the part of me that you are concerned with."

Oscar and Fabian laughed, and Beatrice stood expressionless.

"Now do you find us all what you expected, Mrs. Edgeworth?" said Dulcia.

"She could hardly know what to expect," said Duncan.

"Now, Mr. Edgeworth, don't tell me!" said Dulcia, lifting a finger. "You have not said a word of all the friends who have made your life! Tell that to the marines, if you will, but not to me."

There was a pause.

"It is kind of you all to hide your feelings so well," said Alison. "You must be longing to spurn me as an interloper."

"No, Mrs. Edgeworth! Any feeling of that kind has already faded," said Dulcia.

"It has been rampant, has it? I rather respect you for it. I am all for loyalty to the past."

"I expect you have a tiny feeling of respect for us, for it. But indeed it has not been rampant. It has been suppressed almost as soon as there."

"Not quite as soon? I am glad of that; I should not have liked to interfere with your deeper feelings."

"Mrs. Edgeworth, you have not interfered with them," said Dulcia, on a note of earnestness. "There may have been some feelings for ourselves, simply and rightly kept

133

away from you. The feelings for your concern are what you have seen."

"Is this better or worse than we expected?" said Nance to Grant.

"It is worse: Dulcia has no right to live," said Grant, with unusual asperity.

"I think you have such a charming Christian name, Mrs. Edgeworth," said Beatrice. "I admire it very much."

"Then why not make use of it?"

Duncan gave a faint frown, which was henceforth to greet any breach of convention in his wife.

"What do you think of our harvest decorations, Mrs. Edgeworth?" said Miss Burtenshaw. "We want you to see in them an expression of our welcome."

"I think they are a definite success."

"Have you noticed the decorations, Mr. Jekyll?" said Beatrice, recognising that a church's adornment might hardly detain its rector.

"I say with Mrs. Edgeworth, that their success is definite."

"Oh, we shall be saying everything with Mrs. Edgeworth soon!" said Dulcia, with a sort of groan. "She has come here to impose herself on all of us; I can see that."

"So you do like Alison, Dulcia?" said Sibyl.

"I give in!" said Dulcia; "I give in. I came out this morning ready to resent her; to do my part in the general deprecation; to continue playing what I begin to see a cowardly part. But I am faltering; I am feeling the spell; I admit it."

"You do," said her brother.

"What do you think of her, Almeric?" asked Sibyl.

"She seems considerably better than most people."

"Nance," cried Dulcia, wending her way through the group, "Almeric has fallen! My brother has succumbed! What think you of that?"

"I think it is natural."

"Dear, I am so glad for you," said Dulcia, pressing up.

"I had so dreaded for you—I hardly know what. I am so rejoiced that it was a false premonition."

"It certainly seems an occasion of more joy than we anticipated."

"Dearest, I see it is worse for you in a way. To have the dear place taken by—well, really taken; to say nothing of your own place! But you are generously glad for all concerned."

"I have never seen more clearly, that people make their own places."

"That is a much better way to put it. It was a called for correction."

"Are you going to take an interest in the church, Mrs. Edgeworth?" said Beatrice.

"Am I supposed to? Does it go with my place? Did my predecessor take an interest in it?"

There was a pause.

"Did you—do you mean the first, the late Mrs. Edgeworth?"

"There has only been one before me, hasn't there? I understood I was only the second."

There was some laughter.

"No, she did not take much interest in it," said Miss Burtenshaw. "We will not secure your support under false pretences."

"But you can take your own line, Mrs. Edgeworth," said Dulcia. "You are not bound to any precedent, I think. That does not seem in any way indicated. It might indeed be indicated in the other way. Not that there is anything against either course; there is simply nothing in it at all."

"I am not sensitive about following in her wake. When I am sitting in her chair, and lying in her bed, and married to her husband, there is not much point in making trivial exceptions. I will take her line about the church, as it fits my own inclinations."

"Mrs. Edgeworth, everything in both the rooms has been changed. It almost goes without saying," said Dulcia.

"It would have been done; and it has been done. You do not need us to vouch for it."

There was silence, and Florence and Cassie began to talk.

"Was not the house done up, to receive Mrs. Edgeworth?" said Almeric to his mother. "If it was not, it shows very bad taste."

"I don't know if it was thought of, dear. We did not think of it, did we?"

"It was not our business."

"I must take my wife home," said Duncan. "She had a long day yesterday. The others may follow as they please."

"There are future days," said Fabian.

"Good-bye, Mrs. Edgeworth," said Dulcia, standing forward. "May I say how glad I am—how heartily I endorse the general sentiments to-day?"

"Good-bye, all," said Alison, waving her hand. "I believe I have filled a blank in your lives. I am glad it has only remained for a few months."

"Well, light has been thrown upon our family conditions," said Nance. "I see that some was indicated. I hope I do not exaggerate our appeal?"

"The newcomer was willing to have it thrown," said Gretchen.

"I think it is a good thing to speak of things openly," said Beatrice. "Then nothing can ferment and fester underneath."

"Yes, there are more dark corners in most minds, than in that one," said her cousin.

"More that are kept dark," said Nance.

"Do you not like her, Nance?" said Dulcia, in a surprised manner.

"Yes, we all like her. But I expect her feelings are much as our own. Indeed we know they are, as she reveals them."

"We need not like and understand her less well for that," said Beatrice.

"Indeed no. We meet on a ground of common woman-hood," said Miss Burtenshaw, for some reason changing colour.

"Darling, how wonderfully and beautifully you are behaving!" said Dulcia, suddenly to Nance. "Here we have all been sympathising, and grimly awaiting with you the dread phenomenon! And here we turn round, and show a complete change of face, and turn up as large as life on the other side! I really do feel it for you, though my opinion has to remain as it is. And it would be worse for you, if it did not, wouldn't it?"

"If your opinion is the true one."

"Darling, you are strained and worked up," said Dulcia, in explanation of this.

"So the change in your life has taken place," said Almeric to Grant.

"Yes, and I think my tone has so far been perfect."

"And are you settling down all together?" said Mr. Bode.

"Do not hurry them, Father. They must be a little keyed up as yet. They have taken a full first step."

"So have we all," said Fabian.

"You have struck a time of test," said Miss Burtenshaw. "You will be finding there is compensation."

"How much nearer is your uncle's wife to your age than his?" asked Almeric.

"Two years older, against thirty-nine younger. You heard what Miss Burtenshaw said."

"That is a way to talk! Heard what I said indeed! I heard what you said."

As the Edgeworths took their leave, Gretchen looked after them.

"So that is the child who takes Ellen Edgeworth's place."

"Mrs. Jekyll, Nance reproved me for making some such speech," said Dulcia. "And to my mind justly. She said, and so firmly and simply, that everyone makes his or

137

her own place; and I felt the rebuke to that moment, and was silenced."

"Well, I am not," said Gretchen, turning to Florence. "There are breakers ahead in that house, unless I mistake."

"Well, we must hope you do mistake, Mrs. Jekyll," said Dulcia, her clear voice seeming an advantage, as it had to pierce Gretchen's back.

"The person whom I am sorry for, is that father's pet, Sibyl," said Beatrice.

"I fear there is an element of tragedy there," said her cousin.

"I hardly think so," said Florence; "I doubt if the father has ever made a pet. And she is a girl who will make her own life."

"Mrs. Smollett, I do like your sane, healthy views," said Dulcia. "They are just the thing for this moment. I am prevented from bringing that mother's pet, Nance, forward."

"We will not do that," said Beatrice, "as she would not do it herself."

"That may be a reason for doing it for her," said Miss Burtenshaw.

"And what will your duties be, Miss Jekyll, under this new regime?" said Dulcia. "I should say, what are your good intentions for the family?"

"My duties will hardly exist, as they are not to be different."

"When shall we have your report of the situation, Miss Jekyll?" said Mrs. Bode.

"We shall meet as usual, I think. I must be proceeding into the heart of it."

"Mother, that was deserved," said Dulcia. "Miss Jekyll is giving us no report. And much as we should like one, we would rather have her the loyal friend she is."

"I would rather have the report," said Fabian. "I hope Miss Cassie can adapt herself to conditions."

"There she goes, dear Miss Jekyll!" said Dulcia, shading her eyes. "Walking forward, as though she made nothing of the uncertain future. I think there is a peculiar dignity in service to your equals. No pride of liberty or choice quite comes up to it."

"Peculiar is the word," said Gretchen, turning to go.

Cassie entered the Edgeworths' hall as the family were going in to luncheon.

"I am late, Bethia. We loitered after church."

"These days give us cause for hesitation, ma'am; but we are called upon to act our part in them."

Cassie had spent the night at home, and on entering the dining-room, glanced at the space above the fire.

"I am sorry to have driven away an old friend of yours," said Alison. "But when she saw me, she simply took to her heels and fled. There was nothing I could do about it."

Duncan kept his features still.

"Duncan does not like me to refer to her. But it is not fair that I should not do just that, when he was married to her for a quarter of a century. How does he know she likes him so much better than me? And she is so important here, that I must get on some sort of terms with her. Are you having to repress your feelings at seeing me in her place?"

"It is your place now. And the sight of you arouses its own feelings."

"I suppose you are really the mistress of the house, and no one else has any place at all?"

"I can save you as much of the management as you would like."

"Was my predecessor a capable housekeeper?"

"Alison, we will make an end," said Duncan. "That chapter is closed, and we give our minds to the next."

"But I may be allowed to take an interest in it? It is all fresh and exciting to me, though to you it is so familiar. I hope you do not feel you cannot stay with me, Miss

Jekyll? I should be sensitive about driving away a second member of the house; and you might go further than the landing."

There was silence, and Nance and Sibyl glanced at their father.

"Poor darling, did I worry him by making a friendship too high for me? Did my superior have to be banished to check my growing familiarity? I will try to maintain a respectful distance. Where more than one wife is the custom, I believe there are rules for the treatment of the head wife. If I am too young and ignorant to know them, there is the more reason for me to keep my place."

"I did not disguise from you that I was a widower."

"You did not. You made it clear you were one; but you should have been more careful to give a right impression."

Duncan remained silent, and his mood cast a gloom. Alison, less in training than the rest, sprang from her seat and disappeared. There was a stir, but no one spoke before her husband.

"Grant, go and see if Alison would like any fruit."

Grant went to the drawing-room, where Alison was sitting with a book.

"Why did you run away from us?"

"I felt I would rather be here than there; and I can't understand why no one shared my preference."

"We should not dare to indulge it. I am to ask if you will have some fruit."

"I do not approve of my predecessor's training of her husband."

"I daresay not; but you see it would be better not to talk of her."

"Why should I not talk of her, when she is the constant preoccupation of other people?"

"Not of mine, when you are there."

"I am sorry I disturb your memories, when they are such a sacred part of you."

"You disturb more of me than that, Alison."

"I think I do want some fruit," said Alison, running to the door.

Duncan smiled at his wife, making little of her mood. Nance and Cassie talked to cover any uneasiness. Sibyl looked up to contribute her smile, and glanced from Grant's face to Alison's.

After luncheon they walked in the grounds to show Alison the place. The husband and wife were on easy terms, and the rest of the day was short. In the evening, when Duncan went to the library, he signed to his wife to accompany him, and to Grant not to follow.

"I will have you for what you are, my own. I have been sharing you with too many persons."

"Is it not your custom to share your wives? Have you been more than usually generous?"

"Now let us have done. In the past we know our lines have not met. It is the future we are to share."

Duncan drew his wife towards him, and she sat with her arms about him, crooning a song into his ear. When his eyes closed, she sat on, humming to help his sleep, in youth's pity for the easy weariness of years.

When Grant brought the papers, he was met by a warning gesture. He tip-toed across the room, and conducted a dumb intercourse. Something in the change came through to the sleeper, and his eyelids stirred; and the young man fell on his knees behind a couch, and remained mute and still.

Duncan set himself to a lover's scene, through which Alison suffered from her sense of a listener, and Grant from his own feelings. When Duncan went to bed, tired by the subtle demand of the day, his wife was aided by precedent to remain.

"I will go on with things in my own mind, as you have had enough. It is humbling to be the romantic one. I hope it is what you are used to."

"None of that, as I have said. And don't sit too long,

and forget your husband. I will not be used to that."

As Duncan's steps sounded on the stairs, Grant came from behind the couch. Sibyl, coming to put out the lamps, found her stepmother alone and unoccupied. The latter rose, and taking her arm, walked with her towards the stairs, and Sibyl, mounting them at her side, glanced down into the moonlit room.

CHAPTER X

"HURRAH!" CRIED DULCIA, waving a note above her head. "There is a son born to the Edgeworths! If Alison is held—well, not something of a failure, but not the full success as a consort it was hoped, such feeling will be dispelled to-day."

"If Alison is held a failure, what of the other young women in the place?" said Almeric.

"I am not going to be depressed by you, devoted knight that you are. I am going through the day, sucking all the sweetness from it. For it is lovely and pleasant news, and Nance puts on me the task of diffusing it. The arrival took place in the small hours, and misses the papers."

"Ah, someone is glad of what is good for other people." said Mr. Bode.

"You must have some more breakfast, my child," said his wife.

"Oh, now, Mother dearest, don't you fuss like a dear old hen. I shall not faint by the way. Indeed I suspect I shall come by a good deal of refreshment in the course of my peregrinations. So possess your soul in peace."

"I fail to see any likeness in Mother to a hen," said Almeric, alone in this view, as that of his parents was of smiling sympathy.

"I have no time to weigh my words. So don't fidget and flurry my departure. By bye, parents of mine. By bye, carping brother."

"Good-bye," said Almeric, adhering to the current phrase.

Dulcia ran up the Smolletts' drive, and was shown at her request to their breakfast room.

"Rejoice!" she said. "Rejoice with me! The Edgeworths

have a son! Unto them a son is given! Rejoice with me and all who love them."

There was a pause.

"Fabian was sent for in the middle of the night," said Florence, without a movement of her face.

Dulcia opened her eyes, and flinging herself against the wall, gave herself to mirth.

"I am a prize ass!" she said in choked tones: "I am a drivelling idiot. This will be a joke to tell against myself! I shall be glad of such a good tale, and by no means averse to being the heroine of it. It is an excellent round off to my news."

"I am sorry you have wasted your time over us."

"Wasted!" said Dulcia, again supported by the wall. "Wasted? You and I differ on the relative merits of things! The people who hear my story, will not consider it wasted; and I am the last to wish they should. How you will enjoy making a butt of me, when I am gone! I am more than reconciled to my part."

"You will share our breakfast, Miss Dulcia? You will do that for us?"

"Well, I believe I will, Doctor," said Dulcia, glancing about the table. "I left home after such a very light meal, to be betimes with my news; and now I find it is not news, I am conscious of an emptiness."

"I don't see how people can know yet," said Florence.

"Well, they will wait for their information," said Dulcia, settling her sleeves and addressing herself to the board. "They can wait better than my morning appetite, whetted by a walk and a sense of having taken a fall."

"Your mamma is quite well?" said Fabian, bowing from his place.

"Quite, thank you, though we do not apply that term to her dear, old, workaday personality. And Father too, peace to shades of Papa! And Almeric likewise, though I do not suggest that older people should enquire of his well-being. By Jove, these mushrooms are what they ought to be!"

"People do not know that Mrs. Edgeworth has a son, do they, Robinson?"

"Well, ma'am, Cook was told by the boy who brought the milk from the farm."

"Oh!" said Dulcia, rising. "That determines my interlude for sustenance. I am not going to be anticipated by boys from farms. I must rush on my way, reluctant though I am to leave you and your good cheer."

"You will let us send you, Miss Dulcia? It takes no time to put in the horse."

"No, no; you don't catch me waiting for horses to be put in," said his guest, knowingly shaking her head. "I can walk in fewer minutes than it would take your man to do that, much more drive the distance. So good-bye, and no offence, and thanks to both. And mind you make a butt of me. I definitely enjoin it."

"Now we have to make a butt of Miss Dulcia," said Fabian. "I believe we should have done it, if she had not made a success of it herself."

Dulcia took her way to the rectory, where Gretchen was tending plants in the porch.

"Well, what is your errand?" the latter said, with her can at the requisite angle.

"To bid you rejoice with me, Mrs. Jekyll, and rejoice for yourself too. There is a dear little son at the Edgeworths'!"

"That puts Grant's nose out of joint," said Gretchen, looking into the can.

"I bid you rejoice with him first of all, as I feel he would enjoin it. He will not consider the event in relation to himself."

Gretchen directed a stream to the roots of a plant.

"Oh, Mrs. Jekyll," said Dulcia, in recollection, "I have made such a fool of myself! I went to Dr. and Mrs. Smollett, actually went to them"—she leaned against the porch, and continued brokenly—"and announced the birth of the boy, as if Dr. Smollett had not officiated at it in the small hours."

Gretchen ceased her employment, and joined in the mirth.

"What is the joke?" said her son.

"I cannot tell it again, Mrs. Jekyll," said Dulcia, keeping her eyes from Oscar. "I cannot continue to offer myself as a sacrifice. I give you permission to do it for me, and I know you will not delay; but I will save my face."

"Alison Edgeworth has a boy," said Gretchen, resuming her can. "I wonder how that will fit in with the rumours."

"It is a thing apart," said Oscar.

"It is," said Dulcia. "And it is not a rumour, but a blessed actuality."

"Mr. Edgeworth and Alison were at church the other Sunday," said Gretchen, "and hardly spoke a word the whole time."

"Let us impute that to their feeling for me, rather than for each other," said her son.

"We do not talk in church, Mrs. Jekyll."

"I hope you are both more bright than you appear."

"But I entirely understand, Mrs. Jekyll. We have had a tiny feeling of guilty excitement at the threats of trouble; and the feeling has died down with the threats. Good-bye; and mind you make a victim of me; I leave you to it."

Dulcia went down the garden and on to the house of the Burtenshaws.

"Darlings!" she said, going into their parlour. "You will excuse my including you all in that term; I am too excited to differentiate. Well, darlings all, I have a piece of news. There is a lovely little son at the Edgeworths'." Dulcia's knowledge of the child had increased with her recitals of it, in the way of knowledge. "Come to them in the small hours of the morning!"

"Well, that was a convenient time to choose," said Miss Burtenshaw.

"I am glad," said her cousin slowly; "I think it may be a blessing in the house."

"And in a house that can do with a blessing," said her uncle. "Well, this cooks Grant's goose, doesn't it?"

"Father dear, we are talking of the baby, and not of cooking geese."

"Dear little man!" stated Dulcia.

"Do you think we might use the moment as one of personal intercession?" said Beatrice.

"They seem to be attended to just now," said her cousin.

"Where two or three are gathered together," said Beatrice, with light admonition.

"Well, we can do as we like in our hearts."

The talk went on, and Beatrice stepped aside, so evenly that she hardly seemed to do so, and bent her head, and raised it with a lightened expression.

"I could not have thought of a better piece of news," she said in a cordial tone, "and it comes at just the right time."

"Now I have a subordinate piece of news; well subordinate, but likely to afford you just as much pleasure. I went to the Smolletts', and announced the event, as I have with you; and Dr. Smollett had superintended it in the early morning!" Dulcia's voice failed, and she glanced at the wall.

There was a pause.

"We all do things like that sometimes," said Miss Burtenshaw.

"Ha, ha!" said Alexander. "That was a thing to do."

"Father, it was a very natural oversight."

"I am sure they appreciated the thought, as much as if they needed it, Uncle."

"It is a gift to be able to tell a tale against oneself, a kind of consideration for others."

"Shall you be seeing the Edgeworths to-day?" said Beatrice, with a considerate change of subject.

"Yes, I shall: I had not known it, but I shall. I shall proceed to them at once. It may do them good to see someone who takes a serious view of the occasion, without taking a solemn one. Good-bye, all. Do laugh at me behind my back. I acknowledge your ostensible forbearance."

Dulcia reached the Edgeworths' house as Grant drove up to the door, and waited for him on the steps.

"Now, Grant, I am going to do what you would wish, and congratulate you as heartily as any of the others."

"That is the best way to veil my downfall!"

"I entirely fail to see where the downfall comes in."

"That is the line. Continue on it."

"I am sure you are as eager to see the new arrival as I am."

"I had not thought of him as someone who could be seen. I had better set my teeth, and visit him."

The sisters came to the landing with the nurse and child.

"Come to the nursery, sir, where the light is better."

"I need no further exhibition: I see he exists."

"He is a fine, strong boy."

"No flicker of hope!"

"Nurse does not understand this foolishness," said Dulcia. "You are simply at ease and comfortable here, are you not, Nurse? Now what is the name? I want to be the first to know it."

"Richard, after Father's father," said Nance. "The first sons are named alternately Richard and Duncan."

"Dearest, the fascinating ways of families like yours. Then the name is common property amongst the elect, and I stand revealed as not belonging to them." Dulcia laughed at this position. "Dear Alison! She has attained to dignity indeed."

"I hope she will find it enough," said Sibyl.

"Nance, all is well, from the top to the bottom of the house?"

"I think things are better."

"I could publicly clasp my hands in thankfulness," said Dulcia, performing the action.

"Have you seen Father, Grant?" said Sibyl.

"No; I feel foolish over my delight in being supplanted."

"I suspect you will not find him exacting on this occasion," said Dulcia; "an occasion of the fulfilment of a hope as old as he is."

"He is very aloof over it," said Nance.

"There may be a tiny, tiny regret in all his joy, that this child, who is to be the dearest of his children, does not owe his birth to another."

"He gives no sign of these mixed emotions."

"Now I know what I will do," said Dulcia, stopping in the hall. "I have come to a resolve, and will carry it out. I will go in and congratulate Mr. Edgeworth on his heir!"

She went swiftly forward, glancing back with an excited face, and knocked at the door of the library.

"Come in," called Duncan's voice. "This palaver is not needed."

Dulcia raised her eyebrows towards the spectators, and entering, made a swift advance.

"I am not going to be afraid of you; I am going to treat you as the normal human being I believe you to be, and congratulate you heartily upon your son and heir."

"I thank you. You show me kindness."

"There, I knew you would not eat me; I knew you would accept my felicitations, and be glad to have them. We are all glad in our hearts to have a little notice taken of what is raising us to our own seventh heaven. Now confess your half-guilty pleasure in having this great event in your eyes dealt with in the accepted way."

"I will not deny my feelings."

"There, I said you would be; I was not to be deterred by the general misgivings. I had my own opinion, and would have it borne out. I said you were not a dragon in its lair; and now I reap my reward, and return unscathed." She waved her hand and withdrew, and closed the door before she spoke.

"Successful! Back without harm to life or limb! And

149

with a pleasant little sense of achievement into the bargain! And I am really glad to have had a human word with someone sitting alone and apart, amidst the excitement of the house. Dignity is a quality that is paid for."

"There is a flavour of pathos in Father's acceptance of what Dulcia has to give," said Nance to Grant.

"He had not much choice. We are not really surprised that she has come out unharmed."

"Now, whisperers," said Dulcia, "Sibyl and I will think you are talking about us."

"Alone and apart, amidst the excitement of the house," said Grant. "That fits me."

"It must be a relief in a way to have a certain future," said Dulcia.

"Why is certainty an advantage, when it is on the wrong side? I prefer a ray of hope."

"I think a life of individual effort is fully as dignified as one of inherited ease."

"I do not think so. Your words go right home."

"What are we to do with him, Nance?"

"There are things to be done this morning," said Sibyl. "Two of the maids are ill, on the top of the disturbance of the house."

"Let me attend to an household affair," said Grant.

"I am glad I am here," said Dulcia. "Put me to one of the most disagreeable jobs at once."

CHAPTER XI

"Now was there something wanting in that christening?" said Miss Burtenshaw. "Am I a person of intuition, or a carping individual who does not deserve to be received at the party afterwards? Perhaps it is not for me to say."

"Perhaps not," said Cassie to her brother, "as she continues her way to the party."

"I think there may have been something wanting," said Beatrice, her quiet tone going no further.

"I can't help it," said Dulcia; "I can't help it. There was something wanting. And in this christening, this fulfilled dream of Mr. Edgeworth's youth! There it was, intangible, insistent—*there*."

"You cannot help it, certainly," said Gretchen.

"Well, appearances are deceitful," said Miss Burtenshaw, "or we must hope so."

"Have we not a way of maligning appearances?" said Oscar. "They tend to be the expression of the truth."

"It was I who was maligning them, Mr. Jekyll," said Miss Burtenshaw, standing forward. "I am the guilty one in this case."

"Mr. Jekyll," said Dulcia, "there is something wrong about that marriage. We have turned this way and that, but there is no escape."

"The marriage was destined to failure from the first," said Almeric, "like anything else unnatural and unfit."

"The old man's darling theory falls to pieces, does it?" said Beatrice. "I admit I should not care to make trial of it."

"The dear, enigmatic rector!" said Dulcia. "He is so

dry and sphinx-like, that I defy anyone to get at his essence."

"It is an elusive quantity," said Miss Burtenshaw, in the brisk tone of one not personally inconvenienced.

"I think he often brings out his opinions when he feels they may be helpful," said Beatrice, looking up.

"It is a good thing the baby is a boy," said her cousin, "or it would have been an occasion for tact."

"It is a good thing then, indeed," muttered Almeric.

"It would have taken a fine touch," said his sister, "to steer between congratulation and condolence."

"A better and better thing."

"There would have been no need for anything but congratulation," said Mrs. Bode.

"Oh, I think it is a merciful escape, Mother. Mr. Edgeworth has looked in church of late as if he were keeping himself under a tight hand."

"It is a pity he does not always present that front," said Almeric, "for the sake of those who see him out of church."

"We all know your attitude to Alison, Almeric; and I am glad to see you capable of it."

"It must be plain to the meanest that she is in a difficult place."

"Well, here she is, in that dignified place, be it difficult or not! I have not seen you since your new happiness, Alison. For as a guarantee of happiness we are determined to regard it."

"I am getting used to remedying other people's omissions. It begins to seem quite natural."

"You will feel it your own doing and dignity in the end. Never fear: I shall not for you. Mr. Edgeworth, confess in public your welcome of the little stranger! Never mind. Your confession in private shall be enough."

"Reasonably, as it is now made public," said Nance.

"We do not discuss the members of our family to their faces," said Duncan, smiling.

"Where does Uncle get his ideas?" said Grant.

"Do you feel this will be the first and last issue of this latter union, Nance?" said Dulcia.

"I think Father sees the boy as an only son."

"Well, it is for him to know. Further we will not probe," said Dulcia, ending with a laugh.

"How a woman seems to be apart, when she has a husband and child!" said Sibyl to Almeric.

"Does she? Then a good many women must be apart: I should think more than not."

"What is to be the designation of the youngest member of our community?" said Miss Burtenshaw.

"Yes, what is Baby's name?" said Mrs. Bode, content to speak according to herself.

"Well done, Mother; that does as well and better. Now I am going to announce it; I will not be gainsaid. I was the first to know, and first I will be to make it known. Richard, as his turn falls. And his own son will be Duncan."

"Richard," said Beatrice, speaking half to herself, and then looking up. "I like Duncan better, I think."

"Well, Richard is an empty name to us as yet," said her cousin.

"Miss Jekyll," said Dulcia, "I do congratulate you on another Edgeworth to train from the beginning. It does consolidate your position; it renders it impregnable. I wish we were all as established on the road we have chosen to see as the one to success."

"What road have you chosen?" said her brother.

"The little, humble road of doing what I can for anyone. I have not the least objection to saying it, as I do feel I am making progress."

"Cassie does not train us from the beginning," said Nance. "We attain a stage of reason before we pass on to her."

"Miss Jekyll did not misunderstand me."

"I daresay she did not."

"What have you to say to it all?" said Gretchen to Grant.

153

"I cannot be glad or sorry that I am supplanted, and so I say nothing."

"It seems to me you said most of it."

"Well, Richard," said Grant, "do people try to make an awkwardness between you and me? We will not heed them, the mischief-makers."

"Isn't it just what it ought to be?" said Dulcia. "Nance, did you notice the look your father turned on Grant just then? Love, understanding, almost compunction! It was all there."

"Dulcia," said Sibyl, "could you give a hint to Almeric, not to keep staring at Alison? I am afraid Father will notice."

"Oh, I think there is no harm in that, dear," said Dulcia, not turning her eyes on her brother. "A cat may look at a king; and it is only in that spirit that my poor brother looks at Alison."

"It is in the way a man looks at a woman," said Sibyl in a new tone.

"Well, it must be in a sense; but there is no harm in it. I defy anyone not to look at Alison, so lovely as she is, moving about in her pride of motherhood. I can't keep my eyes from her myself."

"There are other feelings in Alison than those of a mother."

"Well, there could hardly not be. Many other feelings, I daresay. I defy anyone with her endowment not to have them, and any young man not to have them more strongly. My dear, we must take the world as it is."

"Well, Nance," said Mrs. Bode, "I remember you the heroine of a like occasion, as if it were yesterday."

"People who remember things, always remember them as if they were yesterday," said Cassie. "I remember it as if it were twenty-six years ago."

"Miss Jekyll's simple unflinchingness!" said Beatrice, with a smile.

"Yesterday!" said Alison. "That is putting the chapters

154

close, hard though they did follow on each other."

"Alison," said Duncan, in a harsh whisper, "this is not a time for folly."

"It is you who are responsible for the train of people's memories. They must have material for their comparisons."

"Will you exhibit your wit at your own expense?"

"It is at my own expense. I am always kind to your Ellen; kinder than you were to her, if I hear aright."

Duncan grew pale, and his wife spoke in a clear tone.

"I wish I had brought the christening mug. It is the nicest in the family."

"Can I fetch it, Alison?" said Almeric.

"Do, please. It is on the table in the nursery."

"You make use of your guest, Alison," said Sibyl.

"Almeric is an old friend."

"Not of yours. You had not met him a year ago."

"Well, I am one flesh with a person who has known him from birth."

"I wonder if you are."

"Behold the bauble, Alison!"

"The young fellow uses your Christian name, like them all," said Duncan. "You make a point of having it bandied. Not that I care what you choose."

"What name would you have him use? He is accustomed to saying Mrs. Edgeworth to someone else."

"That is no reason why he should not say it to you," said her husband in an almost taunting tone.

"I prefer a distinction to be observed. We need not give an impression that someone has risen from the dead."

"There could be no confusion."

"You can tell him you wish the title to be given to the wife of the moment."

"There can be no objection to that."

"I have stated my objection. I am the only wife who can do so. Do you see our altercation is attracting notice?

Your guests can judge which of your wives plays the better part."

A silence had fallen on those at hand.

"I think there is a certain excitement to be derived from an argument," said Beatrice, in a conversational tone.

"It shows how little we think of it," said her cousin. "We had poor sport from this one, over before we had got at the whys and the wherefores."

"I suppose it is always over in that way, Nance?" said Dulcia. "Your father and Alison get on as well as you now look for?—Dear, I did not mean to probe into what does not call for the light of day. Consider the question unasked."

"The romance of the first months must be a thing by itself."

"And that may have its own touch of what is fit for you. The word, months, gives me a glimpse of what it has all been."

"The question admits of elaboration," said Almeric, "considering it was unasked."

Duncan walked up to his nephew.

"You do wisely to stand aside, boy. We do not need to add to the clatter. It appears to hold its own without us. Can you listen to a word, without words of your own? Or must you swell the babel?"

"May I say once, Uncle, how fit it is to me that you have a son?"

"You bring me to my meaning. I also asked to say what I have to, only once. You have grown up with the girls, and do not need me to speak of them, except to say that they come more above you in my life than you may think. If you incline to one of them, you may not find me in your way. One boy is not much of a prop for the place, and I have had to get used to you. I shall have no more children."

"You see that as certain, Uncle? You and Alison are not on your former terms——"

"When I said I did not want words from you, I said it.

156

A man knows his own life and his own mind; or if you do not, remember there are better men than you, and hear the words of one of them."

"You feel you have made a mistake?"

"What is that to you? Keep your mind on your own mistakes, as they will be enough. And I will lead you to the kittle-kattle, as it is what you are fit for."

The women were making advances to the child, in apparent hope of response, while the nurse held it in smiling understanding.

"Are you one of the people who love a child in the house, Nance?" said Beatrice.

"Yes, I think it does make a difference."

"I am so glad," said Beatrice, as though she had feared another feeling.

"It will be good for Alison to have something to think of," said Sibyl.

"We won't have it put in that way," said Dulcia.

"Why, has she less to think of than anyone else?" said Almeric.

"You neither of you know the life of the house."

"You think that Alison does not always see her way quite clearly?" said Beatrice.

"I think she forgets what Father ought to be in her life."

Beatrice looked at her hostess, and in a moment walked up to her.

"You find your son sheds a great light upon the future."

"Yes, dazzling."

"You know that light is only a shadow of the other Light, which is dazzling indeed, when we turn our eyes to it? You will let me say just that to you? I wanted to so much."

"She thought of what she wanted, rather than of what you did," said Almeric, who was still at hand.

"Your son is not coming to-day, Mrs. Jekyll?" said Beatrice, turning at once.

"You would all have stayed away, if I had advised you," said Duncan.

"That would have been inhospitable advice? We won't stay longer after such a speech," said Dulcia. "Good-bye, all! We don't think a christening calls for our presence in the way of an organised party. We are not thickheads. Come, my parents. Staying to the last moment would be a distinct *faux pas* on this occasion."

"I don't feel I have been quite such an unprofitable servant as usual," said Beatrice. "I did not fall back at the crucial moment. When I see how easy it is just to toss a seed, and trust to its falling on good ground, I am ashamed of my backslidings."

"It is tiresome of exceptions to prove rules," said Miss Burtenshaw.

CHAPTER XII

"WOMEN WALKING, WOMEN talking, women weeping!"
said Duncan. "Doing all they can do. I will thank you to
let me pass, as I am to catch a train this morning. Otherwise
I would ask less. Your chatter may wait, as it is what the
day holds for you."

Alison and Nance and Cassie were talking on the staircase.

"Do you want us to come to breakfast, Father? It is
not quite time."

"Want you to come? What would it do for me? It
would do something for you, as I see it. I want my own
breakfast, as I am pressed. And why say it is not time, when
I tell you my time has come for it? Can you not hear me
speak?"

"Even from the stairs," said his daughter. "Let us take
advantage of his mood. Nothing should count this morning."

"Come in, if you are coming; and go out, if you are
going, and let me hear nothing. So, Sibyl, you appear in
your right mind. What were you doing, weeping and
helping some other woman to weep? I heard your noises
from my room."

"I was talking to Richard's nurse. Father. She is going
to leave, and is very upset. I have only just heard."

"There is no secret about it, I suppose?"

"Sibyl, why were you alone with one of the maids?"
said Cassie, in a sudden, sharp tone.

"For the reason she has told us," said Duncan. "A
woman may speak to another woman in my house. I did
not look to hear foolishness from you, Miss Jekyll."

There was a pause.

"Why is the nurse going?" said Duncan. "Is there anything wrong about her? If there is, see she leaves our house for another, that other people may put up with her, and not ourselves. And fill her place, and make no ado. And do not tell me what is amiss, as I have no wish to hear."

"She is not what we want," said his wife. "I am going to satisfy my maternal instincts, and look after Richard myself."

"Look after him yourself? Be tied to him, morning, noon and night? Your instinct is good for that, when it has lain fallow for your life. It is a scheme you would make. It will take you a week to tire of it."

"Cassie will have an eye on me, and keep me to my duty."

"Why should she do so? What is our brat to her? As it is no duty of yours, it is less of hers. See you engage a nurse, as that chances to be your duty."

"I have a right to look after my own child, if I choose."

"I dispute your words. You are not the fit person. Look on yourself as he would look on you. And it is not your employment. That, as I see it, is to do nothing. And I don't understand why the woman is going. I thought the brat hankered after her."

There was a pause.

"This is no folly of yours, Grant," said Duncan. "So there is this over again, when you are by rights past it. I should be glad to get out of the sight of you, if I did not leave the women of my house."

"You are doing that with your eyes open. You expose rather many to the risk, if you make much of it."

"Be silent. I have no use for your words. It will be for you to be the better for mine, when I have time to give them. Be easy about them: I can keep a rod in pickle."

"We can look after Richard between us," said Alison. "It cannot take more than four women to attend to a child."

"A lot of baffled old maids," observed her husband.

160

"If it does take more, command me," said Grant. "I am to be left in the feminine circle."

"Keep out of the house, where your business is," said Duncan. "Who has taken out the boy this morning, while the nurse sheds her tears?"

"The housemaid, who is fond of him," said his wife.

"Marshall was too upset to go out," said Sibyl.

"So it does take more than four women to attend to a child. I direct you shall engage a fifth, and a sixth, if need be, as soon as is feasible. It is our custom to have a suitable person in the nursery."

"It appears it hardly is, Father," said Nance.

"Alison has made up her mind," said Sibyl. "Let her have her way, Father, and make some occupation for herself."

"And what occupation have you for yourself? It is time you had children of your own, and the right to speak."

"We must all make shift with Richard," said Nance. "It would be a pity to have a nurse, and frustrate the four."

"Miss Jekyll, I did not know you hankered after brats."

"I have been fond of all of yours, Mr. Edgeworth."

"But you have not run about after them. I did not know it was your fancy. Their mother used to say it was not." Duncan now spoke freely of his first wife before the second.

"When Richard reaches a further stage, Cassie will undertake him single-handed," said Nance. "One woman is enough when education is in question."

"We would have less, if we could, for what he will want," said Duncan. "Miss Jekyll will do for him what she fancies, and no more. What use is a boy to a woman? And as I have no concern in your talk, I beg you to continue it without me."

"Cassie, the nurse is not going because of me?" said Grant. "What bee have you got in your bonnet? You are not often so wide off the mark."

"We can't know how it will go on," said Cassie, not meeting his eyes.

"There is Richard coming back in the rain!" said Nance. "He ought to have an umbrella."

"I direct you shall obtain an umbrella, and a second, if need be, as soon as is feasible," said Grant. "It is our custom to have a suitable umbrella in the nursery."

"I will go and meet him," said Nance: "I am feeling rather baffled this morning."

Cassie followed her; Grant went upstairs; and Alison and Sibyl were alone.

"Are you going upstairs with Richard, Alison?"

"No. He has a sufficient escort."

"That is not your reason. It is because you are expecting Almeric."

"Well, in that case it is polite to stay and receive him. We can't press everyone into Richard's service."

"I know you want me to go away."

"You should suppress the knowledge, if you are not going to act upon it."

"I am not going to act upon it; I will not be driven about in my father's house. I was here nearly twenty years before you were."

"I am familiar with that twenty years. I do not regret that I had no part in them. I can leave you to hold this position, if you wish. I am not tenacious of positions in your father's house. That is as well, as mine belongs to somebody else, who seems remarkably tenacious of it."

"Father is in the drawing-room. You will hardly wait for Almeric with him there."

"I would not do anything with him there, this morning."

"Alison, you liked us, when you first came, didn't you?"

"I thought you accepted the stepmother with fortitude. I recall it, when now I observe it failing."

"Would you like to lose Nance and Cassie's friendship?"

"No friendship that is lost has ever been worth having."

"I thought you so much prettier than you thought me," said Sibyl, bursting into tears. "I thought you were beautiful, and I think so now. I know how Father must have felt; and I know how Almeric feels, when you let him. But it will pass, as it has for you and Father." Sibyl raised her eyes to Alison's face. "Grant was the second person you were fond of, wasn't he?"

"You make me out an affectionate creature."

There were sounds of Duncan's leaving the house, with the milder stir of the present days.

"I hear the departure of my first love. Why do you assume he was my first, when your view of me is what it is? And I am deserted by my second, and will leave the third to you."

Almeric entered the hall, and looked up the staircase.

"I am here, Almeric," said Sibyl, coming forward with a drooping head. "Alison has gone up to Richard."

"She had barely gone when I came. She will be coming down."

"She was not going to. She told me to see you for her; but you do not want to talk to a person you have known from a child."

Almeric was silent, and Sibyl started forward and rushed out of the room.

"Can I come in, Alison? The nursery door seems to be locked. Almeric is waiting for you." She spoke in a tone of simple meekness.

"The door locked? How did that happen?" Alison strolled into the passage, glancing back to say a word to Cassie, who was attending to the child. "There is no need to seal the separation with lock and key."

"He is waiting for you," said Sibyl, in the same manner.

"That is returning good for evil. I can't let such forbearance go unrewarded."

Cassie glanced sharply at the door as Sibyl stood within it.

"Go back to what you were doing, Sibyl. You are not

upstairs at this hour. You would be better out of doors."

"I came up with a message for Alison. And you need not speak to me as if I were a child. I am not in a child's position. And if Alison will not keep a nurse, she should look after Richard herself; Father was explicit about it. Though Marshall might do her own work, while she is in the house."

Sibyl drifted to the passage, and catching voices from another room, entered to find Grant and the nurse. Emma Marshall was a short, square woman of thirty-five, with smooth, dark hair, short, blunt features, opaque, dark, drooping eyes, and a moody, aloof expression. She was lifeless within the arm of Grant who was inducing her to dance.

"Grant, you must not be here! Cassie will find you!"

"I have suffered the consequences of that, and will enjoy the preliminaries."

Marshall stood still, as he released her, and did not speak.

"Go downstairs, Grant. Alison is in the drawing-room, and I daresay Nance is with her. If Cassie comes to the landing she is bound to hear."

"She ought not to be surprised. I am doing what is expected of me. Well, Cassie, you have nothing to say that is not said."

Cassie signed to him to go, and turned to the nurse.

"You must leave us to-day, Marshall; I can see no other course. I will give you wages for another month, and you have a home. I do not say it must be your fault, as that is not true; but you must go for your own sake."

"It is no good me saying anything, ma'am."

"Tell Marshall there is nothing against her, Sibyl," said Cassie, going to the door. "I know a good place, where the wages are higher than we give. She can say she is leaving to do better for herself, and feel it is true."

"What good is higher wages, when you leave where you are used to, and a child you are fond of? I don't ask more

164

money than is enough. And what there is between me and Mr. Grant, has nothing in it, like it has had with him and some of the maids. There is reasons behind, as we know, Miss Sibyl, and too many mistresses, as you may find."

"I have to take the house as it is; I can't go to another as you can."

Sibyl went back to the nursery, where Cassie was still with the child.

"I don't see why Marshall is going, Cassie."

"Then you cannot have been attentive at breakfast, or in the other room just now."

"Grant does not seem very guilty about it."

"It would not be his line to make the most of it. And I am afraid he has adapted himself to such positions. Your father seems almost to have done so too."

"I do not think Marshall seems guilty either."

"She may not be so. But you should not gossip with her, Sibyl."

"Will you make an end of treating me as if I were Richard? Father is right, that you will all become lost in the child. You will become children yourselves. And why should I not speak a word to a fellow-creature? He was right there too. There are not too many people in the house for me to talk to."

"Let us have a chat, whenever you like," said Cassie, neither her voice nor her words seeeming her own.

"Have you nothing against Marshall, but Grant's foolishness?"

"You must see that we cannot arrange for her to be kept in his way."

"It would be fairer to get rid of Grant."

"It would; but we cannot find another home for him, as we can for her."

"I think she is very upset about it."

"We did not make the arrangement for anyone to be soothed. If you have an alternative, let us have it. We are obliged to reject your first suggestion."

"We will not quarrel about it."

"We will, on the contrary, if you give any more reason. We cannot do better than take the only course."

"I don't know why you are so disturbed."

"For the reasons that you are. You have given them."

"Well, Richard," said Sibyl, "you grow a big boy, don't you? Nearly as big as sister Sibyl. He is not like any of us, is he?"

"He has the look of your father."

"He reminds me of one of the portraits," said Sibyl in an idle tone: "I can't say which."

CHAPTER XIII

"Who runs may read," said Alison, tossing some letters to Cassie.

Cassie read with a changing face, and both women started at the opening door.

"It is Nance, the one person who does not matter. Fortune favours me so far."

"What is the trouble?" said Nance, receiving the letters, and taking them to the light.

"'Dear Alison,
    "'I have had a letter, which I enclose. I am returning to-morrow.
                                    "'Duncan Edgeworth.'

"What an odd note! Does the other explain it? What childish writing! Is it a child's?

"'Dear Sir,
    "'I feel called upon to write to you, being dismissed for what I could not help, and you will not be able to help either. I have done my duty, all that was given me, with Miss Jekyll and the mistress in and out all day, and me hardly to put a hand on the child, though knowing such things better, as is natural. Master Richard has a piece of white hair on his head like Mr. Grant. For knowing which I am dismissed, and going to a strange place, though it was no fault of mine, as it was through Miss Jekyll or the mistress letting the white show at the roots. And it was taken as prying, which it was not, sir, I assure you. And it is only that he takes after Mr. Grant and the picture, in having a piece in front of his little head, and things must run

in families, as we all know. For which I trust you will thank me, as it gives you to think about the mistress and Mr. Grant, as it has others. Trusting you will not be much upset, and offering my respectful sympathy.

"'Yours respectfully,

"'EMMA MARSHALL.'

"What a predicament! What was her motive? What good can it do her? We were careful to be kind, and gave her a character and presents and everything. I don't understand it."

"We did not understand Marshall," said Cassie.

"Shall we ask for the presents back?" said Alison. "It would have shown juster feeling to return them."

"We can't pretend it is not true," said Cassie. "The stained hair cannot be really disguised. It is something that the child can know nothing."

"Duncan cannot arrive until late. I can rely upon a respite. It is the one thing that seems to matter. We don't often have the first thing we would ask of life: I should feel myself fortunate."

"You should not," said Cassie. "The secret has come to light in a strange way. It might have remained."

"I can't follow Marshall," said Nance. "She seemed to have no initiative. And she can get no advantage. Father will hardly reward her. Why should he be glad to be told? He cannot find it an occasion for gratitude, however it strikes him. Trouble is of course beginning, with Sibyl on the stairs! We must go on talking in an ordinary way."

"She must be told," said Cassie. "There is no help. She must be prepared for your father's return. Questions will be worse than anything."

"The Father's Return!" said Alison. "It sounds like the title of a story; and it is an excellent tale."

"What is all this confabulation?" said Sibyl, almost as she opened the door.

"It has a sufficient reason," said Alison, handing her the letters.

"What are they about? Is Father coming back? Where is the letter he is enclosing? Is anything wrong?"

"I don't think he does feel things are quite as they should be. We have that impression. Read the other letter."

"From Marshall to Father! I suppose it is to Father? Why is she writing to him? To complain of being dismissed? Why did she not ask to see him before he went?"

"Read the letter, Sibyl," said Cassie. "It is the best way to know. And be prepared to be startled."

"What a silly way to write! Why should she do more than she was required to? What? Has he? Has he a piece of white hair like Grant? Is it true?"

"It is true," said Cassie. "And true that she was dismissed when she found it. And true that Grant's folly was made the excuse, though there was something in it. You know now; we need not talk of it."

"It is hard to expect her not to make some observation," said Alison.

"How long have you known? Has he always had it? Oh, I suppose from the first, like Grant." Sibyl looked from Cassie to Alison. "Well, we did not know Marshall; that is clear."

"Everything is clear," said Alison.

"What can we do, Sibyl?" said Nance. "You understand Father best."

"Do? Why, tear it up; burn it; anything. Say that Marshall made it up, and brave it out. Anything so that he cannot be sure. Try to make it a joke against him."

"The laugh is on the other side," said Alison. "And you have not hit on the precise emotion."

"It is not possible, Sibyl," said Cassie. "We should not be in this trouble, if it were."

"Alison, was it that night," said Sibyl, "when I came to the library, and you and Grant—that night soon after you came?"

"This is beside the mark," said Cassie. "We have to think what to do. If it spreads beyond the family, we must take your line, and, as you say, brave it out. But to take it with your father would prolong and emphasise it all. We should have no chance."

"It is such a silly, uneducated letter. Father may not believe it, when he thinks twice."

"It is hardly silly. It had to be uneducated, in the sense of being written by someone without education. And thinking twice must lead to investigation and certainty."

"Well, you may admire it, Cassie," said Sibyl; "I do not."

"I admire it," said Alison. "It is hardly for me to minimise it in any sense. I shall keep it as a memento of a dramatic passage in my life. Not that I shall need reminder. And it is Duncan's property, and this is scarcely the moment to ask for a present."

"What can we do about it?" said Sibyl.

"Nothing, except undo the past."

"I wonder Father stopped to read it."

"We do read letters when they come for us," said Cassie. "There was no loophole there."

"I don't notice a preponderance of loopholes anywhere," said Alison.

"I should think he may not refer to it."

"Oh, yes, Sibyl," said Cassie. "We are in more of a predicament than that."

"Say nothing about it, Alison, and he may not bring it up."

"It is late for that solution. He has brought it up."

"I think you are very brave."

"My virtues are not the part of me under inspection."

"She is," said Cassie; "so brave, that we can depend on her to be braver."

"It seems an odd position for me, to be receiving compliments. I hardly think it is what Duncan would suggest. We do behave differently behind his back."

"We shall all be admiring you, Alison," said Sibyl, in a full, encouraging tone.

"It seems that my husband's view will stand by itself."

"Grant must come home," said Nance.

"Does he know that the child—about the white hair?" said Sibyl.

"He does not know. The fewer who knew, the less the risk," said Cassie. "As it is, the truth is out. Alison knew it first, and told me; and Nance found it out later. Marshall discovered through an oversight; and we told her it was fair to the child to disguise it, until he could decide for himself. She was vague about the family relationships, but we dared not depend on her tongue. We had to make the most of Grant's behaviour, but we tried to keep her good-will. We were not prepared for her being so vindictive. She gave no sign."

"Grant does not get left out of anything," said Alison. "It is Duncan who is rather out of it all. I am quite up in arms for my husband. Well, what is it, Bethia?"

"Young Mr. Bode has called, and is in the drawing-room, ma'am."

"Go down to him, Alison," said Sibyl; "it will make a break."

"I hardly want to pass the time, in view of what I look forward to; but I may as well be seen once again as a respectable matron."

Sibyl looked after her with a sort of light in her eyes.

"I could not show her courage. It seems almost to make up for her mistakes."

"I wish it could really help," said Nance.

"I think it will help. Any fine quality does. Do you really think Father will speak of it?"

"I don't know why you think he may not. It seems what he is coming home for."

"We can only be as kind as we can, to both. I should hate to be a Pharisee at a time like this."

"Our kindness can do nothing for them. It is a good thing they have lost their feeling for each other."

"I don't think Alison ever had much for Father. That may be an excuse for her."

"Hardly one to be brought forward. I could not face Father in her place."

"I don't think she is going to face him," said Cassie, who had moved to the window.

The sisters followed, and looked down at Alison and Almeric, walking at a rapid pace from the house.

"What can that mean?" said Sibyl.

"That Alison feels as I should about meeting Father."

"Will they keep together? Will Alison stay with the Bodes? Has she told Almeric?" said Sibyl, moving uncertainly. "Ought we to go after them? We must prevent any further trouble. It is Father whom we must think of."

"She has evidently told him she has to get away," said Nance. "It is Father whom we are all thinking of."

"It is in the worst taste to take that tone. Do we want the same tragedy over again?"

"I think," said Cassie, "that it is best to let someone in a great difficulty get out of it in any way she has thought of. We hardly have a human right to prevent it. The remedy cannot be worse than the disease. We must leave her her own solution."

"We must send a message to Grant," said Nance.

"We will do so later, if there is need. We shall know, when your father is at home. But she must be left her way. We are fortunate that she has found a way. We could not find one for her."

"It is odd that we think of her and not of Father," said Sibyl.

"Your father has the power; the helpless person has the pity; and it is a poor substitute."

"It is true that tragedy arouses pity and terror," said Nance. "In me terror is getting the upper hand."

Duncan's return approached with the hours; the tension

gathered, and touched the point of reaction; and Cassie and Nance heard his arrival with a feeling akin to weariness. He entered his house with his usual directions, and abated not a jot of his normal manner. The servants had hardly left him when Sibyl ran into his arms.

"Father, don't think it is more than it is; don't think your life is altered! It was a moment of madness years ago. It is not fair it should make a tragedy. Alison has gone, because she is afraid to meet you, Almeric is helping her to hide until she is forgiven. She is giving you a chance to think and understand. It is surely for a man to take it."

Duncan heard with a look of simple resolution. Thought of his wife had little place in his mind. His being was given to fear for the fame of his house. Anything was a matter of course that would save his family name.

"Almeric? Young Bode?" he said, in a voice of direct question. "Has she gone to his house?"

"I don't know; they would not let me follow; but a message to the house might reach her. Let us send and bring her back."

Duncan turned from his daughter, and went out into the night.

In an hour he returned, and went straight to his room. He made no effort to see his family, but met them at dinner in the usual way. He seemed to acquiesce in the silence of the hour. When Bethia had gone he spoke.

"I direct you shall none of you take your eyes from my face until what I say has sunk into your minds. My second wife has left my roof, with a man whose name I need not speak, as he will not henceforth be named. It is enough to say that I found a message at his house. I will have no word of it from any one of you, at this time, at a future time, at any time in our lives, or in your lives after mine. You will not speak her name in my hearing or in my house. I command you to put it from your lips, from your minds, from your memories. You will think of your mother as my wife. I do not ask if you will obey me. Your remaining in my house may be your sign. Your meaning to me is that you will."

He rose to leave the room, and Nance spoke.

"Father, how much of the whole truth is known?"

Duncan turned to meet her eyes, and answered in a quiet, firm tone, with a note of equality and respect.

"The secret you have kept in the house is safe, and should remain. It will hardly pass the lips of any who know it. It will not pass mine, as it has not yours."

CHAPTER XIV

"M<small>R. AND</small> M<small>RS</small>. B<small>ODE</small> and Miss Dulcia are already here, Miss Nance," said Bethia, early the next morning. "The master said you would see your friends as usual."

The sisters and Cassie went to the drawing-room, relieved that the library was not the stage of the meeting. Mrs. Bode was seated on the sofa, weeping into her hands; Mr. Bode was looking from her emotion to Duncan's calm, uncertain what course to take between them. Dulcia stood with her head thrown back, and her foot forward, in a sort of abandonment of fate.

"Mr. Edgeworth, we are here in humility and nothing-ness, to acknowledge the enlistment of one of our own house amongst those beyond the pale! We ask you to see that our conscience is clear as your own, our connection with the unspeakable as involuntary as yours."

"We need not talk of it. We have nothing to do with it, as you tell us. We know too little to make it our affair."

"I never thought I should grieve to be a mother," said Mrs. Bode, barely ceasing to yield to this feeling.

"Mother dear, that is illogical and needless," said Dulcia in gentle, reasoned tones. "Mr. Edgeworth has given us the lead, pointed us the line we should take; and we should follow him gladly, though with heads bent down, facing simply the consequences of any other course."

"We are not left with nothing on the other side," said Mr. Bode, indicating his daughter to Duncan, who did not acknowledge the compensation.

"Father, that may be your view, and likely is; but we cannot expect Mr. Edgeworth to take it, or to give a thought to what, in nature, I try to do for you and Mother. It were not in reason."

"What is to be the result of it all, Father?"

"You are right to ask the question, Nance, and I am right to answer it. I shall seek a divorce from my second wife, and that will be the end. Her son—my son will remain."

There was a pause.

"And, taking it all in all, a just and wise decision," said Dulcia. "We recognise the something more than simple justice. We hear it, and bow our head."

"To think that Dulcia is not the child Mrs. Bode is weeping for!" murmured Nance.

"Now, Mother dear, lift up your head and your heart. Mr. Edgeworth has not roused himself from his own shock and sorrow—yes, the shame; for it must be almost that—to point us our direction, without looking for a touch of resilience and response. We can best repay him by throwing up our heads, facing the four winds squarely, and putting our best foot foremost out of the morass, and also out of his house."

Dulcia suited her actions to her words; her parents followed; Duncan attended them to the hall, and returned to his daughters.

"Father, it is surely the custom for the woman to divorce the man? For the man to allow her to do it, whatever the conditions. We want to avoid plans that will have to be changed."

"What part of the matter is yours? You are not divorcing anyone; you have no one to divorce; it might be the lesser evil for you. I don't ask an old maid's advice. I will have no slur on my name or on your mother's; on yours and your sister's, as it is likely to be your only one." Duncan did not mention his son. "I bring no disgrace upon the innocent. I have no care for what is recognised, or those who recognise it. I have been a rule to myself. And you have soon forgotten what is due to your mother."

"We had to forget it three years ago, Father; and it was very soon. You relied on our putting her aside, and you must not object to it now. What of the friends we were having to-day? Shall we send word we will not expect them?"

"Why should we do so? They will not be unwilling to come."

"They will not, but I am unwilling to have them. We cannot quite pass over the change in the house."

"It does not bear upon us. We are outsiders with regard to it. Do not make your way into other lives. Make shift with your own, if it be a poor one. You will be the hostess, and other things will be as usual. That itself will be as usual, as it now becomes our custom." Duncan left the room.

"The path of duty is the way to glory," said Nance. "Whom do you dread seeing most this afternoon?"

"I dread no one," said Sibyl, wearily: "I don't care how much sport we make for our friends."

"I daresay Father despised us for taking his marriage as we did. Now I think of it, it was despicable. But he behaved like a god, and we simply treated him as one. It shows what it is, never to have any criticism. Gods contrive to have nothing but praise; they definitely arrange it; it is true they are all wise."

"Mother would not like Alison to leave Father, now that she has been his wife," said Sibyl, beginning to weep.

"Take her away where her father cannot hear her," said Cassie. "We cannot prove our loyalty to your mother along that line."

"I cannot picture this afternoon," said Nance. "The guests are coming at Alison's bidding to a house that knows her no more. But I wish we had nothing worse before us."

The something worse was at hand.

Grant returned to the house at luncheon, and walked to the table and took his place.

The meal went its course in outward calm, an hour to the women, a moment to Grant, who saw nothing between it and the ordeal of his youth. Cassie ceased to speak for Bethia's ears, as the support of her broke and failed. The sisters were pale and restless, and Duncan dumb and lowering. It seemed they were fighting with the silence. When Duncan rose and made his usual sign, the familiar action emphasised the terror of the moment.

Grant followed his uncle, and stood waiting for his words. Duncan also waited, doing the worst he could do.

"I will not explain my coming, Uncle. I thought you might not expect me simply to keep away."

"Why explain it, if you were not going to? It is a small thing, and attracts no notice."

"If you tell me to leave the house, I shall not be sorry I have come."

"You would choose that way? Why should you leave house? You have made it your home since you lost your right to it. And you are a small person in it, and remain so."

Grant forced himself to his task.

"Uncle, we were thrown together. We were young. I am as I am."

"You would play the child? You feel you should choose that part? You must choose again. Perhaps you incline to the part of a man?"

"The temptation to which I yielded is common to men."

Duncan rose and struck his nephew a blow in the face.

Grant received it in simple relief that the climax had come and passed.

"I wonder you dare to stand and face me."

"I do not dare: I do it without daring. The weakness that leads to folly, does not involve the strength to meet its results."

"I would listen to talk if I had the patience. As I have not, be advised not to require it of me. If I can hear what must be said, you who must say it, can do so."

"I hardly hope you will believe I was helpless; that I found myself having it behind me, rather than in front."

178

"You have placed yourself beyond the pale of belief."

"I have given you the truth, Uncle."

"When it has come out. So you are a fine fellow to your own mind?"

"Uncle, remember how you first felt to Alison. You could marry her: I could not."

"That was strange about another man's wife! Be still. You say too much."

"I shall meet any obligation for Richard that you think fit."

"What do you think fit? To provide him with a home and a future? That is what is fit. Though indeed you may feel you have done your part. He will hold the place that was yours. It works out that you give him all you had."

"It is a case of poetic justice indeed. You mean you will bring him up as a son in your house? I have a great respect for you, Uncle."

"I will not say the same to you."

"I see that, being as you are, you cannot."

"Being as I am! Do not deceive yourself. You have put yourself outside the pale of other men."

"It was a great shock to me when I heard."

"It should not have been. It was the outcome of what was behind. From whom did you hear?"

"From Cassie, who wrote to me last night."

"What a thing for a woman in my house to touch! You make me glad her father is dead. I would not look her brother in the face."

"Cassie is a woman of the world."

"That would not accustom her to certain things. It would show her them in their place."

"If you will believe me, I had all but forgotten."

"You look for me to think more of you? You make a mistake. But I do not dispute it. Tell me what feeling you have now for this woman."

"I feel nothing for her; and she feels less than nothing for me. It never meant what you have thought."

"Then it was worse than I thought. Your words do you no good."

Duncan was silent, lost in the maze of his own mind. His anger with his nephew lacked its impetus in himself. He saw how his feeling for him had transcended that for his wife, and suffered a sharp and simple self-pity.

"If you could know, Uncle, how little meaning it has had!"

"I will not know it: I will not take that view, the view that nothing can be a man's own. The fact that we shall keep this dark for ever, shows how far we take it, how far we expect it of other men. And we shall keep it for ever, from our family, our friends, our servants, the stranger within our gates. That points to what we think of it."

Grant heard him with an easing heart, seeing he was listening to his own words.

"I will not say I am grateful to you, Uncle."

"Yes, you have to be grateful," said Duncan, looking at the young man with an oddly moved expression. "That is your part. I won't tell you what figure you cut in it. I cannot say I am sorry for you, nor you for yourself; so we will leave you in your gratitude."

"I should like to know if you are glad to have a son to your name."

"I hardly know if I am glad," said Duncan, falling for the first time in his life into a tone of old age. "It is one thing and then another, until I do not know what is what. I should have been glad if Ellen had had a son: that is the son I would have to my name. You think you have done me a service? You have got to that. I am not about to thank you."

"My son must have had the place in the end, a probable son of mine. This only takes us further into the future."

"So I see further than is my right? And again find myself in debt to you?"

"The boy is of your blood. He will serve you instead of me. It is I whom he does not serve." Grant could hardly believe in the tone he could take.

180

"It is for you to talk of his blood. And instead, instead! My wife is instead of my own wife. My son is a substitute. I am too old to have a future, and my present is a sham: I feel as if I were a shadow. Well, I must live in the past, with the rest of the old. Why should I shirk my place? But, Grant, if this makes you a human creature, and you fancy a girl of mine; and she, knowing what she must, happens to fancy you—as anything may come true of a woman—see you make it known to me before you get too far. I have no mind to take more from you. And I ask to be left alone, to the company of an honest man."

Grant left him, suspecting he was still welcome as a son.

The guests arrived in the afternoon, with an almost exaggerated form of their usual manner. They found the family made no attempt at a normal front.

"It is so wise to allow the occasion to be openly a sad one," said Beatrice. "I like the straightforwardness of it. It is quite the best face to put on it, best in the real sense."

"Dear, dear, one can do nothing to help," said her cousin, finding so much less to like, that she made a gesture of wringing her hands.

"What did you expect to be able to do?" said Gretchen.

"We guessed they would wish us to appear," said Dulcia. "So we saw it as our course, sorely though it went against the grain. I pulled the parents up to it, hard though it was with them to appear without their son and advertise their position. We know our disgrace transcends that of this house, and openly accept the difference."

"You need not accept too much," said Gretchen. "No one who is here, can help it."

"Now I knew Miss Jekyll would not remain out of the picture. Through all the family ups and downs she is with them, perhaps more in her element in the downs, accounting herself repaid by their love and loyalty. For some people would ask only to shade. To-day I feel personally grateful to her, representing as I do, the family who provides the villain of the piece." Dulcia deliberately returned to a lighter vein.

"Is Richard quite well?" said Beatrice in an easy tone to Nance.

"Not quite. He may be in sympathy with the trouble in the house."

"He misses his mother, Nance?" said Dulcia, speaking low.

"Only as babies do. He takes to his new nurse. Father will see he suffers nothing."

"An instance of simple generosity, and of the kind that is civilisation's finest flower, that of a man to a woman! It shows no situation is so dark that it cannot be irradiated."

"Did Alison guess the result of taking Almeric from Dulcia?" said Grant.

"No," said Nance, "she knew not what she did. It is Almeric's fault; he must have known."

Duncan moved amongst his guests, with an open increase of his usual gravity: Dulcia glanced from him to her friends, and edged from his path, with a suggestion of being on tiptoe. Beatrice waited for him to be alone, and was at his hand.

"Life is difficult for us sometimes," she observed, in a jerky manner.

Duncan looked at her, and almost bowed.

"We cannot always find our own strength enough."

Duncan did not acknowledge this experience.

"Of course we cannot find it enough," said Beatrice, helped forward by her own stumble; "but some times teach us that more than others. You are face to face with the lesson." She bent on him a swift, low look, murmured her intended words, and giving him a smile of controlled radiance, moved away.

"I did it!" she said, in a tone that partook of the same radiant quality; "I spoke the word I was resolved to speak. I have not to feel I withheld it."

"Wonderful, darling!" said Dulcia, patting her back,

in rather perfunctory congratulation. "And wonderful of Mr. Edgeworth too! Indeed I would assign him the harder part. He stoops to conquer in many ways to-day."

Beatrice looked as if this new light did little towards dimming her own.

"Courage, Grant!" said Dulcia. "You feel this dreadful day will never be over. I was feeling the same, and behold, it is running its course. It will determine itself in time."

"Thank you; but why is it dreadful? Alison wanted to leave my uncle, and I am not sure he greatly wanted her to stay. What is wrong with the arrangement?"

"She leaves her son," said Dulcia, striking a serious note on the other side.

"She can hardly find fault with his fortunes."

Dulcia shook her head at this view, and passed on, keeping Grant's hand until it pulled away, and showing the increasing unrestraint which he had observed in her.

"Well, a brave face upon it all, my Nance! As dignified and gracious as if nothing had befallen! I could almost hail the opportunity for you, though I cannot emulate your front: I feel a thought pulled down and humbled. However your heart knoweth its own bitterness, there is not a trace of it in your bearing. And there is one little piece of compensation. We see you again in your mother's place. Your easy dignity in relinquishing the position remains one of our memories."

"I think resuming the position has its own difficulty."

"Darling, you are too wonderful and resilient," said Dulcia, her eyes roving about. "And I do believe in the purification of suffering. Now where are your father and Sibyl, that we may make our farewells? We do not leave this house to-day, without shaking the hands of every member, lucky as we are to be permitted to shake them."

"Here are the truants!" said Miss Burtenshaw. "Arrived in time for us to part from the family complete!"

There fell a silence, which, when Duncan and Sibyl had passed, returned and remained.

"It is tactful to regard the family as complete, I suppose?"

"Well, dear Miss Burtenshaw, perhaps tactful is hardly the word," said Dulcia, contorting her brow.

"We are not supposed to keep referring to the family blank."

"I suppose your mentioning the family complete, did constitute a reference to it," said Beatrice in a mild tone.

"Now, anyone might have done what you have," said Dulcia, putting her arm in her friend's. "We have all come thundering down at times: I suspect myself of more than one crash."

"I am not conscious of having done anything," said Miss Burtenshaw, staring before her.

"And neither have you," said her father. "You have done nothing. Talk about a mountain out of a molehill! We shall be afraid to open our mouths."

"Good-bye, Mr. Edgeworth. So many thanks," said Beatrice, her social manner disposing of any allusiveness.

"Good-bye, Edgeworth," said Mr. Bode. "We have the support of feeling we are still your friends."

"Nothing has happened between us."

"Nothing at all, Mr. Edgeworth!" said Dulcia, giving him her hand, with a straight look into his eyes.

"How about your share of it all?" said Oscar to his sister.

"It is not so much. Things will be as they were after Ellen died, except for the child. And his father would send him to his mother, if it were not for the place."

"If it is not too much for you, it is of no account. Other people's troubles are what they deserve. Ah, how they deserve them!"

"Look at the rector, saying a family word to his sister, as if he were one of us," said Dulcia, not changing the direction of her companions' eyes.

"Well, good-bye all," said Gretchen. "There doesn't seem much else that can happen."

"There doesn't," said Grant; "unless Uncle marries a third time."

"You keep out of it, in that case," said Gretchen, causing Nance and Grant to meet each other's eyes.

"Will you arrange for dinner to be punctual, Nance?" said Duncan, making a bridge between himself and his nephew. "I may have some matters to attend to. Grant, I have seen you appearing as a nobody, and the sight gives me to wonder if anything could be done to make you less so, for all our sakes. Would it help the matter for you to leave the Bar, and settle here as my agent? I am in my later years, and the boy will be young for my life. The Bar has no need for you, that has been shown; and my man retired this year, and leaves an empty and easy pair of shoes. I can put up with greenness, as I provide the experience." Duncan's easy voice both covered and revealed his feeling.

"I should like it of all things, Uncle. I love the place; but suppose Richard does not want me, when he is a man?"

"I am coming to that. It is what I should be coming to. You seem a simple sort of fellow." Duncan's voice had risen with the new light on his future. "I will provide in my will for your salary to be paid, whether or no you keep the post. It seems that what I don't arrange, will run amuck. Does that make up your mind, as you can't make it up yourself?"

"It does indeed, Uncle. I could ask no more than to have my home with you and the girls, and to watch the boy's progress."

"The girls are used to you, poor young women; and knowing what they must, gives them the chance to improve you, which women are happy to like in men. And any connection with them disposes me to serve you, as you are a second-rate figure by yourself. But the brat takes your place, and will one day be over you. His progress brings him nearer. It passes me why you talk of it."

CHAPTER XV

"Nance, it is over," said Grant, handing the paper to his cousin. "It is complete and absolute, and Uncle begins the third chapter in his life. It seems a mistake for him to go to Aunt Maria. They say nothing revives a habit like the place where it started."

"We seem to have gone back to the first chapter: I have a feeling that Mother has only just died."

"So has Uncle. You must have noticed it, when he took such pains that you should. Her portrait is to go back to the dining-room; he has written to Bethia. It would hardly be worth while to move it again, if it were not to be a permanent arrangement. When it went to the landing, I was permitted the task. Bethia is the next thing to Uncle himself."

"Bethia could not have moved it to the landing; there are things that could not be. Alison would seem like a dream if it were not for the child."

"Nance, it is still a secret, and will always be?"

"I believe there may be a rumour. I suppose that had to come. It is astonishing how little one thinks about it. Bethia said something in my hearing, meaning either to warn me or to wound. One thing is, that no one can say anything to our faces; and Dulcia herself would not breathe it to Father. In a way we are safe. What incredible things happen in this house!"

"Nothing can happen to us outside it. We have no life elsewhere. I want to ask you a question, Nance: I think some people call it the question. Do you think you could marry me? You know about my wild oats; and that is said to be so important, though I should have thought it would be a mistake. There is nothing for you to find out: there really is not, though it does seem strange, when you think of what has come to light. I shall have no secrets from you. My very last one transpired, you see. Things do point to our marrying."

"Father has said something, has he? You were glad not to be cast off, but to be demanded as a son is too much difference. He must be one of those people, who make more fuss over little things than big ones."

"You have not given me your answer. You can't say you do not love me. We could not have lived in this house for all these years, without mutual affection; Uncle would have made it impossible: I think he has a right to expect us to marry."

"There are the reasons against it, that always hold good. I feel to you as a sister, and there is someone else."

"Then God bless you, Nance. Your happiness is all that counts. I see it is all that does. Do you think Sibyl would marry me? I know there is someone else; but he is out of the case."

"Grant, what are you doing?"

Grant altered his tone.

"I want to settle down; and I am not out for romance. You may say I have not kept myself for it. Uncle wants me to marry one of you, and would do more for me if I did."

"You have not always considered what he would like."

"Nance, I see you could not marry me; that it would not be for the happiness of either. Even at this moment you are not studying my happiness. But Sibyl could surely be happy with me, if she could be with Almeric. I shall not give her Dulcia for a sister, and I do not think men superior to women, which very few men can say. It's being simple of them does not make them any better. A quiet respect and affection is the best foundation; and although she can't have respect for me, if she has not affection, she is very unaffectionate."

Nance did not speak for a moment.

"She might be better, married to you, than as she is

now. If you make it clear to her what your feelings are."

"She will not expect my heart at her feet, when her heart is not at disposal at all. It is odd that she and Alison both prefer Almeric to me. It is a salutary lesson, just as your refusing me has been. I shall be very much improved by the time I marry. I hope I shall not always be refused. If I have to tell Uncle that neither of his daughters will spend her life with me, he will not think I am worth a larger salary. He knows they have both spent their lives with him, and what he is like to live with. You won't tell Sibyl I have proposed to you? She might not like to marry a rejected man; though of course I like to marry a rejected woman; the cases are not the same."

Grant went to the schoolroom, where Sibyl was with Cassie, and sat down at her side.

"Will you please leave us, Cassie?"

"Have you anything especial to say?"

"The thing a man only says once."

Cassie glanced from one to the other, and left them.

"Sibyl, if I ask you to marry me, you will give me some hope? I know men are satisfied, if they can only have some hope. You can't go on being a comfort to Uncle, if you will not be my wife. He wants me to marry one of his girls, and Nance and I are not suited. We should make such an awkward pair, and you and I would be a charming couple; and that is so seldom seen, that it would comfort anyone. We ought to think of Uncle as well as ourselves; and this seems the only way of thinking of all three."

"Grant, you are joking; and it is a simple jest."

"You know it is not one of my jokes. You must know them all by now. And my jokes are not simple. When have I asked you to marry me? Of course I am your cousin, and there is someone else; but those are conventional objections."

Sibyl stared at him, and did not speak. Then she looked about her, as though seeing another world rise from the ruins of her own.

"Grant, have you ever had your place taken with some-one who was all your life?"

"Should I propose to you, if I had? And I don't think you have either, quite apart from not being able to bear to think so. Almeric had too little to give you, to be your life. I must speak jealously of him; it is only natural."

"I know it is undignified to yield to a feeling that is not returned."

"You must return my feeling, or you could not say that to me. Would my arm be where it is, if it had no right to be? When Uncle comes home, let me tell him I am his son. My being his nephew will dispose of the question of what I am to call him; and that is such a silly problem for a man. Everything points to our marrying."

"How would things be with us, Grant?"

"I can offer my wife every comfort: I have a right to propose to a woman. And I can offer her more comfort, if she is Uncle's daughter, and so have more right to propose to her."

"Some women would not marry you, if they knew what I know."

"Well, I would not marry them, so I can't see that it matters. And the difference in my past is that it happened at home. It only shows I am at heart a family man. Nothing has gone deep with me; and you cannot say the same."

"Perhaps it did not go as deep as I thought."

"You have made me the happiest man alive: I felt I was right to hope. I am glad I shan't have to go away to get over a disappointment, when I should be settling down as Uncle's agent. He would despise me for being refused, and for not carrying it off better. You see, he has no knowledge of being refused. He seems always to have been accepted."

"Your mistakes have lost you the place that was your own; and some women would use a worse word than mistakes."

"How trying you seem to find some women! I know a man's early mistakes alter his life, and that mine have done it. But with the money I have of my own, we shall have enough for comfort with a little contrivance, which is known to be the happiest state."

"I believe it is a grief to Father, that you will not come after him."

"Nothing binds people so close, as a shared sorrow. I have noticed we are getting closer."

When Duncan returned to his house, he was once again met by Sibyl.

"Father, you have wished that Grant was your son. Now he is going to be. Tell us that you are glad."

"I am glad," said Duncan, putting his hands on her shoulders, and looking with easy feeling into her face. "And your mother would be glad with me. She looked on Grant as her son; and we may say he will be a son to her."

"I felt to her as to a mother, Uncle."

"Oh, words, words. Well, Nance, you remain an old maid, rather than be under this fellow! Miss Jekyll, you and I must not look for much, or we shall find the young ones too simple for us. Well, there is room in the house for its life to spread. You may come to me, boy, and tell me what is in your mind; and I will do what I can, to get most of it out for you. I don't want any of it in mine. One head full will do."

"Nance, Father does not expect us to live in this house?" said Sibyl, when Duncan had gone.

"Why should he not? You offered him Grant as a son."

"He could not have thought I meant it in that sense."

"You seemed to speak sincerely."

"Can't you say a word for us? Can't you say that Mother would think it better for us to have our own home?"

"Father has enlisted Mother on his side. You heard him."

"You would take it seriously, if it were your future at stake."

"I am taking it seriously. I am in a tremble to think that Father is to be thwarted."

"He would not expect me to live with him, with another wife," said Grant; "I ought to be able to settle it."

"I hope not at the expense of changing your wife."

"Would you like to live in this house, as a married woman?" asked Sibyl.

"I don't know why it should be so different from living in it as a single one. Perhaps Grant had better marry me. Father would not mind which daughter made the bond."

"I believe you are jealous."

"Then he had certainly better marry me."

"I believe you think he should have asked you first."

"Well, as the elder, I am entitled to prior dealing."

"I wish I could see some solution. You might try to think."

"I have thought. Father will have to suffer a disappointment."

"Do you think he will mind too much?"

"Not more than you will be able to bear, without preventing it."

"You don't think we ought to live with him?"

"Of course not: I think you should consider your own lives."

"Grant, go and get it over. Then we shall know how it is."

"Grant may not be so eager to make the discovery."

Grant went to his uncle, and found him with his accounts.

"Well, boy, so the girl's portion is not to fall to an upstart. It is strange we have not thought of this. Odd man that I am, I feel your disinheritance, and find myself doing what little I can."

"You show me all kinds of generosity, Uncle. I wish Sibyl were to have a husband equal to her father."

"There is no need for a man to be too much equalled in his own house. Why should you be my equal, after all?"

"We cannot impose upon you so far, as to live here. We must live in a smaller house of our own."

"Why can you not?" said Duncan, looking up, and

then seeming to consider his papers. "It has not troubled you, what you do in my house. What have you to offer my daughter anywhere else?"

"It would be an inconvenience to you and Nance. A different course of life would be running across your own."

"It would not, under my roof, as I should not choose it. I can consider my own convenience: I was not thinking of not doing so."

"Of course not, Uncle. I mean it would be considered a foredoomed experiment. It would be recognised as bad for other people."

"So you are thinking of other people? That is your trouble? How soon are you taking my girl to this small house of your imagining, or I suppose of hers?"

"We feel the ordinary impatience, Uncle."

"We! Why bring in the girl? It is for you to feel impatience, isn't it?"

Duncan got up and walked to the window, breathing with his lips closed. Grant, not seeing what to do, returned to his cousins.

"Well, is it over?" said Nance. "What was it like?"

"I can hardly tell you. Uncle was so much master of himself."

"That indeed tells me nothing. I have only seen him when the self is master of him."

"Poor, darling Father!" said Sibyl. "It will be best for him in the end."

"I don't see why. It will be best for you and Grant. Of Father and me it must be said, that we still have each other."

Duncan sought his nephew as usual in the next days, and, as usual, made no demand on his daughters, giving no sign that he saw the change in the family as calling for other change. But one morning he came to the school-room, where Cassie was alone.

"Well, Cassie, you and I are left behind in the march. We have to follow the example set us, and see to ourselves.

We have seen a deal together, and seen it in the same way. We knew and lost Ellen together, which is the chief thing in my life, and comes high in yours. You are alone, and I am alone." His voice quavered for a moment. "And we shall not be at a loss for talk of the past. Shall we have regard to these things, and go on as we may, together?"

Cassie heard him with her eyes on his, and now gave him a smile; and he lifted her hand to his lips, and the scene was over.

"Is that the easiest proposal you have made?"

"You are a chattering woman! Wanting to gossip at once! Be content with the gossip you will raise. Well, we have something to say for ourselves. Other people have had enough to say to us."

"What will Nance say to it?"

"What should she say? What has it to do with her? We are not answerable to her, I hope, for the way of our lives. She is answerable to us for the same thing. You have been a second mother to her. She and her sister can see you in their mother's place."

"She has been a good friend to me: I hope I do the part of a friend by her."

"You have always done it, and it rests with you to continue to do so. I cannot be troubled with your doubts or hers. I shall not concern myself with them."

"You will, when they are mine."

"Oh, I shall, shall I?" said Duncan, pausing to adjust himself to the new tone of his life. "Well, I shall then, if you say it. It shall be so."

"Will you tell them? I could not screw my courage to such a pitch."

"Your courage? What is there about them, to make such talk? They are ordinary sort of boy and girl, as I see them: I wish they were less so."

"Then I will expect them to know."

"Expect of them what you like, if you will make mention of it. I will tell them what you expect, and bid them look to it. We are over them, and have what we wish from them, I hope."

Duncan went to the drawing-room and found Grant and Sibyl.

"Where is Nance?"

"I don't know, Father."

"Do you know, boy?"

"I am afraid not, Uncle."

"Then will you put yourselves about to find her? One of you go one way, and one another. And when you come upon her, bring her to me, and see you both accompany her. I have something to say which I propose to say only once."

Nance was in the library with Oscar, who had called on Duncan, and found him occupied; and followed Grant to her father.

"I would have you know that I am making a change in my life: I have had enough of changes in yours. The woman who has been your best friend and your mother's, is to be more to you. I do not expect you to follow with your wits, and so will put it again in words. Miss Jekyll has consented to be my wife. Consider what I have said, and also consider your conduct." Duncan turned and left them.

"Oh, can he mean it?" said Nance.

"He seems to mean it; but is there a mistake? Did Cassie fail to make herself clear? Uncle has evidently proposed to her."

"Cassie would not have left it like that," said Sibyl. "She has always been fonder of Father than other people have."

"Uncle seems to have contracted a habit of proposing. Perhaps he proposes to the first woman he meets after he is free. It is absurd of him to pretend he does not think much of women. His feelings for them completely run away with him. It is a mercy Miss Burtenshaw and Dulcia have not been about."

"Mother; Alison; Cassie!" said Nance. "He would not have proposed to Miss Burtenshaw. Well, I can claim it is not I who have set him the example this time. I think he let fall that he was following you. I hardly realised that the young took the lead in this house."

"Can you imagine Uncle proposing to Cassie?"

"I cannot; I will not do what is too much for me."

"I suppose he spoke up like a man. After all, practice makes perfect."

"Nance, it is not because Grant and I are leaving him?"

"It may be. But if it is, he has soon found his compensation."

"Cassie will be a change after Alison."

"Change is hardly the word for Cassie. I suppose he thought he would resort this time to the accustomed. There is really nothing surprising in it: I wonder if we are really surprised."

"Yes, Nance," said Grant. "We did not foresee it. We were astonished. We did not believe it. But evidently we believe it now."

"Poor Father!" said Sibyl. "We might be nicer about it."

"I don't think we are below the standard in these things. There has been a certain demand upon us."

"Nance, you will bear the brunt of it," said Grant.

"There will be no brunt from Cassie. And I am used to yielding my position as mistress of the house."

"Cassie has always liked Father," said Sibyl. "He is so much nicer to her, than to anyone else. She has much more reason for liking him. I don't suppose there is deep feeling on either side."

"I wonder what is their reason for marrying," said Nance, "as the natural one seems disposed of."

"Father wants a companion; Cassie wants a certain future. You talk as if you were a child, Nance."

"Well, that is to be my position. I hope to be a dutiful child to these my parents."

Cassie came into the room with a transparent assumption of ease.

"Cassie darling, we are glad," said Sibyl.

"Cassie knows we are glad, when Father marries. But we have no hidden feelings."

"Cassie, it was nice of you not to reject Uncle. I have lately imagined myself in the position of being rejected; and it would not be respectful to think of him in it."

"It is not an experience he seems to encounter. And I have found him a good friend, apart from my normal wish to marry him. His life has had its rougher side."

"Cassie, be careful. Are you mistaking pity for love?"

"We both have a life behind us. It will be a help to the life in front, and a reason for it."

"I don't think you are expecting too much, which is said to be the great danger. You do not sound as if you could not help yourself."

"You are the one woman, who will enable the portrait to be left in the dining-room," said Nance. "Father could hardly have it moved again."

"I see he had no choice but to marry me."

"Mother would have liked it to be you," said Sibyl, kneeling by Cassie's chair. "I daresay she thought of it before she died."

"I am sure she did not," said Cassie, laughing. "If the matter had come to her mind, she would not have thought your father would marry again."

"Once I should not have thought so either," said Nance.

"Neither should I," said Cassie. "And in a way we were right. He has never attempted to fill her place."

"You have attained a real understanding of him," said Grant. "You are quite right to marry. So many people would have thought he had: I thought I had recognised one or two attempts myself. He should be regarded as absolutely faithful to Aunt Ellen's memory. He may be thought even less so, when he is married to you; and of course that is absurd."

"It seems I am destined to recapture the rights of youth," said Nance.

"I am thankful I am to keep one of you; and it is the one I would choose."

"Cassie, take care," said Grant. "A parent should be impartial."

"Who should be impartial?" said Duncan, driven to the scene by curiosity concerning it. "Cassie and I have an equal respect for all of you, if that will do. You are reasonably worthy people."

"Father, we are glad," said Sibyl.

"What have you to be glad of, that you should come bamboozling me? You keep your thoughts to your own man, and learn from him to whom you belong. Grant, do you care for a word governed by reason? Or must you have the girl at your heels?"

Grant and Sibyl followed Duncan, and Nance turned to Cassie.

"Cassie, I must ask it once. Our relation is not yet altered. Why do you want to marry Father?"

"I want a provision for my future. Oscar must build his own life, when my mother dies. And I have lived with your father for twenty years. It is not remarkable that I can spend some more with him."

"Did you expect him to propose to you? I should not have thought he would have such a good idea. He has only had worse ones."

"The idea was his own. If it had been mine, he would have had it earlier."

Bethia appeared at the door.

"Mrs. Jekyll and Mr. Jekyll are here, ma'am," she said, with a light on her face.

"You are glad Miss Jekyll is to be the mistress, Bethia?"

"There is cause for gladness at last, Miss Nance."

"Well, Cassie," said Oscar, "so Duncan wishes to enter our family?"

"You have decided to be Number Three?" said

Gretchen, staring at her daughter. "Well, you are used to managing his house, and bringing up his children; and you have the mistakes of two to guide you."

"Nance and Richard are an ill-assorted pair."

"There is not so much reason why they should be alike. What does Nance say to losing her place? I suppose she is getting accustomed to it."

"Nance and I can do anything together. And she does not care for managing her father's house."

"Well, he is good at getting other people to manage it. I am glad you are to be rid of two of them. You don't want a houseful of other women's children."

"My life has depended on other women and their children."

"Well, you are the one to bring happiness to them all," said Gretchen, embracing her daughter. "They are not doing wrong in getting you to be over them. Your place is anywhere over the rest."

CHAPTER XVI

"WELL, WE HAVE seen Sibyl turned from a maiden into a matron by a few magic words," said Beatrice. "Magic is of course hardly the word. I wonder if it will change her in other ways."

"We can only hope not," said Miss Burtenshaw, walking on in personal immunity from such risks.

"The wedding I should have liked to see," said Dulcia, "is Mr. Edgeworth's to Miss Jekyll. Marriage rather, I would say. Wedding seems too light a word for that union. The two dear, experienced life-worn people! I should have been a reverential witness of their simple acquiescence at the altar. But it seemed it was not to be."

"It was not, as they wanted the ceremony private," said Gretchen. "We see why people have that wish."

"I don't want to be unfair to Grant and Sibyl, but it is not on them that my eyes are about to rest. You would hardly believe with what high romance that older couple is fraught to me. It showed such simple high-mindedness in Cassie, to become the third Mrs. Edgeworth, without any beating about the bush."

"If we do not believe it, we are stubborn," said Oscar, "especially as Dulcia appears to have private information about the betrothal scene."

"I confess that becoming the third Mrs. Anything is not an idea that appeals to me," said Beatrice.

"If there can be a third, it seems there might be a thirteenth," agreed her cousin.

"I don't see any reason," said Florence.

"Now look at them, the dear, grey-haired pair!" said Dulcia. "And at Nance, becoming young again! Letting herself wholeheartedly become so, in selflessness hardly conscious, it goes so deep. Could one tell, by looking at her, simply seconding those above her, that she herself held that place? I could become lyrical. If I make myself absurd, it seems to me a very small matter."

"I wondered it did not seem so to Almeric," said Oscar. "But I see why now."

"A very grave thing," said Fabian.

"You have a daughter less, Mr. Edgeworth," said Beatrice. "Do you begin to feel your loss?"

"He has lost but one for many boys and girls," quoted Dulcia. "Well, if that is a thought frank and premature, let us say he has gained a son."

"Grant has been my son for many years."

"But I do not regret my speech, Mr. Edgeworth. It provoked yours, and one of a rare kind for you. It was worth your little pulling up of me."

"Is Richard to join the proceedings?" said Beatrice to Cassie.

"No. He could take no part in them."

"But when he can," said Dulcia. "Miss Jekyll will be the first to place him in the fore."

"It is a great responsibility for you to have his bringing up," continued Beatrice.

"It is a usual thing for a woman to bring up a child."

"Miss Jekyll, we must pick a bone with you," said Dulcia. "Our not picking it would argue an insensibility. You did not permit us to view your marriage."

"And so you missed its surface results," said Nance.

"Oh, I mean Mrs. Edgeworth! What an obvious fall! But really a good many people have borne that name." Dulcia gave a laugh. "Mrs. Edgeworth will not think the joke in bad taste."

"It is good to know that," said Oscar to Nance.

"No wonder both Alison and Sibyl saw Almeric as indispensable," said Nance. "It is surprising we did not all do so."

"Now here is a little Mrs. Edgeworth, whom we are

all too fond of to call by that name," said Dulcia, caressing Sibyl. "Too familiarly fond of, perhaps I should say, after my address of her elder."

"It must be nice to marry without changing one's name," said Miss Burtenshaw. "Marriage without tears we might call it."

"What do you feel about that, Sibyl?" said Dulcia, in a tone of interest. "Do you feel it better or not, to keep your name?"

"I am fond of my name; and it will be coupled with Grant's now. I am Mrs. Grant Edgeworth."

"I ought to have a lesson in the use of people's names."

"Has she not had one?" said Fabian.

"I said to Mrs. Edgeworth, Miss Jekyll that was, that Richard's bringing up was a responsibility," said Beatrice. "And she scouted the idea."

"Well, dear Beatrice," said Dulcia, "perhaps it was not the line to take with one of her experience."

"She is too used to that kind of responsibility to be troubled by it," said Miss Burtenshaw.

"I think we are always troubled by it, if we undertake it in our own strength."

"But why should you think Mrs. Edgeworth would do that?"

Beatrice stood with opened eyes.

"That is most unfair," said Oscar to Nance. "Cassie clearly does that."

"Nance, I have been imagining the cosy family party you will be," said Dulcia. "And I can honestly say, I look for you to find it all congeniality and happiness."

"It is good of you to conceive of a perfect future for me. What can you do for Father, shut up with women?"

"He will throw his whole heart into the boy," suggested Dulcia.

"You admit a varied light on your stage?"

"I suppose Alison is never mentioned now?"

"Never in Father's hearing. The rest of us speak of her of course. I hope you hear they are still happy?"

"I am sure you do hope it. Yes, Almeric writes that all is well with them. To us it can only be well in a certain sense. We do not identify ourselves with their course."

"It is a pity you cannot have them to stay: I see it is hardly possible."

"I know you do feel it a pity. But it is not in the question in your father's lifetime."

"We could tell you when he is going away, to save the tedium of waiting for his death."

"The ups and downs of your life leave you always yourself. But it would not be feasible. There would be the encounter with Cassie; and that is what should not be. To sense the shock of what had happened, and at the same time her personal indebtedness, would be too subtle a strain. I feel, simply, we should not expose her to it."

"Father and Cassie may go away together."

"No, dearest, I am firm, dearly though my parents would like me to falter," said Dulcia, with a sigh for her rigid exclusion of her brother from the open doors of his early home. "Now let us forget our dubious pair, and bid God-speed to the other."

"Good-bye, Father dearest," said Sibyl. "Good-bye, darling Nance and Cassie."

"I wish she had put Cassie's name first," said Beatrice in a low tone. "I just wish it; that is all. I can't give a reason."

"Good-bye, my daughter; good-bye, my son," said Duncan, standing with his arms through those of Nance and his wife. "Do not hasten back on our account. You leave enough of us and to spare."

"All good wishes from my heart!" said Miss Burten-shaw, starting a little forward.

"Dear, they did appreciate it," said Dulcia, speaking in reference to her friend's increased colour, but passing over a further increase.

"Good-bye. May your union be blessed," said Beatrice, in a low voice.

"You are fortunate, Grant," said Oscar. "You have come near to marrying your sister, the obvious woman for a man to marry."

"Mr. Jekyll, on the face of it, and in the abstract, a union between you and your sister would be ideal," said Dulcia.

"Unions are not abstract," said Fabian.

"Good-bye, precious ones," said Dulcia. "Things will never be quite the same again. I can't help a little bit of self creeping in at the last."

"Not quite the best moment," said Beatrice, lightly, but with a thought of her last encounter with her friend.

"This is a marriage in which we can rejoice," said Mrs. Bode, wiping her eyes as she expressed her feeling.

"Yes, Mother dear. But we will not be subject to the past to-day, relentless pursuer though it be."

"What should we do without our daughter?" said Mr. Bode, right that they would do differently.

"I don't find the need to rejoice," said Duncan. "If the boy and girl see no reason for it, it is for no one to do it for them."

"We do it with them," said Beatrice.

The carriage drove away with the married pair. The men accompanied their host to the library, and the six women left the house.

"Mrs. Jekyll," said Dulcia. "I am buoyed up by the sense that Cassie is finally attached to Nance. If we were leaving her alone, I should have my own private heartache for her."

"A wedding's sorrows!" said Beatrice.

"It is not only Nance, whom she is supposed to be attached to."

"You are pleased about the marriage, Mrs. Jekyll?"

"I am pleased about almost any marriage, for a woman who is not provided for."

"But Cassie is so equal—forgive me, Mrs. Jekyll; 'Mrs. Edgeworth' does not come somehow—to managing that side of things for herself."

"She has proved it better lately."

"You are one of those women who feel a woman is not fulfilled if she does not marry, Mrs. Jekyll?" said Beatrice, stepping nearer.

"I feel she is not fulfilled, if she never serves herself."

"Her brother would not have failed in chivalry," said Dulcia. "We feel no doubt on that score."

"He already supports one woman, and a hardy one, if she is eighty."

"We cannot imagine ourselves without you, Mrs. Jekyll," said Miss Burtenshaw, as she imagined it.

"For a time I shall be here, and then it won't be left to your imagination." Gretchen glanced round to see if her son were following.

"No, Mrs. Jekyll, he has not yet torn himself from his cronies," said Miss Burtenshaw, swinging along.

"It is a change for him to have a talk with men," said Beatrice.

"Yes; he is generally with an old woman or little boys."

"Mrs. Jekyll," said Dulcia gravely, "we don't think any creature in the world compares with an experienced woman. It has been my own opinion from a child."

"That is understandable," said Miss Burtenshaw, almost laughing.

"Grant is less of a match for Duncan's daughter, now there is a son," said Gretchen.

"Duncan!" said Dulcia, pausing. "Of course he is your son-in-law, Mrs. Jekyll! What a topsy-turvying of recognised relationships!"

"The place might have gone down through Duncan's child after all," said Florence.

"But it would not have gone down through the direct male line, Mrs. Smollett," said Dulcia, on a serious note.

"And that means a great deal to a man of Mr. Edge-worth's type and tradition."

"It does not mean much to a girl of Sibyl's," said Gretchen. "She would as soon it went down in the indirect."

"I really don't think so, Mrs. Jekyll," said Dulcia. "Cynicism never has its way with me."

"I should like to say that I agree with Dulcia," said Beatrice.

"What do you think, Miss Burtenshaw?" said Mrs. Bode.

"Oh, I don't grudge the world its worldliness," said Miss Burtenshaw, with a sense that Oscar was now behind.

"Of course, Mr. Jekyll, Mr. Edgeworth is now your brother-in-law," said Dulcia. "We have been trying to catch up with the general post, and getting, I admit, a little breathless."

"Yes, that is the case."

"Of course they have always been friends," said Beatrice.

"I don't mean there is any essential difference in their relationship. I hardly need to say that."

"You have left your sister in her new home, Mr. Jekyll?" said Miss Burtenshaw.

"It hardly seems a new home for her to me."

"It is a new home, for all that," said Gretchen.

"Yes, Mrs. Jekyll; that has the essential truth," said Dulcia. "It is like you to come to face with things."

"It must be a step of a kind, to be one of the family," said Miss Burtenshaw, "though not in any especial direction."

"Our ways part here," said Florence. "Three of us go on together."

"I really go with you," said Dulcia. "But I detect a faint inclination to be the number mentioned; and so will proceed with our redoubtable cousins, leaving my mother to your tolerance and care. Now do you know what I nearly said? I nearly said, Rosamund and Beatrice. And I consider it a trip to take such a forward step without permission. But have things so far progressed, dear Miss Burtenshaw, that I may consider myself on those terms? You have long been Rosamund in my mind."

"As I call you Dulcia, it is only fair you should return the compliment."

"And age makes no difference, when an intimacy has reached a point: I never consider you so overwhelmingly my senior, except in wisdom."

Beatrice walked at their side, smiling rather formally over the pact.

"It does not alter one jot my relation with you," whispered Dulcia, squeezing her arm. "It just adds another to it, of the same kind, but with the difference that marks them both as what they are. You haven't the tiniest feeling?"

"Of course I have not; I am most glad," said Beatrice, frowning to herself after her words.

"It would be an odd thing to mind," said her cousin. "We cannot all remain on formal terms for ever."

"The odd, little things are those we catch ourselves minding," said Dulcia. "I know I have caught myself right out."

"I am most glad," repeated Beatrice, "in spite of my first little feeling of surprise and friendly competitiveness. If competitiveness can be called friendly, which I am afraid mine could not. Talking of Christian names——" She hurried on—"I don't know what Mr. Jekyll was thinking of, when he said good-bye. He called me by my Christian name as loud as you please. I did not quite know where to turn my eyes."

"I hope you turned them on his face," said her cousin, "as that would have been pretty behaved. He has heard the name so often, that it was a forgivable slip, even if it was a little casual."

"Yes, he said it quite casually and easily, as if he had thought of me like that. Well, he is quite welcome to, if he likes: I have no objection."

"We must not have objections to our friends' little carelessnesses: they have to put up with ours. I am sure he did not intend to be perfunctory."

"I am sure I have no desire to call him by his Christian name. It has barely got into my mind what it is. It would not slip out in a moment of unawareness, as mine did from him. He will not have to put up with that little carelessness. I am afraid I cannot cry him quits."

"Well, whatever either of you feel to him, or he to you, you are both worthy to be called by your Christian names by him," said Dulcia, "a position which I should never arrogate to myself. Now I must fly, or my parents will be pacing the room. You don't know what a glimpse of my face means to them at this moment."

With this setting out of relative situations, Dulcia hastened on her way.

"Well, girls," said Alexander. "I forget where you were going, and why I didn't go."

"To Sibyl Edgeworth's wedding, Father, which leaves her still Sibyl Edgeworth. I told her it was marriage without tears. You did not go, because we were too many to present ourselves in a bunch."

"And so you chose to leave me out! Well, I hope this marriage will lay the rumours: I hope it will be without tears. I suppose you haven't any news? One never knows what will come out of that family."

"No news; except that Beatrice was very cheered by being addressed by Mr. Jekyll by her Christian name. It was an inadvertence which she took up with the most thorough-going seriousness."

"I was not cheered at all," said Beatrice, who put more vigour into these untruths, which she was not to retract; "and I hardly know what you mean by 'taking up'. It did not make any difference to me. I merely mentioned it, as it happened to take place. We must talk about something."

"We must, of course," said her uncle. "And was that

all? He didn't go any further? Well, that wasn't a great deal to go on."

" 'Taking up! Go on!' " said Beatrice, shaking her head. "I don't pretend to keep pace with you. I am getting quite into a fog."

"Well, we have come to one mind about it," said her cousin.

"I was never of any other mind."

"Well, if you are of one mind, why bicker. And how did Cassie look, as mistress of the ceremonies?"

"Dignified and gracious, as her life of more than merely domestic experience has made her," said his daughter. "And, Father, you seem a person for slips about Christian names."

"I always think of her as Cassie: I shouldn't say it to her face, of course."

"Well, that was what Mr. Jekyll did to me," said Beatrice, turning as she spoke to leave the room. "He was not content with merely thinking of me by it."

"Mr. Jekyll did not mean any perfunctoriness at all," said her cousin, in a voice that followed her. "No more than you did, Father."

CHAPTER XVII

"A LETTER FROM Sibyl," said Duncan. "Why does a woman just married think it is good to hear about her? And do the pair put themselves together to show up their simplicity? Otherwise the habit leaves me at a loss. You read it, one of you women. I do not read letters from a man unable to speak from his own mouth."

"They are leaving Italy to-day, Father, and beginning the journey home. It will take them a week."

"They would see things better when they had eyes for something beside each other. And the time will be here soon enough, for it to be worth their while to wait."

"Sibyl has lost her diamond brooch! The one you gave her for a wedding present. What a sad thing!"

"Well, she is the only person who will feel the loss, except that she needed the improvement it made in her."

"They came home one night, and found it gone. They took every step to recover it, but with no result."

"Of course they found it gone, when they had lost it. They wouldn't have found it to their hand, would they? The step they could take, would be to go back and live their lives again, and leave it under lock and key. Is there anything else they found it worth while to say?"

"Indeed there is, Father. An important thing, which you may like to read for yourself."

"I should not; or why should I ask you to do so?"

"They are to have a child in the spring, and are both very happy about it, and hope you are too."

"Why should it alter my happiness? I shall have my own in the meantime, and appear as November passing as May. And why make a mouth over saying it? Your being an old maid is no reason why we should make you more so. It had better have been you than either Cassie or Sibyl, as you are younger than the one, and older than the other. And there are enough brats about to make the future. The one upstairs begins to threaten our peace. No, keep the letter. Why should I carry it with me?"

"I hope you will have a daughter, Cassie," said Nance. "A second brat of the same kind would indeed threaten our peace. Father could not be blamed, if his feelings were too much for him; and we have never faced him in that state, without blaming him?"

Duncan was not to suffer this test. His real and supposed sons were never beneath his roof together. A complete and simple tragedy fell on his house.

A day or two later Cassie was awakened by a violent knocking at her door, and found Bethia at her bed.

"Will you please get up, ma'am? Master Richard will not wake! Nurse will not leave him, and begs you to come at once."

Cassie ran upstairs and was assailed by fumes of gas, and realised they had their source in the room where the child lay. The room itself was full, though the windows were opened wide. The nurse was kneeling by the crib, where the boy seemed to be asleep. Cassie touched his hands and limbs, and ran to find her husband. He had heard the stir, and met her; and they went together to the bed, stood together with their eyes on the child, and sent a urgent message to Fabian, knowing that he was dead.

"Where does the gas turn on?" said Duncan.

"Behind the cupboard, sir, where you cannot see it from here. He must have got out of bed, and turned it on. I never thought of such a thing. He is at an age when no one can tell how much he knows."

"Were not the windows open? The fumes should have found an escape."

"I don't know what to think, sir: I must have deceived myself. I was sure I opened them, and put the latches in their cases. But they were shut; I will tell you the truth."

"Did the child sleep alone?"

"For the last few weeks, sir, since he was wakeful at nights. He sleeps better by himself, and I could hear the least sound."

"Did you not smell the gas?"

"Yes, sir; it woke me, and I came to him at once."

"He could surely not have managed the windows," said Cassie.

"He had seen me doing them, ma'am. He must have climbed on a chair: there is one out of place. I have never known him do such a thing, but he must have noticed more than I thought."

"He must begin some time to do anything fresh," said Duncan, breaking off, as he realised the child would do nothing again. "You are right to be honest, my good woman. It is the way to help."

Fabian entered the room, and went to the child's bed. The moment of waiting was as tense as if they had hoped. He turned at once, and spoke to Duncan.

"There is nothing to be done; he has not breathed for hours. He had no suffering in all his life. We can't many of us say as much as that."

"We most of us could, if we came to our end as he has. You need not put things as they are not. It does nothing. I will take the women away, and meet you again. I direct that things shall be left as they are. Admittance will be easy for anyone whose business is here. We will behave as becomes us, as we are placed."

The family met at breakfast, stunned and silent, but with a sense that they might have had a fuller grief. Duncan's aloofness from his supposed son, his tacit discouragement of interest in him, enhanced, as it seemed, by his consistent thought for his welfare, had prevented feeling from gathering about him, as it might have about another child; and they suffered from the pathos of the helpless death, and from the threat of the world's judgment, rather than any actual sorrow.

"The nurse is honest," said Fabian, "a much better woman than the last. She may have had a lapse of memory, but she is not that kind. The boy must have climbed out of bed, and played with the gas and the windows. He had seen such things done, and wanted to do them; had probably watched on purpose. It was impossible to think of it; no blame attaches to anyone; but there is nothing else it could have been."

"We must send a telegram to Grant and Sibyl," said Duncan.

"Is there any need, Father? They will be home in three days."

"I said we must send a telegram. That is a way of saying there is need. They will be home to-morrow evening." Duncan's manner showed he might have been more deeply shaken.

Bethia appeared, revealing by her face that she identified herself with the family.

"Mrs. Jekyll and Mr. Oscar hope you will see them, ma'am."

"Well, so there is trouble again," said Gretchen. "And of a kind you can't pretend to keep to yourselves. We have joined your family in time to share it."

"We must stand together," said Duncan.

"We shan't have much chance of anything else. It is something that no one is accountable."

"It was not a thing that should have happened."

"I did not say it was: I should be saying it by myself."

"The child was my charge," said Cassie.

"People won't want to disagree with you. You will find yourself welcome to your place."

"They will say it would not have happened, if he had been my own son."

"They will; but it does not make me wish he had been your own."

"It is a crushing thing," said Cassie. "A helpless child!"

"Don't talk in that witless way," said Duncan. "What difference does his being helpless make? If he had been less helpless, it would not have happened. You speak as if someone had done it on purpose."

"If it were possible, I should think someone had."

"Well, we have seen it was not possible; unless you did it yourself. Women in your state are known to do strange things."

"Men in your state too, Duncan," said Oscar.

Duncan looked at his brother-in-law, and gave a short laugh.

"I hope you subdue that man, Cassie?"

"Yes, yes, she subdues me. A masterful woman: I become a cipher in my own house."

"Will you see Mr. Bode and Miss Bode, ma'am?" said Bethia.

"Yes, yes; let anyone come in," said Duncan. "We are glad of the support of our friends."

"Father dear, no questions!" came Dulcia's voice from the hall.

"Mrs. Edgeworth, I hoped you might command me to some service," said Mr. Bode, doing his utmost with statement.

Dulcia came up to Nance, and stood with her eyes before her, openly controlling the workings of her face.

"We are here to prove we are your friends through thick and thin."

"Which is this?" said Nance.

"Darling, you are worked up and strained."

"An odd person would wonder at it," said Duncan.

"My wife would not come," said Mr. Bode. "You could not bear with us all, and she put herself last, as usual."

"She withdrew from the competition," said Gretchen.

"Dear ones, that is what it was; a competition," said Dulcia. "You may believe it or not, but it was."

"I believe it," said Gretchen. "I dare say all their friends will join it."

"If they do not!" said Dulcia, clenching her fist. "Well, I for one shall think very little of them; I won't go further at the moment; I will wait for the hour of need."

Florence entered the room, without waiting to be shown, and went up to Cassie.

"There is a dear, genuine character!" said Dulcia, with a slight gesture.

"We are not mending matters by being on the top of each other," said Gretchen.

"We may be in a way," said Dulcia: "I feel it does make a difference."

"You feel you are doing some good, do you?"

"Mrs. Jekyll, I do: I feel I am doing all I can, and no one can do more. And I should be deeply ashamed, if I had stayed away. You feel with me, Mrs. Smollett?"

"It was a question of whether I was wanted; and I chose to think I was."

"Miss Fellowes!" said Bethia.

Beatrice came swiftly forward, in semi-mourning garments, and going up to Nance and Cassie, kissed them in a deliberate manner, as if by no means omitting signs of intimacy. Florence covertly, and Gretchen openly, regarded her apparel.

"It is good of you to come, Miss Fellowes," said Duncan. "Our friends are what we thought them."

"If we had stayed away!" breathed Dulcia.

Beatrice looked at Duncan, and opened her mouth, but at the moment her cousin hurried past, in her usual clothes.

"Now you are good to be all together. I let Beatrice get a start, and she took a base advantage. But you do not assume our feelings are in that proportion."

"I am sure they know we feel for them equally," said Beatrice.

"Now is there any job you can put me to?" said Miss Burtenshaw, not turning her eyes on her cousin. "Can I write letters, or go on errands, or do any of the hundred and one things that whisper they must be done?"

"I should be grateful if you would write some letters," said Cassie. "They must be written, and I feel I cannot settle to them."

"And you shall not," said the other, drawing off her gloves. "I feel you are treating me kindly. I ask a favour, and am at once granted it, most rare and congenial treatment."

She and Cassie left the room, and Beatrice stood looking after them.

"Is there anything I can do, Nance?"

"No. Setting you all to wait upon us will not mend matters."

"Dearest, I am going to give you a lead," said Dulcia, taking Beatrice's elbow. "You want to give Nance your familiar—and dear and true message. Now does that break the ice?"

Beatrice turned a smile upon Nance.

"I am ashamed of waiting for the ice to be broken; I am but a feeble witness. But may I second the effort? I do not claim it as mine."

"It is kind of you both," said Nance, not disputing this view of the initiative; "but the message is familiar, as Dulcia said."

"Dear, don't repudiate what may bring you comfort and strength," said the last.

"Why should I repudiate it, any more than either of you? Or do you hesitate to state your reasons?"

"Darling, if it has brought a twinkle to your eyes, it has done its work."

"It is supposed to be cheering, I know."

"Mrs. Edgeworth," said Dulcia, as Cassie returned. "I think questions would be, like comparisons, odious. But it would be a comfort to know if we have any light upon what has befallen us."

"The child must have played with the gas, and shut the windows; unless his nurse forgot to open them. No definite light is possible."

"Mrs. Edgeworth," said Dulcia, standing with one foot forward, "a thought has struck me! Forgive my giving voice to it. It is, that that poor, broken-hearted nurse should not be condemned and sent forth; but should be bidden to stay and work out her atonement."

"She has been bidden to stay," said Duncan. "There is no reason for any other course. She is an innocent woman."

Dulcia drew back, bowing her head with dramatic submission. Beatrice, whose eyes had been upon her, came up.

"I think we should avoid a note of flippancy in dealing with certain things. The more so, that jokes of that kind are so easy, and in their way so effective."

"Oh, a note of flippancy, anything, everything, is grist to my mill, while it brings a smile to Nance's face, and any cheer to this family. I can't be taken to task for putting my opinions, your opinions, any in this world or the next, second to that."

Beatrice drew back, recognising her isolation.

"Mrs. Edgeworth, we have done nothing for you," said Mr. Bode; "but you have done much for us. I can tell my wife that in goodness to your friends you are yourselves."

"Dear Father!" said Dulcia. "Sometimes he does make a success of his little speeches. I wholeheartedly second what he said."

Mr. Bode took his way, assuming the continued need for his daughter, whose feeling was still with him.

Beatrice walked swiftly and silently to Florence.

"Mrs. Smollett, a thought has struck me, which I think should be communicated to someone near the family. Do you know if the sad news has been sent to Alison Edgeworth, Alison Bode, as she is now? Nothing alters the fact that she is the child's mother."

Florence regarded her with level eyes, and turned them to Cassie.

"My dear, has anyone let the child's mother know? If not, I can attend to it."

"A telegram has been sent to her husband, so that he may break it to her."

"But, dear, I am grateful," said Dulcia, edging to Beatrice, perhaps with some feeling of compunction. "That question comes near home, as you may guess. I have suppressed it, uncertain of its opportuneness. You did better."

"I felt the little job should be done. It went a thought against the grain, as I was myself not sure of its being welcome. But it was clearly not a matter for choice; and the effort was soon over."

"Well, I have been allowed to make myself useful," said Miss Burtenshaw, in the hall. "It made me glad I did not delay, to make myself ornamental. And I am to come back this afternoon to be more useful. I feel inclined to hold my head rather high."

"We all had our little duties," said her cousin.

"So we are not to be allowed to omit our farewells after all. We thought we had baulked you, Mr. Edgeworth," said Miss Burtenshaw, turning to her host in comprehension of his view.

"Good-bye, Mr. Edgeworth, good-bye—Cassie," said Dulcia. "I feel it an occasion when any sign of intimacy may be welcome and even—decent. I shall not go so far again."

"I hope not," said Oscar, "considering the impetus needed."

"I am glad Mr. Jekyll is staying with them," said Beatrice; "I don't know how we should feel, if we were leaving them by themselves."

"I certainly cannot know," said her cousin, "as I should not have left them."

"We might not have had the choice."

"I should have had one, as I should have made it."

"We might not have been able to," said Beatrice, continuing at once. "I wonder if there is anything we can do for Mr. Jekyll, as he is leaving his work to-day."

"I do not wonder; I find I can do enough to take every

minute until I return. I did not rush off as you did, without a word, but I made use of the interval."

"I did not rush off. I heard my friends were in trouble, and went at once to them."

"Did it not occur to you that I should wish to go too?"

"I am afraid I was thinking only of them at the moment."

"I am afraid your point of view was limited," her cousin easily agreed.

"Can I help you in anything you have to do?" said Beatrice.

"You can help most of us in most times," said Dulcia. "I for one have been honouring you in my mind to-day, as you stood there in your simple black, enough to show you identified yourself with the family, and yet not enough for complete identification. I was struck by it as the acme of good taste."

Miss Burtenshaw just glanced at her cousin's attire, at this description.

"I am afraid claims for oneself may sometimes creep into one's thoughts for others," said Beatrice.

"We all find that sometimes," said Miss Burtenshaw; "though I cannot be accused of feeling much was due to myself to-day. It is true you did not rush off. You made most deliberate preparations."

"I did not see it as what was due to myself, but as what was due to my friends."

"You did not tell me you were going to adapt yourself in that way."

"It did not seem to me worth speaking about."

"Only worth doing."

"I think, if a thing like that does not occur to one personally, it has no value."

"Value?" said Miss Burtenshaw, slightly contracting her brows.

"I meant, no point in it."

"You are both such necessary people, that competition between you would be absurd," said Dulcia, waving her hand, and desisting in view of the circumstances. "A real *reductio ad absurdum*. Give my love to Mr. Burtenshaw, and to each other, and don't forget the last."

The cousins were silent over this interpretation of their words.

"I am sorry I did not tell you I was going to change my clothes, if you would have liked to know."

"I should not have liked it. It was better I should not. It only struck me as odd, that you should not communicate the idea, in case anyone would like to follow it, especially as you thought it due to our friends. It is a good thing I did not know; or I might have spent time useful to other people, in trimming up myself."

"I am glad you can be so useful to the Edgeworths."

"Yes; I trotted about this morning in my old clothes; and I shall trot round again in them this afternoon, and put forth my best effort, undaunted by them."

CHAPTER XVIII

"Father, it is such a shock and sorrow. We have travelled since the moment we heard. We have wondered and wondered how it could have happened, and if it has been too much."

"We sent you word how it happened. There was no need for you to wonder. And we have not found it too little."

"Yes, but a telegram can't say much. We felt we knew the facts, and nothing more."

"We feel as you do."

"Could you bear to tell us how it was? But you shall not say or hear another word. And Cassie, we have thought of you next to Father. We know it could not be helped. We know he had every care. It was nothing to do with you."

"Of course it was nothing to do with her. What could it have been? The child was the charge of his nurse. He was not Cassie's any more than he was yours. The woman forgot to open the windows, and he played with the gas himself."

"Poor, innocent lamb!" said Sibyl. "Well, it is of no good to dwell on it."

"It is not; but there is no sign you would have us not do so."

"I am glad to see you here, Mrs. Jekyll: I had a feeling you would come to Cassie."

"You are satisfied with a good many things for the occasion."

"Do not pull up the girl," said Duncan: "I beg you will allow her to speak in my house, which is her father's. And what is she to say? Nothing would sound right, would it? She appears to be doing as well as anyone else."

"Do you find our numbers too much, Uncle?" said

Grant, who had been silent. "Sibyl and I will go home, and return later. I should like an hour with you this evening."

"Yes, do, boy; that will be best," said Duncan, putting his hand to his head. "I am muddled up with it all. I did not look for a thing like this to come on my house. I have run it on my own course, but I have run it straight. And who would have thought of me, if I had not thought of myself? Leave me, and return when we are of a sane mind. And I don't look for smoothing of the matter, or for any blowing of it up to the skies. We will see it as it is, or else might talk with the women. And I have had my fill of that."

"We have had no time to go to your house," said Nance; "but we sent word you were coming, so I hope things will be right."

"It does not matter if they are not," said her sister; "it is not worth a thought."

"You are a good girl," said Duncan. "It is a bad home-coming for you, bad and muddled and everything; but no doubt you are busy with your own life in your mind."

"It has been everything to have Cassie at the head of things," said Nance.

"You feel you would have made a poor figure in that place?" said Duncan. "Another of you speaking sense."

"You have never left me in the place long enough, to get the habit of it, Father."

Gretchen gave a laugh.

"You told a girl of mine she found cause for gladness," said Duncan, who bore no criticism of his family; "and you seem to be coming to her mind."

"Father, Grant will be such a support to you," said Sibyl.

"This makes no more need for him to be climbing up to my place. It does not put him at the head of things, when I am gone."

"Cassie is to have a child in the autumn," said Nance.

"We knew before you were married, but we left it for the time."

"Cassie is to have a child?" said Sibyl. "Cassie?"

"Well, why not, girl? She is a woman like yourself, isn't she?" said Duncan.

Sibyl looked from one to another.

"Is it true?" she said.

"Of course it is true. Control yourself, girl, or it will appear that your mind began to work, when your trouble came."

Sibyl seemed as if she did not hear.

"Father, it must be a boy," she said, clasping her hands.

"You are a good girl. Not that we can fill a place."

"Cassie, you have brought hope to us all."

"No, it does not alter things," said Duncan. "Why should you think it does?"

"It does a little, Father. Yes, we may let it a little. Cassie, see it is a son, and do what you can for us all." Sibyl gathered up her things, her face pale. "You will see to it, for all our sakes?"

"We must remember Sibyl is to have a child as well," said Grant.

"That must be her excuse for seeming not to be in her mind."

Cassie and her mother went with Grant and Sibyl to the hall, and Sibyl sat down and fumbled with her shoe, seeming unsure of what she did. Her handbag fell, and broke open as it touched the ground; and some odds and ends slipped out, a handkerchief and gloves, an envelope addressed in printed letters—Grant and the women caught the name, 'Emma Marshall', in the square, clear hand—some coins and travelling accounts. Grant restored them to his wife, and she held up the gloves to Cassie.

"Just four hours in the train! And the ones I was wearing as bad! And seven sad pairs put away! It will be something to be clean again."

"Not very much," said Gretchen.

"Something, as she said," said Duncan from the room.

"You must say kind things of me to Father, Mrs. Jekyll. I am his especial daughter."

"I don't think Uncle looks as knocked about as he might, Cassie," said Grant.

"He is affected by the nature of the tragedy. He feels it is a reproach."

"Cassie, you must give him a son, and all will be well."

"I am tired of this talk of sons; and I would in any case rather have a daughter. And of course, all will not be well, Sibyl."

"I too am sick of the subject of our succession," said Grant. "We are not a reigning house."

"Were you surprised to hear that Cassie was to have a child?" said his wife, as they drove home.

"Yes, at the moment; I had not thought of it as possible. We exaggerate the gulf of years. She is not much over forty."

"I hope all will be well. She is old to have her first child. She must be glad in a way, that it will inherit, if it is a boy."

"Don't harp on that, Sibyl. The way is only cleared by this tragedy. We ought not to think of it as cleared."

"Grant, I don't like Mrs. Jekyll," said Sibyl, bursting into tears. "She seems to impute evil to everyone she sees. I hate to look into her hard, old eyes. I should never believe anything she said."

"She is better than most of us, to my mind. And her eyes are not hard, are they? They remind me of Cassie's, though they are so different."

"Grant, is it true that women in Cassie's state sometimes do strange things?"

"I have heard it said; I have not met a case."

"It is true especially of middle-aged women, isn't it?"

"I do not know; I have not heard it is."

"Do they ever do something strange, and then forget it?"

223

"I have no idea; I don't know why they should."

"If no explanation is found for this, it won't be said, will it"—Sibyl's voice sank to a whisper—"that Cassie might have brought it about for the sake of her own child?"

"Of course not! Cassie! What an idea to have!"

"I somehow thought it had occurred to Father."

"Of course it had not. You have missed your sleep, and got fanciful."

"Something made me think that the fear had come to him, and he wanted to cover it; something that no one would notice, who did not know him well. If it did get to be thought, if it seemed it might be true, she would never be held responsible, not Cassie?"

"It would never be thought. It would not be held to be possible. That is enough. Fancies breed others."

"It could not be said that Father was glad for it to happen?" said Sibyl in a voice that could just be heard. "That Richard was not his child, and he wanted his own to inherit?"

Grant was silent, seeing his wife had no thought for his own place.

"We must not say a word about it," said Sibyl.

"There is nothing to say anything about."

"Promise me you won't breathe a syllable. Not even to Nance, unless you keep nothing from her. Not to anyone else in the world."

"There is nothing to keep from anyone."

"It is good to have you to comfort me: I feel in such a strange mood. I should be thinking anything, if I were alone."

"I don't seem to have done much for your thoughts. But here we are at home. Let us take that by itself, and forget what hastened it. We were wise to choose this house. Is that a shadow in the hall? Have we come to someone else's?"

"Indeed you have not. You have come to your own," said Dulcia, hastening to meet them. "Now I don't care

224

what is thought of me; if I am to be held interfering and officious and everything." She paused to embrace Sibyl, reliant on some feelings counteractive to those she feared. "I was determined you should have a welcome, that somebody should remember you had a life of your own, apart from the trouble. It has been a shame for your homecoming."

"It is so good of you, Dulcia. I was dreading all the emptiness and eeriness. If it were not for the horror of it all, I should have stayed with Father. But I could not bear the sight of him, weighed down by uncertainty and doubt. And we put ideas into each others heads. We know one another too well."

"Sibyl is exhausted and fanciful," said Grant; "I have never seen her so unlike herself."

As he turned to the drawing-room, a figure came unobtrusively from the back, and moving smoothly to the hall, was about to pause at the umbrella stand, and vanish.

"It is Miss Fellowes," he said. "I hope some more of our friends are hidden in the house. I think it is such an unfriendly idea not to be here to welcome us."

"Behold!" said Dulcia, throwing out her hand to Beatrice, who was in some way checked in her progress and at hand. "The immediate result of my venture! I knew it for an auspicious one. If it puts Grant into this spirit, how worth while!"

"I hope you have found plenty to do for us, Miss Fellowes?"

"Behold!" said Dulcia.

"I have been arranging some flowers in the vases," said Beatrice, in a tone of reference to something hardly calling for it.

"It is glad news that our garden produces flowers."

"Those are from our garden."

"We can't think of anything more we can have," said Grant. "If we do, we will ask for it."

"Thank you very much," said Beatrice, quietly.

"It is a great thing to be free from material preoccupations at such a time," said Dulcia, "to be able to give oneself to trouble in peace. Domestic hitches add such a note of sordidness to what should be spiritual, and even in its way ennobling. And in this case, you poor, beloved ones, the touch is not needed. Not that there is anything sordid in what has come about. Nothing could be more simple and accidental. But things are as they are."

"Dulcia," said Sibyl, in a low, half weeping tone, as Grant and Beatrice moved away, "people always say strange things, when something happens, don't they?"

"What is worrying you, dear?"

"If anyone should say to you that someone, that Cassie brought this about for the sake of her own child, you would not believe it? Even if they said she was not responsible as she is now? You would make a stand and deny it?"

"No one would say it! What an idea! Of course I should deny it, but the need would not arise. No one has hinted such a thing, surely? I could not have believed it."

"Not to me, not to my face," whispered Sibyl. "They did not know I heard; I could not help it. I may feel you have made me a promise?"

"Of course, but the promise has no meaning."

"I can't talk to Grant about it all. He would find it too much. Dulcia, you know about the time before he and I came together?"

"I have heard that old rumour, the one about little Richard's white hair. You may depend upon me for honest dealing. You could tell me if it was true; but I will not ask; I will not pry. I did not at the time when it was being done. It is not my milieu, somehow. It was a nine days' wonder, and died away. This brings it to the surface, but once more it will die down. I have thought it fine of you to rise above it. Let sleeping dogs lie."

"It was when I was giving him nothing, and he could not help himself. I was more to blame than he."

"Well, that must be enough for you. Let it be enough.

226

Forget it and go on with your life. I am giving you rather worldly-wise advice, but I am not a prude. I know the world as it is; I will not pretend I do not. You are young for the knowledge, but it seems to me your time has come for it. So face it, and go forward."

"Dulcia, I feel I must say it, what I have tried not to say. Something is borne in upon me, that I cannot carry alone. You know what they said about Cassie, what I heard them say? I can't drive it out of my mind; it keeps coming back; a picture keeps coming of Cassie, creeping up to Richard's bed; with Father behind her, creeping too; and both with a look that says he is not their own, and must yield to another child who will be hers and his. It can't mean anything? It can't mean that Father and Cassie wished that he would die? It can't mean Father did? It is not true that people who have had a shock, have second sight, is it?"

"It is not, but it is true they may need a good night's sleep. I am going to put you into the care of your husband. Grant, here is Sibyl, for you to order to bed! She has vowed to obey you, so command her to her rest. And Beatrice and I will obey the behest too, unspoken though it perforce is, in our case. We have performed our offices, and will depart. Peace goes with us; but no thanks, if you please! That is on all counts forbidden."

"Grant, did Richard suffer?" said Sibyl. "I have not dared to ask, but Dulcia helps me to be brave."

"Dr. Smollett thought not. It would have been like going to sleep."

"Would there have been a moment, when he was conscious of something, and could not overcome it? He was so helpless," said Sibyl, in a tone of acute misery and grief.

"No, dear, no," said Dulcia; "put it out of your mind. In a young child the hold on life is light. The very pathos has its comfort. Now again we essay to leave you. And once again no thanks. We shall not expect to repeat that injunction?"

"It would be on such very slight counts, that they would

227

be possible," said Beatrice, her intention of going seeming about to materialise.

"Sibyl is very much affected by the shock," said Dulcia, as they went home. "I could not have believed it would take her as it has. I am not at liberty to divulge the truth, but no one would believe it, who had not her confidence."

"I suppose it is natural."

"It is not natural: it is morbid and strange. As I said, I should not have believed it."

"I should, you know," said Beatrice, in a frank tone. "I saw she was over-wrought, in all the ways that do not go into words."

"You have no suspicion, happily for your peace. And it did go into words, unhappily for mine."

"I have not much peace on her account, I confess."

"You would have none, if you knew."

"I do not know specifically, of course; but I have a shrewd suspicion."

"No, dear; your suspicions may be shrewd; but you are not on the nail here. No. And I am glad you are not."

"Can I help you in the place you are in?"

"No, I am not going to reveal it. I must be strong. I must not be led into betraying a trust, by such insinuating offers."

"I did not suggest you should reveal it."

"Not specifically, of course," said Dulcia, smiling over the phrase. "But there does lurk a tiny hope of revelation in such approach. In your place, I should be in an inner ferment; I admire your stoical front."

"You judge other people too much by yourself."

"If I do, it is the only sure method of judging them," said Dulcia, with a touch of abandon in her gait.

"You are being a little unlike yourself."

"It is unlike me to keep anything from you; but I am not my own mistress here."

"You should have been enough so, to avoid mention of it."

"I should. It is mean to stimulate curiosity, without the power of gratifying it."

"I am not conscious of more curiosity than you make a point of exciting. A little is due to your effort, isn't it? But has it not been effort in a wrong cause?" Beatrice smiled and swung her umbrella.

"Darling, I won't torment you any more. I have reached a point where revelation is a duty. I was possessed by an imp of mischief, which chooses the most unsuitable times to take possession. All part of its impishness! Telling anything to you is synonymous with silence, and I shall be glad of your advice about Sibyl. You will tell me if I was wise in my counsel, or too worldly wise?"

"Do not tell me anything you feel you should not."

"I have got to the stage of feeling I positively should. Your patience and forbearance reveal you as a suitable repository for my confidence. And it is to be a confidence, utter, unbreakable, eternal, so help us God."

CHAPTER XIX

"ARE THESE ALL the guests of your Dorcas meeting?" asked Alexander. "Or are the Edgeworths to be here?"

"I am sure they will be here," said Dulcia. "They are not the people to shirk what is in their way. That is not the effect that breeding and knowledge of the world have had upon them. They will come out with their faces turned to the music, if I know them: and I know them well."

"Why, is there any music for them to face?"

"The hardest music of all, the music of slandering tongues. But if you do not know, Mr. Burtenshaw, remain in ignorance. It is a case were ignorance is bliss. I could find it in my heart to envy you."

"Speak out plainly, I adjure you. It is no case of bliss to be half told, and then put off. I can't do with whispering and clapping of hands to mouths. I only imagine things worse than the truth."

"They have already been imagined," said his daughter.

"Rosamund," said Alexander, resorting to an earlier phrase, "if you do not speak plainly at once, you will be disobeying me."

"I think there is some rumour about Mr. and Mrs. Edgeworth's causing the death of the child," said Beatrice, in a low tone.

"The death of the child? The son they have lost? I thought it was something about Edgeworth's not being the father, something in that line. I didn't know there was anything else in the wind; I haven't caught a breath."

"If that is what he thought, it was a strange thing to require his daughter to explain," said Miss Burtenshaw, shrugging her shoulders rather hopelessly.

"We all require such things explained," said Fabian.

230

"Well, now," said Alexander, "then this comes first. Was Edgeworth the father of the boy? Well, if he was not, what is it to do with us? You can go on driving yourself mad and getting nothing. Rosamund, put it out of your mind. It is not a fit thing for you to think about."

"Certainly not, if we can't get certainty," said Fabian. "It would be too much for any woman."

"It is only fit for me to speak about," said Miss Burtenshaw, with a light and resigned sigh.

"Well, but the next thing is involved with the first," went on her father. "A couple know a child is not their own, and prevents their child from inheriting; well, it is easy to see how the rumour arose. But it is all conjecture; we can't be satisfied. And we must remember there are ladies in the room."

"These afterthoughts, Father!"

"Satisfied is not the word I should use, Uncle."

"Well, I would, in the sense I was using it. You don't know the meaning of words. And you all seem pretty satisfied in the other sense."

"We are not that, because we may speak the truth. Truth never does harm."

"That is untrue," said Florence; "but truth will do no harm in this case, if we can get at it."

"I wonder what we should do, if we found the rumour was true," said Dulcia. "Would it be going too far to imagine it for a moment, for the sake of getting a morbid shiver?"

"It would be a waste of time," said Florence.

"You are right, Mrs. Smollett. It was a skunkish suggestion."

"Well, I suppose the rumour will die away, and nothing come of it," said Alexander.

"We do not wish anything to come of it, Father."

"I am sure I don't; I am not one for hinting and suggesting, and gloating over the truth, what would be almost welcomed as the truth, anyhow."

"You are right, Mrs. Smollett," said Dulcia. "My foolish words did harm."

There was silence.

"Now I think what we all want to do," said Dulcia, "is to bear witness to our belief in the innocence of the Edgeworths, in thought, word and deed. Hands up, all who hold that belief!"

Some members lifted hands, and perceiving the response was not unanimous, dropped them, smiling at themselves. Mrs. Bode supported her daughter, who stood with an air of leadership. Florence turned away, and her husband jotted something in his notebook, as if unaware of the proceedings. Alexander flung up his hand, and leaned back to maintain the position.

"Mrs. Smollett, you second us?" said Dulcia. "You of all people the friend of our friends! Your support was a *sine qua non*."

"That is what it is," said Florence.

Fabian shut his book and put it in his pocket.

"Mrs. Smollett, it was well meant," said Dulcia in a faltering tone. "I felt I owed some atonement."

"I owed none."

"So your suspicions have made you a great game!" said a voice at the door, as Gretchen entered with her son.

There was silence.

"I suppose we could hear a pin drop," muttered Fabian to his wife. "But nobody seems to drop one."

"We did not see you, dear Mrs. Jekyll," said Dulcia.

"A difficult and thankless part, the pin," said Fabian.

"It was I who saw you."

"Then you saw us bearing witness to our belief in your daughter and her husband."

"You found it noble in yourselves to acquit your friends of what you put on to them. It shows you are not far from the same thing."

"Mrs. Jekyll, you are not yourself," said Dulcia,

guiding Gretchen to a seat, and proffering a cup of tea as though to a patient.

"This goes a long way to mend matters."

"There are no matters to mend. Rumours and reports arise, and have no more in them than a cloud of dust. We were dispelling the cloud, when you came. I vouch for it that the last particles vanished, as you entered."

"That is how I caught a glimpse of them, I suppose."

"Mrs. Smollett, I ask for your help. You can swear that no breath of scandal attaches to our friends?"

"I had not thought of scandal in that connection."

Beatrice came up with tea for Oscar.

"That is the way, my dear," said her uncle. "You do what you can, and set an example."

"I hardly think Mrs. Jekyll would thank us, if we all followed her example," said his daughter, laughing.

"I would show the spirit was willing."

"But the flesh is weak, Father dear."

"Thank you. It is sugared, is it?" said Oscar.

"One large lump and one small, and a tablespoonful of milk," said Beatrice, moving away.

"I don't wonder you are definite about it, Mr. Jekyll," said Dulcia. "It is the one break you have in a long stretch of duty."

"Meals come in all lives," said Gretchen.

"Mrs. Jekyll, you are yourself. Hail to your authentic touch!"

"Here are the Edgeworths!" said Alexander.

Duncan and his wife and daughter entered, with Grant and Sibyl in the rear.

"You are in time to know the hearts of your friends," said Gretchen at once. "They have acquitted you of the death of your child, after accusing you of it."

"It sounds as if it had been a waste of time," said Nance.

"Who could think a friend would cause the death of a child?" said Sibyl. "It is a contradiction in terms."

"The contradiction was not as sound as that," said Gretchen.

"There has been some village gossip, has there?" said Duncan.

"Mr. Edgeworth," said Dulcia, "that is what there has been. The merest, lightest gossip, blown away like a piece of thistledown. It has been dispersed when you entered. It was the final dispersing that Mrs. Jekyll saw."

"Thistledown in dispersing goes a good many ways," said Gretchen.

"I should like to go into the village," said Dulcia, "and bruit your fair name abroad from one end to the other, to leave no corner unpenetrated by the light of your house. Woe would be to him who should gainsay me!"

"Let us leave the village its rumours," said Sibyl. "This one is not the first or the last. Don't deprive the bumpkins of their diversions."

"No one in his mind would give an ear to rumour about your family," said Alexander. "I am one of the ordinary people, and I swear to it."

"I am not that. No, no," said Fabian.

"All this swearing!" said Beatrice, with a wryness in her smile.

"Well, we will say 'Yea, yea,' and 'Nay, nay'," said Alexander.

"Burtenshaw should beware of family influence," said Oscar to Nance.

"Should the work of the meeting be going on, or is it a social occasion?" said Duncan. "We wished to accept your invitation, but not to hinder your routine."

"Thank you, Mr. Edgeworth," said Miss Burtenshaw; "I don't know when the orphanage will get its winter petticoats, if we go on like this."

"We hope before the winter," said Duncan.

"Beatrice, you and I must set an example."

"I have been going on with a petticoat in the intervals," said Beatrice, lifting the garment.

"One orphan off our minds," said Fabian.

"Grant, you are silent this afternoon," said Dulc͏ "And as for Mrs. Edgeworth, if I may be Irish, there has not been a sound out of her this blessed day."

"Mrs. Edgeworth," said Alexander, "Dulcia is right. We are waiting to hear your voice. We want to hear it as much as we have ever wanted to."

"Thistledown is in the air," said Gretchen. "It does hang about."

"We should be going," said Cassie.

"We also should be putting things together," said Beatrice, expressing her departure in its own terms. "We have not done much. I must ask permission to take my petticoat home."

"I will take mine," said Mrs. Bode.

"Now, Mother, don't undertake more than you will carry out," said Dulcia, with serious warning.

"The petticoat will be none the worse for a change of air," said Fabian.

"Dr. Smollett, you would be surprised how much worse they are. That is why we had to instigate the system of permission."

"I do not understand the constitution of a petticoat."

"Not its pre-natal one, anyhow," said Dulcia, clearly.

"Shall I take mine?" said Florence, looking at it.

"I will not have one about," said her husband. "They are puny things and outside my sphere of knowledge."

"No, do not ask me, Rosamund," said Dulcia, putting her hands behind her. "I am going to be firm. I know I should not touch it, and I will not enter upon the farce of taking it. And one petticoat is enough in a family."

"All this running off without a thought for the orphans!" said Fabian.

"I am quite stiff with sitting for so long," said Alexander.

"There was no reason for you to stay," said his daughter.

"Oh, wasn't there? There was then," said Alexander, putting his face close to hers. "There was that scrap with old Gretchen. It had me petrified. I can't get it out of my head."

"I don't care to have it in my head," said Florence.

"Mrs. Smollett," said Dulcia, "would you say we gave our friends the impression that we whole-heartedly believed in them?"

"I should say I did, and that is my concern."

"We could wish Mrs. Smollett were less aloof," said Beatrice, smiling.

The Edgeworths and Gretchen walked away together.

"Things have gone far," said Nance. "How far, I suppose we shall never be told."

Duncan proceeded in silence, his breath deep.

"What impossible things come into people's minds!" said Sibyl. "Who would guess the thoughts of decent men and women?"

"People commit crimes for small reasons," said Gretchen, "and I suppose they realise it. They never think other people far from themselves."

"Father, don't listen," said Sibyl. "People are not as bad as that. They only like to gossip. Our friends are as good as we are. We will not be left with no faith in anyone or anything."

"I am going to the village shop," said Cassie. "Mother and I will follow."

The mother and daughter entered the shop, and as they approached the counter, a woman drew back to give them place.

"It is Marshall!" said Cassie. "I have wondered if we should meet again. Tell me what you can of yourself, Marshall. I have wished I had followed your movements."

"I am here for a while, ma'am, to see my friends, before I go away to be married."

"I have been married without going away. And Miss Sibyl is married to Mr. Grant. I expect you have heard of our changes and our troubles?"

"Yes, ma'am; everyone has told me how it is different."

"Don't let us take your place," said Gretchen; "we must follow in turn."

The woman took a money order from an envelope and asked to have it changed. The others recognised the envelope as the counterpart of that which Sibyl had dropped on the night of her return. This one bore a postmark, but no other difference.

"Have you heard from Miss Sibyl lately?" said Gretchen.

"I do not hear from anyone, ma'am. I thought I was forgotten."

"You must come and see them all, and tell them of the man you are to marry. Why not come with us today? Bygones are bygones, and we will none of us throw up the past. You are right that all is different."

"Thank you, ma'am," said Marshall, putting away her change.

"You are rich," said Gretchen, with a smile, seeing other orders in the envelope.

"I earned the money, ma'am," said the woman, drawing back.

"I should like you to have some things of Richard's," said Cassie, as they reached the house. "You were fond of him, and you may find them useful in the future."

"Thank you, ma'am. I was sorry to leave him, and didn't think I ought; but I shouldn't have met the man, if I had stayed; and it is him I think of now."

"All's well that ends well," said Gretchen. "The man will last you longer. Now you will have tea here with us, and go down later with Bethia."

"I will fetch the things," said Cassie. "They are in the nursery chest."

"Can I go for you, ma'am? You will want to pour out tea. I shall be down in a minute."

"Does she know where to go?" said Gretchen. "The nursery has been changed. Did you tell her it was a storey higher?" She broke off as her daughter did not hear, and listened to the steps mounting the stairs.

"Come with me, Cassie," said she in another manner. "I shall not keep you long. Don't question me. Do as I say."

Cassie obeyed by earlier habit an earlier tone, and they entered the room where Marshall was standing at the chest.

"Well, this is an ill-fated room," said Gretchen, sitting down. "We will not leave you alone in it. You have heard of the thing that happened here?"

"Yes, ma'am, I have; the poor little boy!"

"The nurse was more careless than you would have been. She left him asleep with the windows shut. He could never have fastened them himself."

"No, ma'am, not with those latches."

"But he must have turned on the gas."

"Yes, ma'am, he must," said Marshall, moving to glance at the fittings behind the cupboard. "That is what it must have been."

"There was no gas in the house when you were here?"

"No, ma'am. I went to the housemaid's sink for hot water. I call the nurse fortunate now."

Gretchen went to the door and locked it, and returned with the key.

"So you succeeded the first time?" she said.

Marshall stared at her, barely following.

"You only tried once?" said Gretchen, looking almost quizzically into her face.

The woman recoiled, her eyes held.

"Now listen," said Gretchen, restraining Cassie, who gave a cry and started forward. "If you do not tell the truth, you are in the last danger. If you tell it, you are safe. You understand?"

Marshall bent her head, her eyes on the old woman's.

"You need not look at me as if I were a snake. There are people nearer to that. I see you will save yourself, as others would."

Marshall broke into weeping.

"I never wanted to do it. It wasn't me that thought of it. I should never think of these things. I was told it would be worse for me, if I didn't. And it was a lot of money, and my man was ill. I couldn't see how I was not to. And I was frightened I should never get out of the house. It wasn't worth it to me."

"Who was it who paid you to do it?"

"I don't know, ma'am; I am speaking honest; the letter had no name. And the envelope that brought the money had no writing."

"Have you the letter?"

"No, ma'am. It said I was to burn it, and I did."

"It is not the first time you have done harm to this house. You wrote that letter to your master about the child. What was in your mind that time?"

"Nothing, ma'am; I did not think of it. It was Miss Sibyl who wrote to me to do it. It is no good not to tell, as you will only find out. You will tell her I couldn't help it. She sent me money, and made me more angry at being sent away. But the money was not much, and it did not seem very bad."

"You were to do something worse, indeed. Was this last letter written in large, printed letters, like the envelope?"

"Yes, ma'am," said Marshall, staring at Gretchen, as though seeing no good in any denial.

"And you kept the envelope to keep the orders in?"

"Yes, ma'am; I didn't think of harm coming from that."

"There was a deal of good coming from it," said Gretchen, going to the door. "They are all in the drawing-room. I suppose they didn't like the Dorcas tea. They will soon forget it, as I have. Cassie, take her other arm; I am not as strong as I was. Marshall, give no trouble, and you have nothing to fear."

The three women went to the drawing-room, locked together. Gretchen was resolute, Cassie shaken, and

Marshall slavish and terrified. The eyes of all turned towards them.

"What is this?" said Duncan.

"The solution of the mystery," said Gretchen, "the truth of what happened in your house! Your nurse shut your windows, and your child turned on the gas! This is the person who did both!"

There was a silence.

"How do you know?" said Duncan.

"I will tell you later. It is enough that I do know. I suppose you want the suspicion lifted from yourself and your wife? You remember you have one account already with this woman."

"You wrote me that letter a year ago," said Duncan to the nurse.

"I did not think of it, sir. I did not want to do it. It was Miss Sibyl who wrote to me to do it, and sent the money. She said it was right to take revenge. And I was afraid not to obey her; I was always afraid of Miss Sibyl."

Duncan and Nance turned to Sibyl, who had fallen backwards on the couch. Cassie moved instinctively towards her, but her mother held her back.

"People don't look round for something to fall on when they faint. She is only in an awkward place. The truth has come out about her early doings, and few of us like that." Gretchen's tone was almost kind.

"Well, let us get back to the main thing," said Grant.

Gretchen took the envelope from Marshall's bag, and showed it, with the orders folded to its shape.

"This came to Marshall with the money. A letter came to her before, telling her to do what she did. There is no trace to be followed. It is a home-made envelope, addressed in a printed hand. Someone has covered his tracks. But it is enough to have suspicion lifted from the innocent."

Sibyl stirred on the sofa, unable to be still without support.

"Get up and talk of your early mischief," said Gretchen. "To know all is to forgive all."

Sibyl gave a drawn out wail.

"I know it was a mean thing to do; I was too wretched to think. I was so young and alone, and no one was kind. They seemed to think it was wrong to love Almeric, and all it meant was misery. I thought Alison would go away, if Father knew: I did not think of her taking Almeric. No one will know what that time was."

"You knew it was Miss Sibyl, who sent you the money to write that letter?" said Duncan to the nurse.

"She wrote herself, sir, and put her name."

"Yes, I did, Father," said Sibyl, with a note of eagerness. "I told you, I had to do something. It was foolish to write myself, and sign the letter. It does not make things better to be stupid. It has made it come out, and given you a shock you might have been saved. But I am not a person who should do subtle things; I know myself now."

Duncan allowed her hand to rest in his, and kept his eyes on Marshall.

"You do not know who it was, who paid you to do this second thing?"

"No, sir, if it was not Miss Sibyl. I did not want to do it; I hated to be cruel; but the letter said I should suffer if I would not, and I was afraid. And I wanted the money for my man."

"Can we get on the track of the person?" said Duncan. "Is it safe to have such a creature at large, with some grudge against us?"

"Would anyone commit a second crime in the same quarter?" said Nance.

"What object could there have been in the first?"

"Let us think," said Sibyl, putting her hand to her head, while Cassie and Nance looked at her, and looked away. "Anyone with anything to gain, for himself, or anyone else, would have had one. That is, you, Father"—she gave a little laugh—"or Cassie; or Mrs. Jekyll or Oscar, for

Cassie. I can't think of anyone else, and that does not take us further."

"Was Marshall willing to write this letter for you?"

"Yes, Father. She was anxious for revenge for herself. If I had not known that, I should not have put it on her."

"Be silent. The moral line is not yours," Duncan turned again to the nurse. "Marshall, had you still a feeling of revenge, when this behest was laid upon you?"

"I had not done anything to be sent away for, sir," said the woman, barely following his words.

Duncan addressed his family.

"This seems to me a primitive creature, in the grip of a bitterness of spirit. It is likely that the crime is her own, and that she contrived the envelope in case of discovery. Such people have their own cunning. And the earlier episode gave the suggestion. Was there a postmark on the envelope?"

"A London postmark, that tells nothing," said Gretchen.

"Is it our duty to follow up the crime for the sake of the innocent?"

"She was promised her safety, if she spoke the truth. We have no proof that she has not spoken it. She has given us a good deal."

"Then go, poor creature," said Duncan, with relief both formed and formless at his heart; "and in your future life be human, if you cannot be a woman. Your traces will be kept, and further crime will recoil upon you."

Marshall went weeping to the hall, accompanied by Nance and Grant, and Duncan turned to Gretchen.

"Mrs. Jekyll, a word! Did you contrive this story to avert suspicion from Cassie? It would be understandable in a mother; I should understand it." There was an odd hope in Duncan's tone. "I do not judge a mother as if she were a man. The truth should not go beyond this house."

"It should not, Mrs. Jekyll," said Sibyl earnestly.

Gretchen gave a laugh that carried conviction to Duncan.

"What is your proof that the woman was guilty?" he said.

"I promised to give it, and therefore I will. She went direct to the nursery, though it was a different room when she was here. She knew the window latches, which were altered when the change was made. She knew where the gas turned on, when gas was brought to the village since she went. She was easily brought to confessions. What would you call proof? No one saw her do it, of course."

"It is proof," said Duncan, turning to the window and tapping his hands upon the sill. "We owe you our gratitude."

"Do you want any more?" said Gretchen, taking advantage of his back to direct her eyes to Sibyl.

"No, Mrs. Jekyll," said Sibyl.

"So that is what you did with your brooch," said Gretchen, guiding her backwards with her hand, and speaking with her face close to hers. "You sold it and sent the money to Marshall. And you made your envelope yourself, and printed your letters; and you tried more than once to get it all to your liking. And this time you were past the folly of using your own name. Now, if there is danger in the future to Cassie or Cassie's child, remember the secret will not die with an old woman."

Grant and Nance came back, and Duncan turned to meet them.

"Father," said Sibyl, taking his arm, with a feeling that boldness would serve her as well as anything else, "you will not think of what I did, when I was so alone and wretched? It was partly that I felt you should know the truth. I did not feel to Grant as I do now. You will forgive your especial daughter and Mother's?"

"Nance was Aunt Ellen's especial daughter," said Grant, as if voicing a mechanical thought.

Gretchen turned on him a look of pity.

"It was a thing your mother's daughter and mine could do. I have to face the truth. Your husband must also face it."

"We must go home," said Grant. "It is time we went. Come—come——" It seemed he could not use his wife's name. "We should both go now."

"We must spread the truth," said Nance. "If people do not know what to think, they will go on thinking anything."

"I will see they know," said Gretchen, "and then I shall be through. It is my last piece of work. I am not looking for another. And put it from your minds. It is all over."

But it was not all over. An hour later Grant returned and sought his uncle.

Duncan was sitting with his family in a rare mood of disliking to be alone.

"I have had a difference with Sibyl, Uncle. We have parted for the time, probably for ever. She is going to-morrow to Aunt Maria. I don't know if she will return."

"So the girl's early stumble is putting you about like that! When it came from a worse one of your own! Why should a woman's youth be spotless, any more than a man's? You are a good person to want a youth to be perfect. What would happen if she looked at yours? I'd as soon have a girl's young days to peer at as a boy's. And a boy's pernicketiness no longer becomes you."

Grant was silent.

"Go back to your wife, and to the house where she is to have your child. What business have you anywhere else?"

"I hoped you would let me stay, and live here as I used. Things are at an end between Sibyl and me. I shall of course be responsible for her support."

"Or would you look for her to see to yours? If you don't like a woman's ways, why did you marry? The girl has had more than one glimpse of a man's, thanks to you. And has now had another, as you tell me."

"Let them live their own lives, Father," said Nance. "If Sibyl knows her mind, and Grant keeps her in comfort, what need is there for anyone to judge?"

"I will have no daughter of mine apart from her husband; and no daughter of mine need try to talk for me. I am able to talk for myself."

"You cannot arrange for what daughters of yours do. If you could, things would be different. Father, let it go for the time. Let us live each day by itself."

"You worry me and see I have no peace, old man as I am. I will not try to withstand you. You are too much for me. It has all been too much."

CHAPTER XX

GRETCHEN'S WORDS OF herself seemed a prophecy, as such words will in the old. The next weeks, aided by a spell of cold and a normal carelessness, brought her to her end.

She met it with matter-of-factness, as a normal thing, and showed a desire to deal with its problems herself. Her goods were disposed and her burial directed, while she lay waiting for her will and her brain to die with her body.

Beatrice was admitted at times with counsel she dared not give, and was never to know that her purpose of brightening a deathbed had been fulfilled.

The end seemed smooth and sudden, as Gretchen was herself to her last breath.

"You will soon be free of me," she said on the day of her death to her son, "and be able to live with a wife like other men. It has been hard on you to have my support, and I know plenty who have thought so; but I don't know what I should have done without a home; and none of them offered me one. But my time is up, and my place ready for another."

"Mother, don't try to be so unusual," said Cassie.

"You will not gain by my going," said Gretchen. "But I love you better, because you live apart. It is a great thing to be separated. Your brother will soon find he loves me better."

The words seemed to have a difference, and Oscar and his sister came to the bed.

"I hope the boys will behave at the funeral," said Gretchen. "They have never gone to church without me; but I shall not be able to help it, when I am dead." She gave an uncertain laugh. "People will say it is a good thing I am not there, and they will feel it is a good thing."

She lay looking at the light, as if she did not see it, and it was soon clear that she did not see. There seemed simply to be a pause, before her son and daughter left her.

"Mother did not live her last moments well," said Cassie.

"You had to see no change," said Fabian.

"I certainly saw no improvement. But I don't mind people's not being at their noblest at the last. It is the least useful time."

"She seemed to have nothing to repent of," said Oscar. "But she has something now. After a life of hiding her preference for you, she might have died with her secret."

"For you, she was at her noblest, Miss Cassie," said Fabian, smiling, and then changing to an incidental, condoning tone. "Yes, Miss Dulcia and Miss Beatrice are in the house. I believe they came with some flowers."

"Shall we have to see them? Mother has died in the nick of time."

Dulcia came from the hall, with Beatrice a step behind.

"I am going to talk in an ordinary way. Something tells me you would prefer that vehicle of sympathy to an encroachment upon a sacrosanct. I am glad I brought the flowers when I did. It is a small thing in itself, but a big one to me."

"Mrs. Jekyll was in peace?" asked Beatrice in an oddly jerky tone.

"Unusually at ease," said Oscar. "She showed my sister favouritism with her last breath."

"Mr. Jekyll, you take me at my word," said Dulcia, "and follow me gladly. Sometimes one's instinct does tell one truth."

"Who is that crying?" said Beatrice, as they crossed the hall.

"One of the lads. They were very attached to my mother."

"Dear little fellows!" said Dulcia. "It shows how Mrs.

Jekyll was really beloved in her own home. Not that I ever met one of those who doubted it."

"Is anyone with him?" said Beatrice, coming to a pause.

"The cook, a comfortable soul. She will soon have them happy. They really think it right for the old to die; they must be amazed that my mother lived so long."

"I am so glad they are not alone," said Beatrice.

"Are you not coming with us, Mr. Jekyll?" said Dulcia, pausing in the doorway. "We ask you to do so."

"I am staying here for a while. My sister is going home."

"Well, if he must stay, he must," said Beatrice, glancing backwards with a sigh.

"Mr. Jekyll!" said Dulcia, moving back. "You have refused me one request! Will you grant me another? Will you undertake not to think of Mrs. Jekyll's last words to you—well, as her last words? You will speed me with a lighter heart, if you grant me that."

"I will undertake anything about them. I have many other words to remember."

"Thank you. I might have known; I did know; but still, thank you."

Cassie took leave of her brother, and left the house; and Beatrice and Dulcia simply set off at her side.

"This is where our paths diverge," she said. "I must not take you out of your way."

The two walked on.

"Nothing doing, Mrs. Edgeworth!" said Dulcia.

"It is really needlessly kind."

"It is. We are neither of us under the delusion that we are doing anything for you, in pacing by your side. But the fact that you would prefer to be alone is a reason why you should not be. You will look back and see it."

Cassie walked on in silence.

"Dear Mrs. Edgeworth," said Dulcia, "we are talking lightsomely of set purpose. You know we are not oblivious of this last milestone in your life."

Cassie gave an assurance of the transparence of their disguise.

"It is impossible to say anything that helps," said Beatrice, "anything of a usual kind, though many things ought to be usual that are not."

"Go on, dear, go on," whispered Dulcia. "The moment!"

"Now, here are my gates, and I can release you. Thank you very much for your company."

"My gates!" said Dulcia. "Even at this moment it gives me satisfaction to hear you say it. You little thought, when you first entered them, that you would live to call them that, so unselfconsciously."

Beatrice walked through the gates, and Dulcia glanced at her and followed.

"Am I to be escorted to the door?"

"To the door, and not a step beyond," said Dulcia. "We shall not respond to any pressure to come in, so you need not think so. That is, you may freely give the unavoidable invitation, without fear of its having any result."

Cassie paused at the steps, and then mounted them with her companions.

"The door is shut, but I can hear Bethia's step. Will you not really come in?"

"Good-bye, Mrs. Edgeworth," said Beatrice, offering her hand; "I am so glad to think of you at home."

"Good-bye, Mrs. Edgeworth," said Dulcia, doing the same, and turning and running down the steps.

Cassie went into the library, where Duncan and Grant were together.

"Duncan, my mother died while I was at the house. Oscar and Fabian were with us. She was herself up to the last."

"Ah! poor woman, poor woman!" said Duncan, rising and putting his hands on her shoulders. "Yes, I will take you to the other woman. I remember losing my mother; I have lost a good woman more than once. Nance, here is Cassie, out of sorts and out of heart. So listen to her, and let her talk herself out. She hasn't come to you, for you to be of no good to her. See you are of some use as a woman, as you can be of none as anything else."

"It has happened at last, Nance," said Cassie. "We had no hope, and really did not want it. And Mother knew, and had a heart of hatred at the end."

"I am glad she died as she lived. The temptations of a deathbed might have been too much. Did Father tell you that his sister was dead? I wonder if she yielded to them."

"This deathbed had its own temptations, and my mother yielded."

"Well, people are too much above themselves at the last. They repent of their sins, and forgive other people, as if there were all that difference between them. I am glad she could not forgive, as no one can really. Do you suppose Aunt Maria forgave Father for what he was as a boy?"

"Cassie, I am upset that you are an orphan," said Grant, coming in. "I have found how difficult it·is lately. Uncle no longer attempts to be a parent to me. Could you sink your own troubles in mine? It is the best way to forget."

"He will never be reconciled to your living apart from Sibyl. And he feels her place is here, if you are not together."

"It is a deadlock. I can't afford to run my house and make her allowance. I have no business to exist. My only use is to make a fourth at cards, when I am just better than a dummy."

In the course of this pastime later in the day, Oscar spoke to Duncan.

"Have I your leave to propose to Nance, Edgeworth? I believe it is the custom to approach the father, before the person more concerned."

Duncan looked up from his hand.

"A reasonable custom, if it had any meaning. But wouldn't you let one woman get to her grave, before you concern yourself with another?"

"No, I would not, in this case."

"Well, you seem to me as good a man as most. But I had hoped for more for her. Though I don't know why, when she has seen nothing and nobody."

"I am a better man than most."

"In that case you may see if she will have you, though it is odd you should think yourself a person to take her fancy. And she has a better home than you can give her."

"She is not the mistress of it."

"No; your sister is that."

The game continued.

"Would you look for my daughter to shepherd a flock of brats?" asked Duncan in a pause.

"That comes to an end. What it brought in, will be covered by her allowance, if it is the same as you made to her sister."

"You may refer to my other daughter by her name, if you wish to become her brother-in-law."

"The same as you made to Sibyl. I do wish to become so. The allowance would balance the teaching. The profit did not come to much."

"Well, in that case perhaps it would," said Duncan. "So our game, and your deal, Smollett."

"You think it a good plan, Smollett?"

"Don't chatter to the dealer," said Duncan, watching the cards. "You are right to arrange to live with a woman. You seem to be cut out for it."

"Just not too good to be true," said Fabian.

"I suppose I shan't have you on my hands, like this man, Oscar?" said Duncan, using the other's Christian name for the first time, and indicating his nephew. "Your wife will be able to bear the sight of you for more than a month? I will hope so, if you tidy up your house after the urchins. But you don't want praising up like a girl, do you?"

"Sibyl and I parted by my wish as well as hers," said Grant.

"And you think it becomes you to say so? You think I can never bear enough? I have seen to it that you should think it. But I will thank myself for no more. Here is a letter, which I desire you shall read and return; and as that is so, you will do both. You and Nance may consider it together, and consider also your own future."

Grant read the letter while his companions looked at their cards.

"My dear Father,

"You will hear from Aunt Maria's lawyer that she has left me all she had.

"There was no question of undue influence. I did what I could for her last days, as no one else thought of her.

"The old plan was, as you knew, though we did not, that the money should go to the sons and daughters of her brothers, in the proportion of two to one. This would mean that Grant and a son of Cassie's would each have about eight hundred a year, and Nance and I four; the figures being modified in the case of Cassie's having a daughter. Aunt Maria had a right to do as she wished, as most of the money was her husband's.

"If I am to live apart from all I have known, I shall definitely keep the whole. If Grant and I come together, I shall transfer it by deed of gift in the old proportion, keeping what would have been my own. Grant and I together would take at least twelve hundred a year. The lawyer tells me I am in my rights in either course. There are advantages for me on either side.

"Your loving daughter,
"Sibyl Edgeworth."

CHAPTER XXI

"Have I come to this meeting in a cheerful spirit or not?" said Dulcia. "On the one hand there is the loss of Mrs. Jekyll; but on the other the emergence, crystal clear, of the name of Edgeworth from the murk and darkness which threatened it. I take my seat between two stools; but not on the chair by vested right yours, Mrs. Smollett."

"It amazes me that people should catch up such a rumour," said Alexander. "I don't think the murk and darkness only threatened the Edgeworths."

"I don't know who the people were, Father; I am glad I have not met them."

"What amazes me, is the blank Mrs. Jekyll's death has left," said Dulcia. "You would hardly believe how I am affected by it. Harsh and grim as she may have seemed to most, I always caught the light of something steady and steel-true beneath. I think there never breathed a person, who walked on earth more unguessed at. Well, let us say: 'Better so'."

"Why should we say it?" said Florence. "It was a pity, if it was the case."

"The person who is in my mind, is Mr. Jekyll," said Beatrice. "The thought of him, sitting alone in the rectory, does recur to one. It will."

"Don't, Beatrice; it is too much," said Dulcia, looking aside with a shiver.

"If it is too much just to think of, what must it be to suffer?" said Beatrice gravely.

"We all have interludes in our lives," said her cousin, "and we must hope this will not be a long one."

"It is hardly of the nature of an interlude, is it? It will be an ever-present sorrow, always there."

"You spoke of his being alone in the rectory. There is no need for him always to be that," said Miss Burtenshaw, with no personal desire to contribute to this necessity.

"I think anyone who joins his life, will come closer to him for a comprehension of what he has behind."

"Oh, it is too soon to dispose of the poor man yet. Don't be in such a hurry to snap him up, to get him snapped up," said Alexander. "And sitting alone in the rectory! He is probably playing cards with Edgeworth and Smollett."

"Get him snapped up, Father! We should not display such haste in our match-making, if we were engaged with it. Our intentions would have to be better disguised."

"Or we should defeat our own object," said Beatrice. "And such things would have no meaning, if they did not come about of themselves. And we have no intention of that kind, of course."

"Mr. Jekyll may be left to his own ideas for his own life," said Miss Burtenshaw, satisfied with these.

"Why are we so sure he is not contented as a bachelor?" said Florence.

"Somehow one is sure of it," said Beatrice, looking round.

"Yes, somehow it comes through," said her cousin; "just that thing."

"It is a good thing it is such an interesting thing to know."

Dulcia gathered herself together, and running forward, struck Florence a playful blow.

"Here is Mr. Jekyll coming!" said Mrs. Bode.

"Yes, Mother dear; but let him come in like anyone else. No need to announce him with that touch of particularity."

Oscar came into the hall.

"I am here to reveal that I have made an advance in life, and become an uncle!"

"Oh!" breathed Dulcia. "Oh, I can't keep it back.

If only Mrs. Jekyll had lived just to this moment!"

"I congratulate you, indeed," said Beatrice, bringing his cup with a promptness and smoothness which seemed somehow incompatible.

"Well, now, first of all," said Miss Burtenshaw, offering a teaspoon which her cousin had forgotten, without noticing the latter's movement toward it, "let us hear whether the hero of the occasion is a hero or a heroine."

"And let us hear even before that, how Mrs. Edgeworth is."

"I think we have really heard. No news is good news."

"My sister is well, and the baby is a boy."

"Hope has dawned," cried Dulcia. "Mr. and Mrs. Edgeworth looked forward to the succession of their heir. Dear Cassie! It is well done."

"Their anticipations may stop short of his succession," said Fabian.

"I had been looking forward to its being a girl," said Miss Burtenshaw, selecting the sex to which to Oscar's knowledge she herself belonged. "I had even decided its name."

"And what was that?"

"It is of no good now: I will keep it for the advent of the daughter."

"I know what I should have liked the name to be, if it had been a girl," said Dulcia. "I will say it. Why not? Sibyl."

"It would have been a good name in that event," said Oscar; "but we have to decide the matter in view of its being a boy."

"Which would you have chosen yourself, Mr. Jekyll?" said Miss Burtenshaw. "Are you with me in preferring a member of the gentler sex?"

"I expect it depended upon Mrs. Edgeworth's preferences," said Beatrice, in the gentle tone of a member of this sex.

"I had no feeling, and I think my sister had not much.

Things were clear before us; and we wished no more."

There was a silence.

"Mr. Jekyll," said Dulcia, "as you have touched on the matter of your own volition, do you mind a straight question? It is prompted by comradeship and not by curiosity. How did you feel, when you knew the arrow of slander had attacked your sister, when the difficult idea came home?"

"You have asked the question before you know if I mind it."

There was laughter, in which that of the cousins sounded reluctant and clear.

"Now I am not going to be made to feel a blunderbuss, however you would all enjoy it. I know that feeling of guilty pleasure in another's discomfiture. I am going to repeat the question, unabashed and undeterred. The rector would not be out amongst us, if the subject any longer had him on the raw. Mr. Jekyll, what was your feeling, when the truth pierced your consciousness? It must have been slow in doing so."

"That there was something about my sister, which would show it was not truth."

"Well put," said Alexander. "That is how we all felt. If anyone had asked the question, we should have given that answer."

"The answer went without saying," said Beatrice.

"And the question, with Dulcia here," said Oscar to Fabian.

Beatrice glanced at Oscar, and then smiled towards Dulcia in gentle condonement.

"And how about the arrow of slander's attacking Edgeworth?" said Alexander. "Do any of us care about that?"

"I do," said Dulcia; "I care about it even more, in the proportion in which a man's suffering is always more pathetic to me than a woman's. Mr. Edgeworth and I have long been friends; he has held out a hand to me as he has not to most: and I have felt from my heart for that proud and humbled spirit. And from my heart I rejoice that it can rear its head."

"I will return to my sister," said Oscar, "and come back to hear your decision on the name."

"Let us get this flannel out of your path," said Miss Burtenshaw; "I don't know why you should be bothered by a dozen potential petticoats."

"Let me move it, Miss Burtenshaw."

"No, I have nothing to say to a woman afraid to use her hands. She would not be much good in a parish. And the flannel is not in your province. You will be offering to lay hands on your nephew next."

"As far as I have observed the two things, they are hardly distinguishable," said Oscar, causing the intended laughter to follow his retreat.

"Well, that was an exciting interruption," said someone.

"And Mr. Jekyll did not seem in the least conscious that it was exciting," said another. "That is what is so nice about him."

"He seemed really pleased about his sister's child. It helps one to realise what he would be like as a father," said Beatrice, with her usual thought for others, as she was herself independent of aid.

"I don't want to imagine him a father," said Dulcia; "I like him to be as he is, single, clean-cut, definite— himself."

"It certainly is rather premature," agreed Miss Burtenshaw, content with preliminary steps.

"We ought to be thinking of the name," said someone else. "Mr. Jekyll put it upon us, and will expect some decision."

"Yes, we ought," said Dulcia. "It struck me that he made the suggestion in all seriousness."

"What of Duncan, after his father?" said Mrs. Bode.

"No, Mother, hardly. That austere and perhaps rather hide-bound figure does not call for an understudy. Let us leave him, the one Duncan."

"Or Oscar, after his uncle?" said Beatrice, lightly.

"That name should wait for a son of his own," said Miss Burtenshaw, who had advanced in fancy.

"We are determined to provide him with a family," said Florence.

"What of Richard, after the brother he will never see?" said Mrs. Bode.

"Mother dear, you are fruitful in suggestions; but no; emphatically no. Cassie would never tolerate the suggestion of replacement. I know her well enough to know that, intimate though we shall never be. One of my early aspirations has fallen to the ground."

"We have thought of naming the child after his father, his uncle, and his brother," said Florence. "Are we required to go further?"

"Mrs. Smollett, now!" said Dulcia, holding up a finger.

"What of William, the name of Cassie's father?"

"You may have hit it, Mrs. Smollett. Little William Edgeworth! By that name Baby Edgeworth may walk in our midst. And a good solid old name too, suitable from king to peasant."

"I suspect it is as king, that this young man will take his place in the house," said Beatrice.

"We ought to get on with our work," said someone. "Mr. Jekyll will come back and find us idle."

The cousins took up their sewing, and desisted, as though wrought up in some way.

"It would certainly be pleasant to see Mr. Jekyll a father," said Mrs. Bode.

"Yes, his qualities fit him for fatherhood," said Miss Burtenshaw, now with simple terseness.

"Here he is, coming with Nance," said Florence, bending her eyes on her work.

Beatrice rose and began to fold her own.

"What are you going to do?" said her cousin at once.

"Catch Mr. Jekyll, and compel him to a lightning

survey of the choir accounts. He gave me orders not to let him escape."

"Well, what is the name?" said Oscar.

"William, after his maternal grandfather!"

"My reliance upon feminine intuition is justified."

"Is that the name?" said Dulcia. "Mrs. Smollett, you knew it all! Don't sit there, looking as if butter would not melt in your mouth."

Florence disregarded this injunction, and continued to sew, and Oscar proceeded.

"You are kind to concern yourselves with the name. Of course you have not met William Edgeworth. If you had, you might hardly think him worth a thought."

"You may have babies yourself one day, Mr. Jekyll," said Mrs. Bode.

"Yes, yes, Mother dear; but we are not ignorant of that, because we do not say it."

"Then I shall not let people show them to me. A parson must keep his respect for human nature."

"He will never get it out," said Nance. "I shall have to take his part upon myself, or continue with no part at all. We are here to reveal the revelation which has arisen between us. He has sought my hand, and I have by no means refused it."

"As you show an interest in William," said Oscar, "we can feel no doubt that you will extend it to us."

There was a pause, and then Dulcia ran to Nance.

"Darling, it is perfect, fundamentally and classically perfect! The reason why we did not think of it, is that it is fit and true, like the sun and showers, and calls for no ordinary notice. Out of all that has conspired to crush you, this rises up your own!"

"I am so very glad," said Beatrice, with quiet feeling.

"A wish of mine has come true, that the lady of the rectory should be taken from our midst," said Miss Burtenshaw, with briskness and truth.

"I wondered how many of you had guessed," said

Florence. "Some of you have said things, that seemed to indicate suspicion."

"I admit it has not the thrill of a real piece of news to me," said Miss Burtenshaw, who was indeed without inner excitement.

"I had no suspicion," said Beatrice, in a quiet, full tone.

"Idiot that I am," said Dulcia, "I had my suspicions all the wrong way round! How can I have been such a booby? Nothing will persuade me to give myself and somebody else away. So don't any of you expect it."

"Perhaps you will give yourself away to me, when we are at home," smiled Mrs. Bode.

"No, Mother, you are not safe. You might not remember that someone is involuntarily, and even humiliatingly involved. I cannot risk one of your breaches of faith."

"There is surely no humiliation in an unconscious part," said Florence.

"But it would be so easy to imagine it was not unconscious, Mrs. Smollett. That would arise almost inevitably from revelation. It must not be risked."

"It would be rather nice to be involved in romance, without any trouble for oneself," said Miss Burtenshaw.

"We shall all be insulted, if we are not the heroines of Dulcia's imagination," said her cousin.

"Now I see no more work will be done to-day," said the former; "so I will dismiss the meeting. I feel quite excited. It is amusing of people to marry and entertain us. I quite feel they have done it for that purpose. We ought to offer them a vote of thanks."

"And we will offer one," said Dulcia, in a graver tone. "We thank Nance and her future husband for coming out of the sad story woven around them and theirs, and giving us a happy ending to carry away."

"I am going to excuse Mr. Jekyll the accounts," said Beatrice. "I was dense enough to be unconscious that romance of any kind was in the air. I did not get as far even as Dulcia, who seems to have had her own ideas."

"I get more and more ashamed of them."

"I do not feel ashamed," said Miss Burtenshaw. "I feel rather inclined to vaunt myself and become puffed up. But I will take my detached self home to my duties."

"I will do the same," said Beatrice, looking towards Florence, as she spoke, and then going quietly and quickly to her side. "Would you send this package to Sibyl, Mrs. Smollett? I don't like to disturb Nance. I feel it would not be quite fair to-day."

"Oh, certainly," said Florence, looking at a sheaf of booklets, which Beatrice, recollecting the convention, now transferred to Fabian. "I will send it to-night."

"Do we know her address?" said Fabian. "Her aunt is dead, and she may have gone somewhere else."

"Then would you please give it to Mrs. Edgeworth, or to anyone else in the house?"

"Is it of general application?"

"Yes—yes—of universal," said Beatrice, moving away.

"Is it correct to apply these titles to our friends?" said Fabian, turning them over. "It would be pretty in us to keep some of them to ourselves." He started at a swift, light step.

"Will you please give me the packet?" said Beatrice, holding out her hand.

Fabian adjusted the band and complied, his eyes down.

"Thank you very much," said Beatrice, in a gentle, friendly tone. "This has been an exciting meeting for us, hasn't it, with this revelation? I think Mr. Jekyll and Nance make a very well-matched couple."

"Yes, yes, a perfect pair."

"Well, as nearly perfect as can be," said Beatrice, with the failings of humanity perhaps fresh in her mind. "They have these lovely autumn days for their engagement; I feel so glad for them."

"I find them tiring," said Florence.

"Now I do not; I am purely exhilarated by them. They

act on me like a tonic. It is in the spring that I flag."
Beatrice gave her hand again to each.

" 'The year's at the spring—All's right with the world',"
murmured Fabian.

"Darlings, good-bye," said Dulcia, bound to attend the
cousins. "And a very particular kind of congratulation.
You may understand me or not, as truth dictates. I know
you do both rejoice from your hearts."

"I have wondered if this would happen in the end," said
Mrs. Bode.

"In the end! We honour your avoidance of the delicate
and difficult, Mother. But there was rather too much of a
hint of them. Mr. Jekyll would naturally hold himself
from advances to a woman, that could not be consum-
mated."

"I have never believed that a parson is less popular
when he marries," said Oscar; "and I see I am right. Of
course, anyone would look down on a man for being no
one's choice, and look up to him for being Nance's."

"Do you know what I thought? It is too absurd to need
to be a secret," said Dulcia, leaning back in mirth at the
idea that had found her favour. "I thought that either
Beatrice or Miss Burtenshaw was the rector's choice!
There is my theory, for weal or woe to me!"

"A very sound theory," said Oscar. "I ought to marry
both, as I could not do without either. But neither would
have time to marry me; I could not spare it to them. They
must put it to more useful purposes."

"Oh, if they could hear you!"

"I think it was so nice of Mr. Jekyll to put things like
that, about two women, suggested to him in that way,"
said someone. "I think nothing stamps the quality of a
man as much as things like that."

"Mr. Jekyll's quality is stamped," said Dulcia.

Miss Burtenshaw and Beatrice walked home, with their
arms linked and their feet in step, bound by mutual
sympathy, mutual relief that neither was preferred to her

friends, and a deep, almost subconscious gladness that their life was to remain unchanged.

"You girls seem as satisfied, as if you were to be brides yourselves," said Alexander. "Rushing off without me, as if you had something to be excited about! I had all I could do to catch you up."

"A good deal more satisfied than that, Father," said Miss Burtenshaw, leading the way into the house, and looking for the letters. "I don't know if there is some sort of feeling of escape in the spinster population"—She tore an envelope—"when this sort of thing happens. Perhaps there is."

"There is the actuality, anyhow," said Beatrice.

"Actuality, fiddlesticks! You would neither have refused him, if he had asked you, annoyed though you may be at my saying so."

But his daughter and niece were so far from being annoyed, that they fell back in fits of laughter.

"I must tell Nance," said the former in a choked voice; "I must share the fun; sorry as I am to tell tales against you, Father."

"Mr. Jekyll should share it too," said Beatrice, her voice calm, considering her late emotion.

"For heaven's sake don't tell him I said everyone wanted him to propose to them."

"Oh, not everyone, Father," said his daughter, her voice freshly impeded. "Beatrice and I! That makes it so much better. *Both* of us! That is best." She sat up and wiped her eyes. "Poor Mr. Jekyll! To be divided like a batch of loaves! He is really more than that."

CHAPTER XXII

"CASSIE, I HAVE told Oscar," said Nance. "It was not suitable for our first secret. I am a believer in secrets between husbands and wives, but they are better when they arise naturally after marriage."

"It is probably a discussion in which there is nothing to discuss," said Oscar. "So experience in making sermons may be a help."

"Of course there is nothing to discuss," said Grant. "As I could not live with my wife, without her money, I should not be able to live with her, with it; and I am not able."

"The two things are not the same. It is the difference that makes you go through this form. When the matter is once at an end, it must never arise."

"It is at an end. It has not really arisen."

"Father thinks it has," said Nance. "He believes it is on foot at the moment. He will be coming to hear the foregone conclusion. It will not occur to him that we may give up our inheritance. How can it, when he has known us from our birth? Will anyone dare to tell him? I shall not dare to hear."

Duncan entered the room in his occasional genial manner, causing Grant to grow pale.

"Well, we are to send for Sibyl—good girl as she is to want to come back—and set off again together. We may put our stumble from our minds, unless it does one of us good to remember." He turned and took his son from his wife, leaving in the mind of his nephew the knowledge, that here was the thing of all he had forgiven, which he was never to forgive. "Well, William, you have cause to thank your sister, and will do so when you have the English.

And meanwhile the rest of us have it. Someone should write to-day, and it may be the one it should be." He left the room after a bare moment within it.

"I did not dare to say it," said Grant; "I shall never dare. He could not face the truth, even so small a part. He has borne enough from me, and must bear no more. He will never know that the wrong I have done him, has saved him in the end." His voice changed and sounded as if he were alone. "So it is decided in the other way. Sibyl will come back, and will be my wife; and we shall be together till we die. If I have a son, she will be his mother; if I have a daughter, a daughter who will grow to be a woman, she will be her child."

The others were silent, as they watched him move away.

"Well, what of it, Nance?" said Oscar.

"Money is the root of evil. I am glad of my inheritance, even as things are. It is the root of as much evil in me as that."

"Grant will have his own share and Sibyl's. It is something on the other side."

"I see the evil appearing."

"Twelve hundred a year on that side."

"More and more evil!"

"It is a good thing he does not deprive William of his portion."

"As that would really be depriving Father, on the top of everything else. Eight hundred a year extra on the wrong side might have been the last straw. I should indeed hardly call it a straw."

"How do you feel about meeting your sister?"

"My natural affection is asserting itself. Or I am imagining it is, because affection seems so much better than avarice. The evil probably includes self-deception."

"You are getting used to what you know of her. We get used to anything. That will be a help to Grant."

"The wrong is never the only thing a wrong-doer has done," said Cassie. "That is the pathos of criminals. No class has a greater. Grant has met other things in Sibyl, and will meet them again."

"We shall be feeling he has too much," said Nance.

"Sibyl has been through emotional strain, in a life in which succession had loomed too large. She never had a normal moral sense, and she was not in a normal place."

"Grant will have her as well as all the rest."

"We need not be ashamed of wanting Sibyl back. It is not a good thing to cast her off, for any reason."

"We are not ashamed of it. We hardly have it to be ashamed of."

"It is natural to find a thing easier," said Oscar, "when we have compensation."

"Well, we are always ashamed of what is natural. We should not be ashamed of anything exacting or artificial. Nothing should help us to understand Sibyl, better than our welcome of her. We can all do something against our nature for gain. Except, of course, Father. No wonder he is set above us all. That is his place."

"Your share of the gain is not much. It does not make all that difference."

"The difference between struggle and ease, the difference that counts to thinking people. I cannot be ranked with Father."

"I suppose Grant should be."

"He will not be by us, as he has the compensation."

"So has your father, in effect."

"Father does have things both ways. He can be a sorrowing widower and a happy husband at the same time. And he is always a martyr and a ruler."

"Did you expect me to come to Grant's help? Or did you know I was afraid of your father?"

"I know it now, as you know things about me. The moment has to come, when neither is what the other thought, and nothing can be the same again. It is better to get it over."

"You feel that Grant is being sacrificed to the rest of us?"

"I can hardly help feeling that, but he is really being sacrificed to Father. And what could we expect? Think of what he has done to Father, when no one else dares to speak to him! It is proper that his whole life should be spoiled. He felt himself that it was the only thing."

A week later Sibyl came back.

Duncan made more account of the event, than of any within their memories. He shook off the burden of years, and showed himself as Ellen had known him. Every detail of the preparations had to pass under his eye.

"We shall christen the boy, and return to the house," he said to his daughter on the day. "Then your sister will reach home to find her friends awaiting her." Duncan never spoke of a child as a brat, after the death of his reputed son.

"It is a very good plan for the welcome, Father."

"There is no plan: there will be no welcome. Your sister is not very safe. The boy is to be christened, and she returns from a visit on the occasion."

"That is to be it? I daresay it is best."

"You daresay what is best? That is to be what?"

"The plan for the day."

"There is to be no plan! How does one make a thing clear?"

"I see it is best to make nothing of it, Father."

"Nothing of what?"

"Of Sibyl's being away so soon after her marrige."

"You would have tried to make something of it, left to yourself?"

"It did not occur to me that it could be passed over. But I think it is a good plan—good idea."

"Plan! Plan! Plan! Do you feel your engagement alters your place?"

"I think I do, Father, though you are the first to say it."

"The income you owe to your sister, also puts you up?"

"Incomes always do that at first. By the way, Grant is going to the church from his own house."

"He must learn that that house is his home."

"He has been living there these last weeks."

"Do you suppose I don't know that?"

"You spoke as if you did not."

"I am glad you listen to my words: I should not always think it."

Nance tried to give a turn to the talk.

"I shall be told by everyone to-day, that they remember me in clothes like William's."

"That becomes long ago. Your parson should be coming for you."

"It is to be the next celebration."

"What is there to celebrate in putting out a daughter late? We were better to hush it up."

"We have hushed enough things up," said Nance under her breath.

Duncan strode from the room, colliding with his wife, and passed her without a word.

"Cassie, Father is himself to-day. It is the last occasion for his fulfilment."

"Keep out of his way until the guests are here. No man can be himself with guests."

"At last he has a wife who knows him."

"I wish that need not be, but it is impossible to help it. It does not seem fair, when he does not know me. What a silly thing it is, to complain of being misunderstood!"

"Do you dread meeting Sibyl, Cassie?"

"You know better than to say that. We are glad to have her back, and that her difference with Grant is over."

The christening could only seem an occasion from the past, on which the same people fell into the same places. The cousins showed a rather festive aspect, maintaining a personal standard independent of Oscar's situation. Sibyl came her last stage by carriage, to save meeting a train, and to avoid a private encounter with her husband.

"Dear child! It was a thoughtful idea," said Mrs. Bode.

"Different too, from the old Sibyl, Mother. We should take it as a happy augury."

Sibyl ran up the steps, and into her father's arms, recalling to Nance and Cassie a moment of yet another scene. Duncan responded, and at once gave place to the husband; and the couple embraced, and stood together, before Sibyl turned aside.

"Where is Nance?"

"Here, with her welcome!" said Dulcia.

"And how are you, Dulcia?"

"Nothing and nowhere, while nearer and dearer wait," said the latter, her hand held for guidance. "Now so much for the sister's embrace. Then there is another relative, waiting with her welcome, someone who will anyhow do her utmost in the part, for the reward of recognition. We see the two Mrs. Edgeworths greet each other."

"How are you, Cassie? And how is my new brother?"

Sibyl took the child from the nurse, and Cassie started forward.

"Look at our clear-thinking, level-headed Cassie, grudging her treasure to other arms for an instant!" said Dulcia. "To think what instincts might have lain fallow, did lie fallow for too long! Well, they have their outlet while there is time."

"I rather grudge Cassie to a domestic life," said Florence.

"Yes, do you know, so do I, Mrs. Smollett," said Miss Burtenshaw, half laughing.

"I think you hardly judge soundly, Mrs. Smollett," said Dulcia, "clear though it is that nothing in your own life prompts the view." She looked at Florence's face, and laughed. "You hate me, Mrs. Smollett, don't you?"

Florence did not speak.

"Don't you, Mrs. Smollett?" repeated Dulcia, her eyes twinkling on Florence's face, before they moved to Nance. "I take silence for consent. Nance, it is good not to see you aloof amongst happy pairs, though it was aloof with head held high. Nothing could have given your dignity more of a chance, in a way. But to-day I had almost said, 'If but your mother were with you'!"

"Remember what you quite said about Cassie. We are a family where you have to be careful."

"My dear, it is my nature to be simply myself. I hold no brief for edited personalities; and I am sure you do not. You would not wish me different."

"How are Almeric and Alison?"

"Well, if you will let it again be said; and happy, if I may say that too. My parents take an interest in their grand-daughter, and one cannot in reason check them. Judgment is tempered with mercy."

"It seems that mercy has the upper hand."

"Well, as it is extended to yourself, you will be forgiving. We shall see your father a patriarch in his house. But it will lose—— No one can doubt my loyalty to Cassie—much of its sense of fulfilment."

"He has never got over my mother's death."

"It is a tribute to her, and a tribute to Cassie, and a tribute—I will say that too—to Alison. With you there is no need to give a dog a bad name and hang him."

"It is a tribute to my mother. No one else can help it."

"Dear, there is no feeling of bitterness creeping into your relation with Cassie? It has now been put to the supreme test. But you are right to smile at the idea. It is laughable."

"We will go home," said Florence, "and leave the united family."

"I think the slight constraint of re-union is often smoothed by the presence of outsiders," said Dulcia; "provided they are not outsiders in a second sense."

"I feel I have recovered a daughter," said Mr. Bode, who was walking with Sibyl.

"Yes, Father dear," said Dulcia, looking at him from her distance, and moving up and down on her feet, "that is nice and welcoming, but goes a little far. There is a gulf between the two families after all, and the hint of connection is hardly to be brought forward."

"You are going to settle down, Sibyl?" said Beatrice, "and not run away again?"

"I want to settle down for ever, and see all I can of all of you."

"And of someone else too," said Dulcia. "I think marriage has smoothed and softened our little Sibyl."

"I have known it a mellowing thing," said Miss Burtenshaw.

"Now, do you know," said Dulcia, looking at the cousins, "I am going to do a thing I had sworn I would never do; and tell you what I would have cut my tongue out, rather than reveal. I thought—don't look at me while I say it—that Mr. Jekyll had centred his affections on one of you, and that you were, like Barkis, willing!"

The pair looked at her in neutral enquiry.

"One of us? But which one?" said Miss Burtenshaw.

"That I left to fate, or you, or Mr. Jekyll, or all at once. I admit I imagined either of you in the place."

"But surely that was the whole point," said Miss Burtenshaw, looking puzzled. "What one it was."

"He could not have married both," said Beatrice, "especially as he was going to marry Nance."

"Oh, I was wrong! I was a dodderer; but what I am leading up to, will be my excuse. It is an ill wind, etcetera; and I want to tell you his words, when he knew the idea had detained some of us."

"Some of you?" queried Miss Burtenshaw. "Did more than one person seek to provide him with a harem?"

"Oh!" said Beatrice, in amused recollection. "Did not Uncle have something of the same idea?"

"Charity begins at home," laughed her cousin.

"It is a good thing he did not live in the days of the celibacy of the clergy. Poor Mr. Jekyll too, who might almost have done so until lately!"

"Hear me out, hear me out! And then judge of my

words, or rather of his. His reply was, that he could not marry either, as he wanted you both for more useful purpose. Was that not a perfect answer in all its aspects? Chivalrous and unassuming, and, in view of what might have been, completely sensitive?"

"Good as it went, but a plain negative would have done," said Miss Burtenshaw.

"Do you think the baby shows any likeness to his uncle?" said Beatrice, hardly detained by the topic.

"I have longed to see Mr. Jekyll a family man," said her cousin, defining any feeling that might have escaped.

"What I long for more—Let us say it low and grave," said Dulcia, doing as she said, "is to see Nance a mother."

"I shall be content to see her a bride," said Miss Burtenshaw. "She it is of all my girls, whose bridehood I have looked forward to the most."

"You two dear ones! How wrong I have been!"

"Why, did you think we grudged Nance the fulfilment of her natural desires?" said Beatrice.

"Yes, it is a simple, natural thing. Everyone should have it, who wants it," said her cousin.

"It is not quite so ordinary as that, to be the choice of Mr. Jekyll."

"It is not indeed," said Miss Burtenshaw, cordially. 'It is the fulfilment and fitting of two personalities, and dear, important personalities too."

"We will go now, Fabian," said Florence.

"We follow, Mrs. Smollett," said Dulcia, with a movement of clicking her heels and saluting.

"My wife has little to wish for you, Mrs. Edgeworth," said Mr. Bode, "and that means there is little to be wished."

"Yes, that is right, parents dear; but enough; you are safe so far," said their daughter, marshalling them onward. "We cannot but be on precarious ground under this roof. I applaud your tact in making your visits few and far between."

"We leave you here, Mr. Jekyll, a member of the family?" said Beatrice.

"For the moment; I am soon to add one of them to my own family."

"And a family just as good in its sound and simple way," said Dulcia, following her parents.

"Will Sibyl and Grant be with us to-night?" said Cassie. "Duncan, will you answer what I ask you?"

"It is not I whom you should ask."

"Sibyl decides for herself, does she? I must get out of the way of thinking of her as a child."

"Do your best towards it. She has got out of the way of thinking of you as what you were."

"Father, why not come back with Grant and me? If you would rather not, I will stay here with you."

"It is time you were with your husband."

"Oscar is staying," said Nance. "Will one be enough for you, Father?"

"Why should it be that one, in that case? But I am not a dotard, to be able to put sense into only one of your fellows at a time."

"Sibyl and I can easily go home," said Grant, finding the words come before he thought.

"You have not seemed to do that so easily."

"Of course you will stay," said Cassie. "We must be together this evening."

The meal passed almost without words, Duncan's reaction from his long strain causing him to shed from the head of the table an almost tangible gloom. Cassie and Oscar's efforts at talk seemed weighted into the silence. The hour drew Grant and Sibyl together, as nothing else could have done. The old alliance in the face of Duncan's oppression rose between them. Something in Duncan suggested an aversion from their numbers; and the three young people found themselves drifting to the schoolroom, as though the old conditions carried the old customs.

"We can't be too thankful that Mother is dead," said

Nance, hurrying into another silence. "It will be enough to leave Cassie alone with Father. How difficult it would be, if people did not die! Think of the numbers who die, and all the good that is done! They never seem to die, without doing something for someone. No wonder they hate so to do it, and plan to be immortal. It is a mercy that both Aunt Maria and Oscar's mother are dead. And think what a bad thing for us Father's life has been!"

"And ours for Father," said her sister.

"I have been so ashamed of being alive and well, and having to be housed and clothed and fed and provided for. It really is not reasonable. No wonder phrases like 'vile bodies' arise. When people have to be provided for, death is the only thing."

"We are not touching any real truth," said Sibyl.

"It does not do to touch real truth," said Grant, breaking off with a flush creeping over his face.

"The Victorians were openly ashamed of being well," said Nance. "I don't know why we called them hypocrites."

"I had no idea that Aunt Maria had left her money to me."

"The Victorians never talked about their wills," said Grant, turning fully to his wife.

"They would not give the pleasure of anticipation, as well as the actual goods they were to give up," said Nance. "Death does sound dreadful, put like that."

"We did not want Mother to die," said Sibyl.

"We were fond enough of her, to want her to have her life, even though it had to be lived with Father. It shows what we think of life."

"Why did Aunt Maria not leave her money to Uncle?"

"She was not very fond of him. She left it out when she was ill. She thought him overbearing, and Mother too good for him."

"What dreadful thoughts for a death-bed!" said Nance. "About Father too!"

274

"I think I see how she got her impression," said Grant, in his natural manner.

"But people so often forgive at the last. When they have to forgive inheritance, they can easily pass over some human weakness. That may be what brought in the custom of deathbed forgiveness."

"What did she think of Uncle's later marriages?"

"She seemed surprised that so many women accepted him," said Sibyl.

"It does suggest there is something in him, one has not seen."

"We should really be sorry, if he died," said Sibyl.

"Of course, he is a rule to himself. I have heard him say so," said Nance. "Perhaps he never told Aunt Maria, and people are not observant in families."

"If you please, Miss Nance," said Bethia, "the master wishes to know if you are all out of the house."

"Why did he send to the schoolroom to enquire? That is in the house."

"I came up at my own initiative, miss. Have you a message?"

"We are in the house, and will repair to the drawing-room."

"You are coming down. Yes, miss."

"You two go first. You are masters of your actions."

"I am not," said Grant. "I may be presuming on the past. Have I any right behind the scenes?"

"Come along: I am not afraid of Father."

"That must simply be an exaggeration," said Nance, forgetting it was only of her father, that her sister need not be afraid.

"Well," said Duncan, "have you made up your minds to which houses you belong? In that case consider your places in them."

"You are right, we should be going, Uncle."

"Can't you follow a simple word? Go then, for all the sense we can find in you."

275

"I am so happy to be in the place where you are, Father," said Sibyl.

"You come bamboozling me, when your part is second fiddle to your husband."

"We shall both see you to-morrow."

"I don't know why. It is time for you to stay in your house, and manage it."

"You would like me to come in, Cassie?"

"Of course, women must run after each other. It passes me why it is said that they don't incline to their own sex. It puzzles men that they should, I suppose; poor fellows, to fancy there is any use for their sense!"

A silence fell, and seemed it would not break.

"You have no liking for this man's company, Nance?" said Duncan, with a gesture towards Oscar. "You give no sign that you would pass your life in it."

"I wanted to be with Sibyl on her first evening, Father."

"What have I said? And you did what you wanted, didn't you? Oscar, you keep a hand over her, or she will have you under hers. A masterful girl from the beginning! And her mother's fancy for some reason, and Cassie's too."

"And mine," said Oscar.

"Yes, that is how it would take you. As it has better men. Well, I am here to give you a word when you need it. You are all at my hand to be taught."

MORE ABOUT PENGUINS
AND PELICANS

For further information about books available from Penguins please write to Dept EP, Penguin Books Ltd, Harmondsworth, Middlesex UB7 0DA.

In the U.S.A.: For a complete list of books available from Penguins in the United States write to Dept CS, Penguin Books, 625 Madison Avenue, New York, New York 10022.

In Canada: For a complete list of books available from Penguins in Canada write to Penguin Books Canada Ltd, 2801 John Street, Markham, Ontario, L3R 1B4.

In Australia: For a complete list of books available from Penguins in Australia write to the Marketing Department, Penguin Books Australia Ltd, P.O. Box 257, Ringwood, Victoria 3134.

In New Zealand: For a complete list of books available from Penguins in New Zealand write to the Marketing Department, Penguin Books (N.Z.) Ltd, P.O. Box 4019, Auckland 10.

A GOD AND HIS GIFTS

Ivy Compton-Burnett

'She saw life in the relentless terms of Greek tragedy, its cruelties, ironies – above all its passions – played out against a background of triviality and ennui' – Anthony Powell

A God and his Gifts was the last of Ivy Compton-Burnett's novels to be published in her lifetime and is considered by many to be one of her best. Set in the claustrophobic world of Edwardian upper-class family life, it is the story of the self-willed and arrogant Hereward Egerton. In his marriage to Ada Merton he maintains a veneer of respectability but through his intimate relationships with her sister, Emmeline, and his son's future wife, Hetty, he steps beyond the bounds of conventional morality with both comic and tragic results . . .

'An acting out of powerful impulses that run counter to an accepted morality – brutal truth-telling, repressed family hatreds and loves' – Storm Jameson in the *Spectator*

'One of the most brilliant and original novelists in the English language' – *Daily Telegraph*

Forthcoming:
A FAMILY AND A FORTUNE

ROSAMOND LEHMANN

DUSTY ANSWER

Enormous acclaim, 'hysterically good reviews' and thousands of letters, including ones from Galsworthy and Compton Mackenzie, greeted the publication of this novel.

The *Sunday Times* wrote: 'This is a remarkable book. It is not often that one can say with confidence of a first novel by a young writer that it reveals new possibilities for literature.'

Dusty Answer is Judith Earle's story – her solitary childhood spent dreaming in her enchanted house by the river, her awkward, intense experiences at Cambridge rounded with passion and disillusionment, and her travels abroad with her elegant, sophisticated mother. Above all, the novel is about Judith's consuming relationship with a family of cousins whose inroads into the dreams and preoccupations of her young womanhood make *Dusty Answer* so uniquely and tenderly subtle and true.

THE ECHOING GROVE

In a novel that is as subtle as it is extraordinarily imaginative Rosamond Lehmann explores the human heart. Her story concerns three characters – Rickie Masters, his wife Madeleine and her sister Dinah – and their fatally interrelated lives are unfolded through their eyes and through their experience. In showing us the rivalry which divides the two sisters and the love which unites Rickie to them, Rosamond Lehmann reveals in her beautifully structured novel a deep and sensitive understanding of both the sublimity and the pain of personal relationships.

'No English writer has told of the pains of women in love more truly or more movingly than Rosamond Lehmann' – Marghanita Laski

'She uses words with the enjoyment and mastery with which Renoir used paint' – Rebecca West in the *Sunday Times*

ELIZABETH BOWEN

A selection

EVA TROUT

Few writers can match the brilliance of Elizabeth Bowen's prose. And here the formal grace of her style, her flair for mischievous social comedy and the subtlety of her dialogue go into creating one of her most formidable – and moving – heroines.

'Resonant, beautiful and often very funny . . . Eva is triumphantly real, a creation of great imaginative tenderness . . . Elizabeth Bowen is a splendid artist, intelligent, generous and acutely aware, who has been telling her readers for many years that love is a necessity, and that its loss or absence is the greatest tragedy man knows' – Julian Webb in the *Financial Times*

'Rarely have I come across a novel in which sexual frustration (and sexuality) have been so richly and powerfully conveyed' – Roger Baker in *Books and Bookmen*

THE LITTLE GIRLS

In 1914 they had been eleven years old, three little girls at St Agatha's, a day school on the South Coast. Fifty years later, Dinah, beautiful as ever, advertises in the national newspapers to find the other two – Clare, now established with a successful business, and Sheila, a married woman, glossy, chic and correct.

In this brilliantly orchestrated novel, as subtle and compelling as a mystery story, Elizabeth Bowen asks: can friendship be taken up where it left off? What are the revelations – and the dangers – in summoning up childhood?

'There is that recurring shiver of delight . . . for this story is poetic in its awareness, its stimulus, its beauty of writing; and as full of clues, hints and half-revealed secrets as any thriller' – *Scotsman*

VALMOUTH AND OTHER NOVELS

VALMOUTH/PRANCING NIGGER/CONCERNING THE ECCENTRICITIES OF CARDINAL PIRELLI

Ronald Firbank

Beneath soft deeps of velvet sky dotted with cognac clouds, lies the world of Ronald Firbank . . . There her ladyship languishes on the jaguar-skin sofa, robed in jewelled pyjamas; a negro boy roams the gold city streets, searching for sherbet but dreaming of butterflies; there, closeted in a chasuble, his Eminence baptizes the blue-eyed police-pup of the Duquesa DunEden . . .

'A world, in the last resort absolutely original; one that causes a cavalcade of wish-fulfilment myths to sweep gaily past the reader's vision' – Anthony Powell

STORY OF THE EYE

Georges Bataille

Widely regarded as the greatest sexual/pornographic novel of this century, *Story of the Eye* was first published in 1928, and in it Bataille explores his own sexual obsessions.

This edition also includes Susan Sontag's essay, 'The Pornographic Imagination', which discusses this and other erotic classics, together with Roland Barthes's essay on *Story of the Eye*.

A LIFE

Italo Svevo

First published in 1893, *Una Vita* and its author remained in obscurity for over thirty years until James Joyce hailed Svevo as a major literary discovery. As in all his works, Svevo is concerned here with the bourgeois soul, and its inability to will or act. His heroes are typically men of business, but with cultural pretensions, and he depicts them in their free time when they are not working. It is less important to Svevo whether they have spare money or not: the important thing is that they always have time to spare. How they lose it, use it or kill it forms his major theme – worked with all the quixotic genius of which he was capable.

THE TRAGIC MUSE
Henry James

Henry James published *The Tragic Muse* in 1890 at the beginning of his intense, but disastrous, flirtation with the theatre. Its themes reflect those preoccupations and, although this is the most 'English' of his novels, James concentrates his debate on the artistic life, in a masterly example of the 'all dramatic, all scenic'.

JOSEPH AND HIS BROTHERS
Thomas Mann

As Germany dissolved into the nightmare of Nazism, Thomas Mann was at work on this novel. This epic recasting of the famous biblical tale is a magnificent reconstruction of the ancient Near East. It stretches back past the days of the patriarchs to the dawn of civilization itself, and constitutes one of Thomas Mann's major achievements.

THE HOUSE OF MIRTH
Edith Wharton

First published in 1905, when it profoundly shocked society, *The House of Mirth* is a novel of manners that helped to carve out for the author an area of social fiction into which not even Henry James could trespass. 'A passionate social prophet' wrote Edmund Wilson, 'is precisely what Edith Wharton became. At her strongest and most characteristic, she is a brilliant example of the writer who relieves an emotional strain by denouncing his generation.'

King Penguin

A selection

LIVES OF GIRLS AND WOMEN
Alice Munro

Del Jordan's scrapbook of memories records a young girl changing from childhood to adolescence. Through the people she encounters – her mother selling encyclopedias; her aunts, two lives devoted to Uncle Craig; Garnet, her first taste of love; and her best friend Naomi relentlessly pursuing marriage – Del becomes aware of her own potential and the excitement of her unknown independence . . .

'A superb account of complex childhood perceptions and experiences' – *Guardian*

A SPY IN THE HOUSE OF LOVE
Anaïs Nin

A brilliant analysis of a woman whose affairs with four men express the duplicity and the fragmentation of self involved in the search for love. 'Her sense of woman is unique . . . her reputation grows . . . she excites male readers and incites female readers. She is readable and she comes against life with a vital artistry and boldness' – *The New York Times Book Review*

HOUSEKEEPING
Marilynne Robinson

A drifter until she comes to the lakeside town of Fingerbone, Sylvia makes a determined effort to keep house for Ruth and Lucille, left alone after their mother's suicide. But her efforts are fitful and doomed; Lucille, armed with dress patterns, nail polish, and new friends, moves out, and Ruth is drawn irretrievably into Sylvie's shadowy, impermanent world.

'I found myself reading slowly, then more slowly – this is not a novel to be hurried through, for every sentence is a delight' – Doris Lessing

King Penguin

A selection

ASH ON A YOUNG MAN'S SLEEVE
Dannie Abse

Sharp, sad and romantic, Dannie Abse's reminiscences weave the private fortunes of a Jewish family in Cardiff into the troubled tapestry of the times. Unemployment, the rise of Hitler and Mussolini, the Spanish Civil War, the fate of the European Jews; all these themes are the more real for being seen through the angry, irreverent eyes of youth.

'Acutely remembered, admirably told . . . a clever, moving evocation' – Angus Wilson in the *Observer*

BLACK LIST, SECTION H
Francis Stuart

In 'an imaginative fiction in which only real people appear', Francis Stuart looms like a Dostoyevskian figure: married to Maud Gonne's daughter, IRA gunrunner and prisoner in the Civil War, living with whores in Paris, farming, roaming Europe and writing novels. Gambler, rebel, mystic, delinquent – in 1940 he arrives in Hitler's Germany to join the black list of the guilty and damned.

'The strangest book of a strange career . . . Stuart is of Rimbaud's damned and illumined company' – Robert Nye

'A preposterous, dissimulating, macho-machiavellian novelist, but he has a rare streak of genius' – Alan Ross in the *London Magazine*

BIRTHSTONE
D. M. Thomas

Specially revised for this King Penguin edition, this novel explores the magical effects of the birthstone Men-an-Tol on three people – Jo, Hector and Lola – as they settle into a holiday cottage on the Cornish coast. With his characteristic brilliance and wit, the author of *The White Hotel* gives us 'fantasy as Freud envisaged it, powerful enough to counter reality, working like free association and allowing the unconscious to take over' – *London Review of Books*

A Choice of Penguin Fiction

FALLING IN PLACE
Ann Beattie

It's a hot, sullen summer on America's East Coast. As John and Louise Knapp bicker at their weekend marriage; as twelve-year-old Parker makes another trip to the shrink in New York; as Cynthia the English teacher clings to her freaky lover Spangle – Ann Beattie invades Updike and Cheever territory to give us a cinematic, brilliantly comic view of America's affluent hell.

'Wonderfully funny' – *The Times*

MOTHER'S HELPER
Maureen Freely

The Pyle–Carpenter household comes complete with three children who can do what they like as long as they have Thought It Through, an intercom that never turns off, with Weekly Family Councils and with the television padlocked into a bag. Like Kay Carpenter herself, it was a totally liberated, principled, caring, warm, nurturing nucleus . . . And at first, Laura was completely fooled.

'A novel to weep over or laugh with. Whichever will stop you going mad' – *Literary Review*

DAUGHTERS OF PASSION
Julia O'Faolain

Anger, passion, tenderness . . . nine evocative stories from the author of *No Country for Young Men*. Julia O'Faolain never falters as she moves through situations both strange and familiar – the seduction of a lonely nanny in Paris, a family embarrassed by an unwelcome guest, the sharply focused memories of an imprisoned hunger-striker under pressure to eat. It is a brilliant, compulsive foray into a landscape of passion from a writer at the height of her powers.